TERRARIUM

It is, after all, not man but
the universe that is subtle.

—BARRY HOLSTUN LOPEZ

This book is for
Murray Sperber
and for
Fred Pfeil—
camerados

TERRARIUM

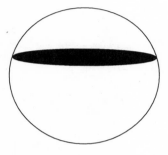

Scott Russell Sanders

Indiana University Press

BLOOMINGTON AND INDIANAPOLIS

This is a work of fiction. All the characters and events portrayed
in this book are fictional, and any resemblance to real people
or incidents is purely coincidental.

© 1985 by Scott Russell Sanders

Afterword © 1995 by Scott Russell Sanders

The paper used in this publication meets the minimum requirements of
American National Standard for Information Sciences—Permanence of
Paper for Printed Library Materials, ANSI Z39.48-1984.

MANUFACTURED IN THE UNITED STATES OF AMERICA

Library of Congress Cataloging-in-Publication Data

Sanders, Scott R. (Scott Russell), date
Terrarium / Scott Russell Sanders.
p.   cm.
ISBN 0-253-32956-6 (cloth). — ISBN 0-253-21021-6 (pbk.)
1. Twenty-first century—Fiction. I. Title.
PS3569.A5137T47   1995
813'.54—dc20   95-4805

1 2 3 4 5   00 99 98 97 96 95

ONE

Phoenix thought of her as the barefooted walker. From the morning when she first loomed into view like an unpredicted planet, she set up fierce tides of desire in him.

On that morning the pressure inside Oregon City and inside his head seemed no greater than usual, no more conducive to visions. A blue wig dangled stylishly about his ears, facepaint disguised his features, and a portfolio of satellite film beneath one arm identified him as a man bound for the office. Chemmies regulated every bodily process that needed regulating. All his life was in order. But when Phoenix emerged from his apartment, ticking off the day's plans in his mind (work, then breeze-tripping for lunch, electro-ball in the afternoon, and eros parlors in the evening), suddenly there she was, a barefooted woman pacing in the wrong direction on the pedbelt. Slap of naked flesh on the conveyor. By matching her stride to the speed of the belt she managed to stay at the same point in the corridor, just opposite his doorway. Bustling along, yet

1

never stirring from her chosen spot, she reminded Phoenix of the conjoined whirl and stillness of a gyroscope.

Surely a madwoman. Escaped from the health patrollers. Phoenix backed rump against his apartment door just as it clicked shut. Embarrassed, he glanced down, but not before catching a glimpse of red hair escaping from the woman's hood, her cheeks showing feverishly through a skimpy glaze of cosmetics, her green gown actually darkened with perspiration below the arms and around the neck. The corridor trapped her scent, forced him to breathe it. Smell of hot animal. Her knees, thrusting against the gown at each step, nudged a raw spot in his brain. Just a beast, a throwback, he thought—and he felt aroused and ashamed.

By lowering his gaze he hoped to give the woman a chance to recover her senses, to withdraw from his life. But down below were those naked feet, slapping the pedbelt, and they sent his gaze skidding back up along her flanks and spine to the hooded face. So he had the misfortune to be staring at her luminous green eyes when she turned on him and said, "It's called walking, you idiot."

Abruptly she stopped her pacing and tugged the hood closer about her face; the conveyor hustled her out of sight.

Phoenix blinked. Gone back to her cave, he thought. Crawled under her rock. Good riddance. He filled his lungs slowly, emptied them. The ventilator banished her smell within seconds. Well, that's over, he decided.

But the image of her face—flushed, practically naked beneath the film of cosmetics—stuck fast in his memory. He went on to work, transferring from pedbelt to escalator to elevator, and eventually to the roller-chair that deposited him at his desk, where he bent as usual over the satellite monitors. But rather than hunt for signs of hurricanes, thermal inversions, radiation storms, for the thousand signs of Terra's assault on the human system, his eyes kept tracing the shape of the woman's face in the cloud patterns, the bulge of hip and breast in the contours of continents.

After work he yearned for something stronger than

breeze-tripping or electro-ball, so he proceeded directly to the gamepark for a day-ending orgy in the eros parlors, where he hoped to wipe the woman's image from his brain. At the door of the eros parlor he drew back, however. The rosy electronic din inside the lovebooths seemed distasteful. So he joined his cronies at the pharmacy, thinking he would take a chemmie. That would surely obliterate all memory of the barefooted walker. But as he tilted the drink toward his lips, something caught in his throat, and he set the chemmie back on the counter. As the shutters came down over the eyes of his companions, he slipped away from the pharmacy and rode straight home.

There was no barefooted woman pacing on the conveyor outside his apartment, of course, since both pedbelts were jammed with riders. Of course, Phoenix reassured himself. What do you expect? Patrollers would have caught her by now. Already be coaxing the beast out of her. Make her a good citizen of the Enclosure, no threat to anyone.

He spread his palm against the lockplate on his door, then stood there for a minute in the opening, glancing sidelong at the double stream of riders. All their feet were covered, their legs motionless, their heads properly hooded and wigged, their bodies hidden beneath gowns, their faces expertly masked. All as it should be. No one returned his wary glance.

It pained him to enter the apartment. The room's orderliness, which had comforted him that morning, oppressed him now. The dials glinted on his console, row after row, perfect circle after perfect circle. The glittering angles of his metal furniture seemed too harsh. Nothing invited his touch. The photo-murals on the wall were just then shifting their kaleidoscopic designs to mark the beginning of a new hour, but they could not be touched, they were only patterns of light. Feeling like an idiot—she had called him that, an idiot—Phoenix stood in the middle of the room, tongue hanging out, sniffing and tasting. Dead air, without taste or smell. Beastly smell she had. Sweat? Green eyes like flares.

He tossed a few pillows on the floor, left a cabinet standing open, and dragged half a dozen costumes from their hangers, but without any real hope of disturbing the order of the place. He oozed a dollop of veg from the food dispenser, sniffed it without appetite, then flung the green stuff down the recycle. Slumped in the softest chair, burning his lips on a cup of hot narco, Phoenix scrutinized the geography of his life, seeking some wild place that might accommodate the longing aroused in him by this barefooted woman.

Days ticked by. Each morning before work he peered out through the spyhole in his door, but with less and less fear—or was it hope?—of seeing her. Just when his life was composing itself again, when the clouds on the satellite monitors were beginning to resemble clouds again instead of lips and ankles, one day he looked out and there she was, pacing along in her sweat-darkened green. The lens of the spyhole made her appear swollen. Her naked feet seemed to dangle from a bulbous torso. Her head, with its fringe of red hair, bobbed ridiculously. Horrible, really, now that he had a good look at her. Wondering how such an unappetizing creature could have enthralled him, Phoenix boldly opened the door. It was a mistake. Her full stare caught him. Moist cheeks behind the glaze of makeup, long-boned feet, swim of legs beneath the gown.

This time she pronounced the words icily: "It's called walking. You should try it. Melt away some of that flab."

By reflex, Phoenix smoothed the gown over his cushiony stomach. Flab? How dare she refer to his body! The chill in her voice told him she had no memory of their earlier meeting. All these days while he had been suffering around Oregon City with her image spiked into his brain, she had salted him away in the vaults of forgetfulness together with a million other once-glimpsed faces.

"Do you mind?" she said, never breaking stride. "There's less traffic here. Fewer pedbelt zombies to compete with."

Looking away down the corridor he shook his head no, then in confusion nodded yes, unsure just what he was answering. The woman kept at her walking, matching the conveyor's pace. Phoenix shilly-shallied in his doorway, immobilized by a sudden vision of himself as he must appear to her: bouffant wig of iridescent blue, face painted to resemble the star of *Video Dancers*, every inch of flesh cloaked in a moodgown. And, yes, to tell the truth, a wee bit heavy in the paunch. He could not bear to look down at the fireworks of color he knew his gown would be making in its vain attempt to express his inner pandemonium.

"I don't mind." He felt his nostrils flare with the scent of her. "Why should I mind?"

"Good question. But there's a lot of drecks who do."

She smiled, and he winced. The smile, the private sharing of words, the eye contact, the exposed face—it was all coming in such a rush, shattering the rules of sexual approach.

Unable to bring himself to name a body part, he stammered, "Your walking things . . ."

"My feet?"

"Yes. Do they hurt?"

"Never. That's why I go barefoot, to keep them tough."

"And why have them tough?"

"So I can walk barefoot."

"But why walk at all?" Phoenix demanded in vexation. Before he could slice into her circular reasoning, passengers trundled around the curve, and the woman, with no attempt at disguising her smile, crossed to the other pedbelt and rode away out of sight.

For a long time he stood in his doorway, hoping. But traffic thickened in the corridor and the woman never reappeared. Or perhaps she did pass again, duly costumed and painted, camouflaged in the crowd. Passing, she might even have seen him, and still not been able to distinguish him from the hundred others who were decked out this morning in iridescent blue wigs, and whose faces were patterned after that video actor. Phoenix felt paltry, lurking there on his threshold, at once conspicuous and invisible.

Finally he surrendered to the day, to work, to an afternoon of lightshows, to an evening of brain-puzzles at the gamepark; and then he surrendered to the return home, to the waterbed, to sleep. Dreams of the barefooted woman stalked through his skull. An extra dose of narco did no good. A bout on the eros couch, with the gauge spun all the way over to visionary delight, offered only mechanical relief. Electronics could not reach the territory in his mind where the woman's image kept burning and burning.

Desire melted away what little order remained in his life. The apartment grew shabby. Friends stopped scheduling daykillers with him when he failed to show up a second time or a third. His costume suffered, at first from neglect and then from his deliberate search for idiosyncracy. He wanted to be visible to the woman when he met her again. So he hauled out unstylish clothes, ones that paid no attention to his body chemistry but just hung upon him in outrageous combinations. His wigs grew increasingly bizarre. His facepaint appeared slapdash, as if applied in the dark by a vindictive cosmetician. Wherever he went in Oregon City the glances of passersby slithered along at his heels.

He wondered how long he could traipse around like this before the health patrollers carted him away for a little hormonal therapy. Perhaps he should even turn himself in for a checkup. Judging by all he had been taught concerning health, he was a profoundly sick man. Yet he did not *feel* sick. He felt exhilarated.

At work the satellite photos looked more than ever like a stew of lips and breasts and trailing hair. His supervisor made him rewrite a third of the eco-warnings and advised him to cut back on the narco. But Phoenix was not applying narco or any other balm to his inflamed heart. Nothing half so vivid as this love-ache had ever seized him before, and he was in no hurry to escape the exquisite pain.

Days off work he spent vainly trying to discover some timetable in the barefooted woman's exercise. But he had no more luck than the ancients had at predicting sunspots. When she did loom into sight, he kept indoors, not yet ready to meet her again. Every night he paced with naked feet around the perimeter of his room. Five steps and then turn, five steps and then turn: the blisters multiplied on his soles. After two weeks of this, questioning his sanity at each step, he could walk for an hour without panting, and his feet began to leather over.

Training on the pedbelt was more risky, only possible at two or three in the morning, when anyone else traveling through the corridor would most likely be as eccentric as he. Soon he was able, with very little puffing, to stay abreast of his room for half an hour. Struggling to defeat the conveyor's ceaseless motion, he did not feel like a gyroscope—he felt like a lunatic.

On one of his three A.M. training sessions he was striding along, engrossed in the study of his feet, when her voice broke over him:

"So you tried it."

Looking up, he met the achingly familiar stare. "Yes," he mumbled. "I kind of wondered what it was like."

"And what do you think of it?"

"Oh, it's interesting." Witlessly he repeated, "Very interesting."

For several seconds the two of them paced side by side, two lunatics out for a stroll. From the corner of his eye Phoenix enjoyed the woman's profile, her skin showing more nakedly than ever through the paint, her legs kicking against the loose fall of gown. Elegant concentration of energy. The eyewall at the center of a typhoon, that's what she was.

"Good for the heart and lungs," she said.

"I suppose so," he agreed, shocked by her language.

"And legs."

He loosed the sexual word without thinking: "Legs."

The woman calmly continued, as if she were in stage seven of the mating ritual. "My name is Teeg Passio."

"Passio?"

"Something wrong with that?"

"It's just a famous name, that's all."

"Famous for the wrong reasons," she said. "My father . . ." she began in a tone of bitterness. There was a spell of silence, broken only by the pad of feet, the rumble of the conveyor. "And don't you have a name?" she eventually asked.

Phoenix could sense the expectant twist of her body as she waited for a response. "Name? Sure, sure. My name's Marshall."

"Only Marshall?"

"The back one's Marshall. Front one's Phoenix. Phoenix Marshall."

Her green eyes seemed to be measuring him. "You're not offended? About exchanging names?"

"No, no, certainly not," Phoenix boasted, with a show of bluffness. "I don't really accept all the . . . well, you know, the formalities."

"Stupid waste of time, aren't they?"

"Stupid, yes indeed."

"All this business about mating rituals," she proclaimed, dismissing his lifelong code of behavior with a sweaty stroke of her greensleeved arms, "and when you can exchange names, and when you can look in another person's eyes, and when your little fingers can touch. Ye gods. Idiocy."

"Idiocy," he mumbled, swept up by those passionate gestures.

"It's like a web, all these rules. Every time you want to open your mouth or lift your hand there's a rule binding you."

Phoenix heard himself agreeing earnestly. "Like a web, exactly. Everywhere you go you get tangled in it."

"Cut loose, is what I say."

"Cut . . . loose?" He stilled his tongue, alarmed by the turmoil her talk was stirring in him. He could feel the sweat trickling down his face, streaking the paint, dampening the collar of his moodgown.

"How often do you walk?" she asked.

"Oh, every day. Sometimes twice a day."

"Any special time?"

His eye was caught by the surge of flame-colored hair around the edges of her hood. His fingers twitched. "Morning," he said, then quickly added, "or night, just about any time. My schedule's flexible. And you?"

Her smile seemed to raise the temperature in the corridor several degrees. "I don't keep a schedule. But maybe we could set a time, meet for a walk. That is, if you—"

"I would. Yes, very much," he said with a rush.

"I know places we can walk without these jackass conveyors getting in the way."

Jackass? he wondered. But all he said was, "Anywhere's fine."

"How about Shasta Gamepark at 1600 tomorrow? South gate?"

"Sure," he agreed, reduced to monosyllables. "Fine."

"Peace." With palm lifted, she began to drift away on the pedbelt.

"Wait," he begged. In a panic he thought for ways to keep her, fearing that such an improbable creature might not survive until tomorrow. "Do you live in Portland Complex?"

She jerked a thumb domeward. "Seven floors above you." Walking again, she kept her place on the belt. Arched above her face the hair formed a red border of turbulence.

"And what brings you through here for exercise?" he asked.

"Looking for a walking partner."

"Oh." Again he scrambled for words. Her bluntness dried up his throat. "And why do you walk?"

The smile again, crippling all his faculties. "I'm in training," she said.

"Training?"

"For going away."

11 October 2026—*Astoria, Oregon*

Teeg and I watch an acorn woodpecker hammer a hole in the trunk of a dead fir, red topknot catching the sun. When the opening is just the right size and roundness, the bird taps an acorn snugly into it. Squirrels cannot dig it out. But the woodpecker can, and will, some February day when the bug population is running low.

Teeg's five-year-old eyes open wide in wonder. "Is it killing the tree, Mommy?" she wants to know.

"The tree is already dead," I tell her, "poisoned from the things people sprayed, and the woodpecker is using it for a cupboard."

And all the open cities are becoming husks, abandoned shells, as people flood into the domes. At least we can salvage the steel and copper, the aluminum and chrome, the bits of Terra tied up in the old places. The dismantling of Portland is nearly complete. Sad, plucked city. Brick streets and wooden houses are all that remain. I mourn by bringing Teeg out here to Astoria for a weekend, where we admire the acorn woodpecker. Astoria, thank God, will not be recycled, for it is built mostly of wood. The salt and wind and birds can have it. We have seen fourteen birds since yesterday morning, six of them able to fly.

TWO

Unlikely as it seemed to Phoenix, Teeg did meet him at the gamepark. Afraid she might not recognize him in the crowd of merrymakers and chemmieguzzlers, he wore the same mask and costume as yesterday. He would have dangled a sign about his neck, if need be, to attract her attention. Who cared a fig about the stares? He stood on a bench to make himself a landmark, high above the passing wigs, and presently he spied her slipping toward him through the crush of people. Facepaint instead of mask, baggy robe kicking at her feet, hood tied crookedly about her head. Thrown-together look, as usual.

"So you came," she announced, with what seemed like mild surprise. She drew him away from the racket of electronic warfare, past the simulators where people lined up to pretend they were piloting rockets or submarines, past the booths where ecstatic customers twitched upon eros couches.

"Zoo time," Teeg muttered, leading him on. She said something else, too, but Phoenix could only make out her

11

bitter tone and not the words, for two opponents were haranguing one another on a nearby shouting stage.

Why so angry? he wondered, following her along the pedbelt. As the conveyor banked around a curve, Teeg swayed to one side and her hip swelled against the fall of her robe. She seemed unconscious of her body. How could he begin mating ritual with a woman who ignored the simplest sexual rules? She might rip off his mask and lick his chin in front of everybody. Who could predict?

Soon they reached a deserted corner of the park, where the pedbelts gave out. Antiquated amusement booths, with shattered windows and dangling wires, were heaped on both sides of a disused footpath.

"This is left from a skategame kids used to play," Teeg explained, patting the scuffed walkway with her foot, "back when kids used their legs."

Legs again. Apparently she would say anything. Blinking at the body-word, Phoenix answered, "I remember, you hunched down like this," and he assumed the bent-knee posture he had perfected as a boy on skates. Looking up, he found amusement in her green eyes, and quickly looked away.

"So you were a skater?" she said, and then she was a squall of questions. What work do you do? Who are your parents? Any children? Ever go outside? How do you like living in Oregon City?

And so he told her about his training in geo-meteorology, his job studying satellite images ("Because I have a good eye for patterns," he boasted shamelessly, "something the cybers still can't match"), and he told her about his mother's death in the 2027 fusion implosion at Texas City, about living with his father who tested chemmies in New Mexico City, then about his father's bad trip and the eleven-year drug coma that followed. He mentioned his twenty-one years of schooling, the move to Oregon City a year ago after his father's death, the days at work and nights at the gamepark. His sperm was duly banked, he told her, but so far as he knew, none had been used. Eugenics probably thought one of him was enough. He admitted that he had begun the mating ritual with a bevy of women, but had rarely pursued it to—he paused, reticent—consummation. He confessed that he knew all about weather but had never stuck so much as his nose outside the Enclosure, confessed, in a voice that surprised him with its urgency, how restless he felt, how lonely, how trapped.

All the while Teeg was nodding yes, yes, that is truly how it is, and between questions she was telling about herself: She had spent most of her childhood in the wilds, traveling about the northwest corner of the continent with her mother, who had been in charge of dismantling Portland, Vancouver, Anchorage, lesser places. Her father was one of the architects of the Enclosure, a monster of rationality.

Teeg's last name finally plunked into a slot in his brain. "Passio? *Gregory* Passio? You're his *daughter*?"

"Yes," she replied. "That's the particular monster. You've heard of him?"

"He was one of my childhood heroes. He and Zuni Franklin. They made me want to be an architect."

"Then why're you a weatherman?"

"I got hung up on third-order topology. When the cyber simulated my buildings, they kept falling down."

"You don't need math for meteorology?" Teeg asked wryly.

"Sure, but not so much, not where I come in. After the cybers spit out the weather maps, I see the patterns. Gestalts. Kind of a right-brain thing."

She looked at him skeptically, the kind of look you would give a food-stick that seemed off-color. What did she think of him? Blue-wigged noodle-brain, or stage-seven lover? Impossible to tell. Talking with her was like tracking a typhoon—you never knew which direction she would take.

"Gregory Passio was my father all right. And not much of one. You could have picked a better hero." She paused. Her facepaint was so thin he could actually follow her turbulent emotions with a sidelong glance. "Don't mix him up with Zuni Franklin. She's a different fish altogether."

"Fish?" he said.

"You know, swimmy-swimmy?" She laced her fingers together and wriggled her joined palms in the air before her. Evidently the confusion still flickered in his eyes, for she explained: "I just meant that Zuni Franklin and my father both helped design the Enclosure, but for very different reasons. She's no monster."

"I don't understand."

"You couldn't," she said bluntly, and she went on to tell Phoenix how her father had made her come inside when she turned thirteen, legal breeding age. And then he had drowned while up supervising the construction of Alaska City. Now she worked mostly outside the dome, back on land, as a troubleshooter repairing tubes and transmitters and auto-machinery. Her ova had been used for eighteen— or perhaps twenty, she forgot—children, all of them grown inside other women. She had been mated three times, she told him, never happily, never long, twice with men and once with a woman.

"Eighteen offspring?" Phoenix whistled. In a steady-state population that was an astonishing number. Worthy of Eve in the old garden.

"That's what comes of having bright parents."

"Is your mother still outside?"

Teeg smiled crookedly. "I guess you could say that."

"Do you see her when you go on repair missions?"

"They killed her."

"Who killed her? What? The wilds?"

Instead of answering, Teeg swung away down the path, back toward the clanging heart of the gamepark.

A few days later they spent an afternoon at the disney, studying the mechanical beasts. "Timber wolf," a sign proclaimed, and there stood a shaggy creature with jaws agape and ribs protruding. Awful, Phoenix thought, as Teeg pressed the button and the wolf's jaws clapped open and shut, howling. But Teeg seemed to take some bitter delight in making the beasts perform. She led him on from "griffin" to "pterodactyl" to "African elephant," pressing every button, her mouth pursed and her eyes hard.

On other days they hiked around the hydroponics district, along hydrogen pipelines marked EXPLOSIVE, down aisles between huge whirling energy-storage wheels. Teeg's ID opened gateway after gateway. With each expedition she led him deeper into the mechanical bowels of the city, down several hundred meters below sea level where minerals and food and power were extracted from the ocean. Was it because of her famous father, Phoenix wondered, that Security allowed her to venture down here among these life-and-death machines? Red-eyed surveillance cameras greeted them at every turn. The few people they met in those lower reaches—technicians intent upon some repair or adjustment—pretended not to see them.

Phoenix discovered parts of Oregon City he had only known about from video. In his increasingly anarchic talks with Teeg, he discovered parts of himself he had never known about at all. Signals kept arriving from forgotten regions of his body, aches at first, then pleasures, as if nerve and muscle were conspiring with heart to make him love her.

Some two weeks after their first walk they descended one afternoon to the bottom-most level of the city, a labyrinth of tunnels reeking with brine. Teeg scooped up a handful of ocean water from one of the desalinization tanks, and said, "You forget the whole city is afloat, until you come down here."

Phoenix suddenly felt queasy, vulnerable, the way he felt when something reminded him of death. Yes, the ocean was always there, ready to burst the human bubbles that floated upon it. He gazed around at the mammoth pumps and extractors, listened to the slosh of water. Afloat. He recalled how Oregon City appeared in the satellite monitors: the central dome, and clustered around it the ring of smaller domes for manufacturing and aquaculture, for cancer wards and corpse freezers and mutant pens, then radiating outward from each dome the pipelines and tubes that linked the city to the rest of the human system. Viewed from the sky, set off against the vast curve of ocean, how fragile it all seemed.

He was relieved when they ascended to the workaday level of Oregon City again, up where the dome shut out sky and ocean, where the honeycombed buildings and pedbelts and shuttles reassured him of the power of mind over matter. Up here, nature did not exist. People everywhere, and the shiny things people had made.

"Do you work in the wilds all by yourself?" he asked her.

"Depends on the job. Sometimes on my own, sometimes with my crew."

"Did your crew mostly grow up outside the way you did?"

"Mostly. But a few of them were insiders, then got fed up. . . ." Her voice broke off sharply.

Phoenix tried to get her to say more about the crew. What would possess someone to work in the wilds? How could they stand the chaos, the filth? But she would not answer, so he let it go.

After a while he said, "That pass of yours seems to get you anywhere."

"I'm a master troubleshooter. That lets me work on any part of the human system, inside or out."

"How did you wangle that?"

"Zuni Franklin arranged it."

"You *knew* her?"

"Know her," Teeg corrected.

Phoenix was awed. It was like knowing Michelangelo, Buckminster Fuller, Alexi Sventov. "How did you ever get to meet her?"

"After my father made me come inside, he dumped me

with her every time he went off on a job. Thought she'd
teach me to love the Enclosure, forget my mother."

"I take it she didn't succeed."

Teeg laughed, a quick laugh that always punched him in
the wind. "No, she didn't teach me that at all."

The shadow of a glider flowed over them, and Phoenix
glanced up at the shiny belly of the machine. No walkers up
there. No walkers anywhere in the city, so far as he could
see, only the streams of cloaked bodies riding pedbelts or
coasting in the aluminum gliders overhead.

"She was a powerful woman," Teeg added.

"I'll say. She conceived this entire city."

"I wasn't thinking of Zuni Franklin," Teeg said impatiently. "I was thinking of my mother."

She stepped onto a pedbelt and he followed close behind.
Other passengers shouldered aside, and turned their masked
faces away. Probably thinking: here were two escapees from
quarantine. Mutants on parole. Phoenix tried to recall his
own mother. But he had only been four when she died, and
all he could remember was a square face with stray hairs
fluttering around it. Implosion. One of the last attempts at
sustaining fusion before they gave up the idea, and she had
been erased. Poof. His father, whom he had gone to observe
occasionally during the eleven-year drug coma, was hump-
nosed and pasty-skinned in his memory, a thing with
sagging mouth waiting forever to die.

After several moments Phoenix realized that he and Teeg
were drifting along, each one lost in a separate reverie, and
he wanted to connect with her again. So he stepped off the
pedbelt at Marconi Plaza and gently tugged at her sleeve so
she would follow.

The plaza was deserted, except for a few children in
power-prams. The fountain at the center, where Teeg and
Phoenix stood for a moment to watch the play of water,
smelled of brine. Shreds of money, torn up and flung there
by some mumbler of wishes, jostled on the surface.

"How have you kept your pass, thinking the way you do?" he asked her.

"They don't know how I think. I do my work well. I've never been caught breaking any machinery or any rules."

"But doesn't Security think it's a risk, letting you go outside?"

"Because I grew up in the wilds?" Teeg gave him one of her unsettling green stares. The paint on her cheeks was cracked and peeling. Paleness underneath. Her actual skin. "They don't have much choice," she said. "Not many people will take the work. Too messy out there, too dangerous. And the few of us who do go out—except the suicidal maniacs—wouldn't mess with the system. We know enough about the defenses to avoid thoughts of sabotage. The most I could do is just stay out there after some job, never come back. Outside, I'm no threat. It's inside the city I'm a threat."

Phoenix felt her eyes searching him for some response, and he pretended to be absorbed in watching his feet, his long-boned and brazenly naked feet, scuffling along beside hers. She had him so scrambled that he had given up even trying to calculate which mating rules they were breaking. Just don't get arrested for indecency, he thought, and otherwise ride the emotional rocket. "Do you think about that sometimes," he asked, "staying outside?"

"Sometimes," she confessed; then after a few more paces she added, "Often. All the time, in fact. In my twenty-nine years I've only lived in the city nine, maybe ten of them. Here's the place that seems alien to me," she said, sweeping both arms overhead, trailing the gauzy sleeves like wings, "and outside is home. Everytime, coming back inside, it's torture."

One moment the dome seemed to Phoenix impossibly high, higher than the sky ever could have been, and the next moment it seemed a brutal weight pressing down on him.

"It's like crawling back inside a bottle," she continued, "a huge sterilized bottle for culturing people."

A feeling of claustrophobia rose in his throat, nearly choking him, like the sour taste of food long-since swallowed and forgotten. He stopped walking, halfway across Marconi Plaza, and the city snapped tight around him. Apartment towers glistened feverishly with the trapped energy of several million lives; the pedbelts and glider-paths sliced the airspace into hectic curves; offices repeated the same honeycomb pattern, like geometrical stuttering, as far as the eye could see. The sudden pressure of the city on his mind was so awful that he did not notice for several seconds the lighter pressure of Teeg's hand on his arm.

"You never felt that before?" she asked gently.

"I guess I did," he answered. "I guess I've always felt that. I just never admitted it before. The frenzy—it's always there, like death, waiting. But I fight it down, hide it away."

"Make things tidy," she suggested.

"Exactly. Tidy, tidy. I put everything in order. And then at night I lie in bed and a crevice opens in my heart, and the dread creeps out, a fog, engulfing me. Death, I suppose. Nothingness." He stopped abruptly, ashamed of his passion.

"Yes?" she urged.

But he was too shaken to say anything more.

Without planning their next walk, they parted in Marconi Plaza. Phoenix rode the belt home, frightened by Teeg, by the crevasses she opened inside him. For the first time in weeks he was aware of the alarmed glances his helter-skelter costume and his bare feet provoked. Surely people would think he was crazed, afloat on a tide of chemmies, reverting to beasthood. Perhaps they would even notify the health patrollers. Rehabilitate him. But he could rehabilitate himself, could fight down the chaos that Teeg had loosed in him.

He didn't care if she was an alluring animal. He didn't care if she really was the daughter of Gregory Passio, or the intimate of Zuni Franklin. She would quickly destroy him if he didn't break free.

Safely back in his room, he scrubbed himself, dressed in his most fashionable moodgown and wig, then applied a fresh mask, painting very carefully, copying the face of a dance champion whose poster hung beside the dressing mirror.

He put everything in the apartment in its place. He ran the sanitizer. He gulped a double dose of balancers.

All that day and the next he rode through Oregon City, visiting eros parlors, attending rhetoric matches, watching electro-ball, clinging to his old entertainments. He played four-dimensional chess with Lon, designed murals with Chie, even resumed lackadaisical mating rituals with two women who had nearly forgotten him. With this one I had progressed to the touching of hands, he learned from the old mating charts, and with that one I had exchanged a five-second stare. But even while he tried to revive the passion that had once driven him into this prolonged sexual dance, he kept feeling the print of Teeg's hand on his arm, kept hearing the sound of her voice, so confident in its anarchism.

After three days of this charade, he gave up and called Teeg. She gazed directly into the vidphone, her face unpainted, her mouth a grim slash.

"I've been sick," he lied to her, turning away in confusion from her exposed face. "Chemistry's been out of kilter."

"Chemistry." She echoed the word as if it were a place he had gone to visit.

"How about a walk today?" he asked.

"Tomorrow," she said. "But let's not walk. I need you to get me some maps."

"Maps?"

"From work." She spoke in a voice as tough as the soles of her feet. "You do use thousand-to-one scale maps for weather grids?"

"Yes."

"Okay, I want the sections for the Oregon coast from 43° to 46°." Her bare face hovered on the vidscreen like a forbidden planet. "Your place. Nineteen o'clock. Any problem with that?"

"No," he answered hastily. "Is microfiche all right?"

"I'd rather have polyfilm prints I could keep."

"What for?"

She merely repeated the latitudes, as if he were a child with a porous memory.

Watching her naked face evaporate from the screen, Phoenix wondered what drove her to ignore the mating rituals, what urgency in her burned through all rules.

At greatest magnification the relief map shone upon the screen as a snarl of dunes, cliffs, inlets, river beds. Each landform was a distinct color, making a crazy-quilt of shades and textures. The disorder of it made Phoenix feel slightly nauseous.

"They don't supply you with maps when you go out for repairs?" he asked.

Teeg was crouching near the screen, haunches on bare heels, tracing the shape of a bay that hooked into the coast like a bent finger of blue. "No. I type in my work coordinates and the cyber guides my shuttle there. I just climb outside the tube and work on transformers, or cables, sometimes on the tube itself. There'll be mountains, maybe. Forests. Sometimes even deserts. But I usually don't have any clue where those things are on a map."

"Usually?"

"Some landmarks I remember from traveling with my mother, especially around the coastal cities south of Portland, the last places she dismantled." Pointing to the map, she crooked her finger to mimic the blue hook of water. "This inlet, for instance. I remember that place. Whale's Mouth Bay, my mother called it. She used to take me wading there. I think it was her favorite place. She took me there the last time we—"

"Wading in the ocean?"

A sudden fury made Teeg's eyes turn smoky, the same fury he had glimpsed on that first day when he had gawked at her bare feet. "Yes, the ocean. The stuff we're floating on, the stuff we're mining and eating and tapping for energy, the stuff we pump through Oregon City every day in billions of liters. What's wrong with wading in it?"

Instead of answering, Phoenix forced himself to look at the chaos on the screen. The only straight lines visible on the map were the tube routes, angling north to Alaska City and south to California City, or trailing away eastward, where further maps would show them reaching the land cities of Wyoming and Iowa, the float cities on Lake Michigan and Erie and Ontario, then farther east to the oldest float cities along the New England coast. At work, Phoenix preferred using a schematic map of the continent, which showed the hundred-odd land cities as bright red circles, the thirty float cities as green squares, the connecting tubes as stripes of black or yellow or blue. This entire scheme was superimposed on a grid of cyber coordinates, and behind it all lurked the shadowy outline of North America.

Queasiness finally made him look away from the screen. "You're going out there someday? To stay?"

Without turning from the map, she said, "The coast is all rocky along there. I remember some kind of yellow-flowering bushes in the spring."

"Are you?" he insisted.

She faced him now. "Who knows?"

"It's madness. Sure death."

"If you don't know what you're doing."

"And you know, do you? A few scrambled childhood memories, and you think you knew how to survive the wilds?"

"I can survive."

"Alone?"

Her fists unclenched, her body relaxed, a quietness came over her. "No, not alone. I'm never alone."

31 December 2026—*Portland, Oregon*

Enclosure Day. The hour had to come in some lifetime, I suppose, yet I wish it had not come in mine. Today, all around the Earth, health patrollers begin sweeping the reluctant ones into sanitation ports. Those who put up no fight are promised citizenship in the Enclosure. And those who resist? Will it be quarantine? The freezers? Oblivion?

The last salvageable pieces of Portland leave today by tube—all except a few materials I squirrel away, tools mostly. I am thinking this might be a place for Teeg and me to hide, later on, after the patrollers are satisfied that the wilds have been scoured clean of people. The winters are mild here. Two great rivers offer passage to the mountains and the sea. One could patch together a decent sort of house from the wooden shells. And in the spring, up in the park, there are roses.

Gregory beams me news that Oregon City is now fully operational, from tritium extractors and ocean thermal exchangers to sani-showers for the three million living units. His fat, greasy lightbulb of a head fairly glows on the screen. I am not cheered. He's also full of chat about that Zuni woman. Visionary of the Enclosure, he calls her. If she can stand him, she's welcome to him. When will Teeg and I be joining him inside? he asks. Never, I think, but do not say the word.

THREE

The only troublesome items Zuni had not allowed the surgeons to replace were her eyes. Both lungs, one kidney, various joints, even the valves of her heart, those she had been content to let go, for they did not seem to be intrinsic parts of her. Let the doctors fiddle with her ears or pancreas, she would not care. But if she ever gave up her eyes, the ones she had used to design the Enclosure, to memorize the contours of earth, to trace the shifting tones of daylight, she would no longer be Zuni Franklin. Would the surgeons consent to be fitted with new hands? They should have realized that an architect lives in her eyes.

So when the drugs no longer cleansed the blight from her retina, she had to put up with dimming vision. And when she announced her plans to retire from the Institute for Global Design at age seventy-six—nine years early— everyone assumed her balky eyesight was to blame.

"Are you afraid blindness would spoil your work at the Institute?" a video reporter asked her.

25

Zuni squinted into the camera lights. "It is true that I no longer see things as I once did."

"You mean you can't see well enough to work on blueprints?"

"I mean that vision changes with age."

"Eyesight?"

"Vision."

The reporter gave up trying to straighten out her replies. Better minds than his had been stymied by Zuni Franklin's ambiguities. "How much longer will you remain at the Institute?" he asked.

"Only a few weeks more. Long enough to wind up my affairs."

"Then you haven't set a final date? You might still be persuaded to stay on and oversee the completed design of Project Transcendence?"

They were seated in Zuni's office, surrounded on three sides by filing cabinets and display screens and consoles. The room was as stark and impersonal as an operating theater. Zuni had deliberately kept any trace of herself from showing, for fear of giving away her masquerade. The fourth wall, of glass, overlooked the towers and plazas, the curving transport belts, the dazzling geometrical shapes of Oregon City, a city she had largely designed. The sky ballet for the afternoon was an electrical storm, so projectors flashed sullen clouds upon the inside of the dome and loudspeakers occasionally muttered with thunder. A creditable imitation of ozone breathed from the fragrance ducts.

"No," she insisted. "I'm definitely retiring. But the precise date depends on the weather."

"Weather? You mean the sky ballet?"

The corners of her mouth turned upward. "I don't really mean anything, do I? Just an old figure of speech, from an old woman."

The reporter cocked his head to one side, listening to editorial directions arriving through his earphones. After a moment he nodded. Then he reversed the tape a few dozen turns. While the camera and recorder idled, he confided in Zuni, "Info thought the reference to weather would needlessly confuse the viewers. Would you mind pretending that our little exchange never took place?"

"Of course," Zuni agreed. Although the reporter was masked and wigged to resemble an elderly newsman who had been famous back in the television era, Zuni could tell from his nervous manner and wavering voice that he was actually quite young, insecure. Awed by the grand old architect of the Enclosure? she thought wryly. She would have to keep him from blundering onto dangerous ground. "I'll be more careful in my choice of words," she told him.

Reassured, the young man brought camera and recorder back to life. "So what are your plans for retirement?"

"Of no interest to the public, I'm afraid."

He laughed politely. "Come now. A person of your stature—"

"Very small, really."

"—of your fame—"

"Undeserved."

The young man forced himself to smile for the cameras. "Are you returning to private architectural practice?" he persisted.

"My plans would be very puzzling to you."

"Will you revise your *Philosophy of Enclosure*?"

"I have written all I care to on that subject."

"But surely you can't just abandon your lifework?" The reporter gestured overhead at the suspended model of the Enclosure, a spherical web of tubes and nodes. Each tube represented a transport artery, each node a land- or floatcity, and the emptiness inside the sphere stood for earth.

"There are others well qualified to carry on my work."

"But what of your mission to liberate humanity from Terra?"

Zuni pressed fingertips to fingertips and gazed at the wizened artificial face. Behind it she sensed the earnest features of the young man. They were all so earnest, these children of the Enclosure. "Humanity's escape from Terra is the logical outcome of all our past history. It will go forward with or without help from me."

"Many people are hoping you will write an autobiography."

Zuni scoffed at that.

"Perhaps you'll travel?"

"I have a journey to make," Zuni conceded.

"To the lunar colonies? The asteroids?"

"Not so far."

"Ah, then you'll be traveling inside the human system here on Terra?"

"On Terra, yes. Where else but here?" Her white hair was bound up neatly into a bun, her replies were neatly bound in a smile. She was notorious for her refusal to wear masks or wigs. The cameras showed her in filtered light, to spare video viewers the shock of seeing her naked face. It was not such an unforgivable eccentricity in a woman who had lived her first forty-odd years outside the Enclosure. Besides, her own face, benignly smiling, crisscrossed by wrinkles like a Martian landscape, was as hard to read as any mask. Like the antiseptic room where she spoke, everything about her was scrubbed clean of self.

"Will you be lecturing?" the reporter suggested. "Teaching young architects?"

"No, I will be learning again, from the wisest instructor."

"From Rupinski? Tei? Sventov?" The reporter named the only Terran architects whose fame rivaled Zuni Franklin's.

"None of those." Yes, she felt the man would certainly be under thirty. No one who had been born much earlier than Enclosure Day, back in 2026, could have spoken those names with such uncomplicated reverence. "You would not know this teacher at all."

"A designer?"

"Yes," she replied, "the greatest of all. But very little known."

* * *

For a week or two the video and newsfax chattered with rumors concerning her future. Zuni Franklin, dismayed by blindness, would have herself vaporized and blown into the air of her beloved Oregon City. On the contrary, she would have her face rebuilt and begin life over as an eros parlor madame. Or perhaps she would venture off into spiritual realms, in search of her dead colleague, Gregory Passio. No, no, she would disguise herself and lurk through every dome and pipeline of the Enclosure, like a queen incognito, inspecting the empire she had helped construct.

Perhaps, some commentators reflected, she was merely impatient to get on with the business of evolution, to push *Homo sapiens* farther from its animal origins, toward the realms of pure energy. She might stow aboard a trans-light ship. She might experiment with chemmies, with trances, with psi-travel. Or she might even be the first to have her brain transplanted into a cyber-field, and thus liberate mind yet further from the entanglements of matter.

Zuni was content to let them guess away, so long as they did not guess the truth. There was little chance of that, since the truth would have seemed to run counter to the drift of her life. For wasn't her name synonymous with the Enclosure? Hadn't she fought harder than anyone, harder even than Gregory Passio, to move humanity inside the global network of cities, to shelter humankind from the disease and chaos of the wilds? During the first two decades of the century, when the poisonous biosphere threatened to extinguish the race, she tirelessly preached the idea of a global shelter. She constructed models of the Enclosure, drew up detailed blueprints, described in mesmerizing language the glories of life inside that perfected world. If Terra is inhospitable, she argued, let us build our own habitat, as we have done on Luna and Venus and the asteroids. We can mine the air and ocean for materials. We can suck energy from sun and wind and tide. We can purify everything that enters our system, and admit only what is useful to us. The Enclosure can be the next home for our race, a wayhouse on our road to transcendence, and everything in it will bear our mindprint.

Knowing such things about Zuni, how could they ever guess her true plans?

6 November 2027—*Vancouver, British Columbia*
The Enclosure Act is not even one year old, and already the wildergoers have withdrawn into the Rockies, the Appalachians, and the Ozarks. Some few apparently still hold out in the Everglades and the bayou country. Beast people, the video calls them. Patrollers have scoured the plains and Gulf Coast and the shores of the Great Lakes. Rumors claim that all babies are stillborn among the renegades. Effect of the toxins? Or health policy? News about the cleansing— another video term—is hard to come by, especially from the other continents.

In his smug messages Gregory informs me that all the plutonium stockpiles have been "liberated" from the Fifth and Sixth World territories, which leaves them weaponless against the Enclosure. They realize the Enclosure's defenses will only grow stronger with each passing month, he says, so the last rebellious tribes are moving inside, coming home. Home! As if that rat-maze of bubbles and pipes and electronic skies and painted faces could ever be home for an animal who has walked on the earth.

FOUR

On the beach at Whale's Mouth Bay, amid boulders and sea gulls, Teeg lay roasting in the sun. Against her naked back and rump the sand felt like a thousand nibbling flames. Salt-laden wind fanned her hair. Even through the breathing-mask she could smell the ocean. Between repair missions, when she was required to stay inside the Enclosure, more than anything else she missed the feel of sun on her skin.

During this trip she quickly finished her assigned job—replacing fuel cells on a signal booster atop Diamond Mountain—and had three hours left over for scouting. Most of the time she used for discovering how hospitable a place the bay might be, testing for radiation, toxins, soil nutrients, the quality of water. These last few minutes of her allotted time she lay basking in the sun, as a celebration for having found the right place at last. She would have to make sure Whale's Mouth had been omitted from the surveillance net. It probably had, since no tubes or laser channels or signal avenues passed anywhere near the place. Just another

piece of real estate long since erased from human reckoning. She hoped so. Phoenix could tell her for sure. And
she would need to spend a week here, later on, to run more
tests on plants and microbes and air before she could assure
the other seekers that this was indeed the place for the
settlement.

Phoenix's maps had led her straight to the bay, her shuttle
flying low and coasting along on compressed air to avoid
the patrollers and the sky-eyes. On each repair mission,
stealing time to explore locations for the settlement, she was
more and more tempted to stay outside alone. But whenever
she wavered, all she had to do was close her eyes, think
about the plans for the settlement, and the faces of the seven
other conspirators would rise within her silence. She was
one of them, a limb of their collective body.

Lying there on the beach, she felt the sweat gathering in
her navel, between her breasts, on the slopes of her thighs.
The crash of surf against the volcanic walls of the bay sent
shudders through her. Occasionally an eddy in the wind
snatched the odors of fir and alder from inshore and filled
her with the pungency of green. Thoughts swung lazy as
hawks through her mind.

A sound pried her eyes open. Two gulls squabbling over a
fish. Life was creeping back into the land, the ocean,
though on nothing like the scale her mother used to tell
about. Her mother. Dead up north in Portland. Murdered.
Will I ever gather the courage to go there, Teeg wondered,
and look at the place where they killed her?

The cliffs surrounding the bay bristled with young trees
and bushes. Life reclaiming the land. The plants seemed
hardier than animals; they recovered more quickly, perhaps
because they had evolved in an atmosphere even more toxic
than the present one. She had noticed on this flight that there
were fewer scars of bare soil in the countryside. Perhaps, as
Zuni always insisted, Enclosure had been the only way of
halting the energy slide, the famine for materials, the
poisoning of the planet. If it *was* halted. An oceanographer

had confided to Teeg (one did not say such things in print or on video) that it might take another fifty years for all the toxins to wash off the land masses into the seas, and perhaps another fifty years before the oceans showed whether they could survive the poisons. "We might already be dead and not know it," he had whispered. "Or then again, the ocean may surprise us with her resilience."

Resilience. She liked that, the springing back of nature. She smeared the sweat across her belly, enjoyed the springiness of her own flesh. Womb inside there, where never babe did dwell. Enclosure. The great domed cities, wombs spun of glass and alloy and geometry. Mother helped provide the materials for them. Zuni and Father helped provide the designs. And I? I want out.

She propped herself on elbows and surveyed the bay. Yes, this was the place to build a colony—hills shouldering down to within a few hundred meters of the shore, then a meadow traversed by a sluggish river, and then the beach of black sand and black volcanic boulders. The north arm of the bay was a massive headland, topped by the ruins of a lighthouse. There was even an abandoned oil pipeline running along the old roadbed nearby, connecting across eighty kilometers of ocean to the tank farm in Oregon City. Ideal for smuggling out equipment and supplies.

When she had first visited this place as a child, on one of those rapturous holidays with her mother, the pipe had still carried oil and the shoreline had been half a kilometer farther west. Snags of the old coast were still visible as gray outcroppings, great broken teeth, farther out in the bay. On one of their recent outings Phoenix had assured her that the polar icepacks had stopped melting. "One more benefit from the transition to solar living," he explained. That meant the new coastline would probably remain stable for a while.

A strand of marsh grass blew along the sand, clung to her ribs like a green wound. She peeled it away and wrapped it about her left thumb. Will Phoenix decide to come out here with us? she wondered. The grass made a vivid ring on her sun-pinked flesh. Sitting up, she hugged her knees. Can he shake himself free of the city? And will the others let him join our circle?

A bank of clouds shut away the sun, and the air grew chill. Teeg rose, slapped sand from her legs and buttocks. Cleaning grit from her back would have to wait until she took an air-shower at the sanitation port. Despite the chill, her body still felt atingle from the sun. She slithered into boots and shimmersuit, tightened the breathing-mask over her face. Through goggles the bay still looked beautiful. Running shadows marked the passage of clouds across the knobby black walls of the cliffs. Surf exploded rhythmically on the boulders. She wanted to make love with that roar in her ears.

Aloft in the shuttle, Teeg hovered for a minute over the beach, before heading inland toward the nearest port. She skimmed across the meadow, sun winking in the river, then she climbed the foothills at a height some ten meters above the tips of spruce and hemlocks. There was joy in balancing the tiny craft on its cushion of air, riding the thermals like a falcon. From above, the slopes looked solid green, a carpet of moss, as if you could walk from treetop to treetop without ever touching the ground. Some patches still showed brown where the last clear-cuts had not yet mended, or where toxins had concentrated. But everywhere the forest was coming back. The oceans provided cheaper substitutes for cellulose, without all the mess of lumbering.

Between the first range of hills and the somber mountains, she could just make out stretches of the old coastal highway. Scraps of concrete and tar showed through the weeds. In places the ocean had backed into valleys and covered the roadbed. A charred clearing beside the road and a scattering of rubble marked the location of a dismantled town, probably some fishing port. The map Phoenix had given her mentioned neither road nor town, identified nothing but landforms and the frail web of tubes.

From the peak of the next range she spied, away down in the mountain-shadowed Willamette Valley, the glowing travel-tube. Its translucent glass pipes, frosty white and glittering like an endless icicle, stretched north towards Vancouver City and south towards the clustered domes of California. Whenever she glimpsed the tube system or the domes from outside, she was amazed at their grace, and she thought of her father. Whatever shape you could reduce to a mathematical formula, he would weep over. But that was the only beauty he had ever learned to see.

While Teeg watched, a freighter poured its flash of blue lights through the northbound tube.

She let the shuttle skip lightly on the updrafts along the far side of the coastal range, dipping down into shadows. The valley stretched away north some two hundred kilometers to Portland, her mother's place, the place of death. Teeg shivered, trying to shut the scene back in its mental cage. Yet I must go there, she thought, go and face whatever remains of her.

In the shadowed valley she looked for the yellow beacon that marked a gateway to the Enclosure, her thoughts drifting, as they often did, from her mother to Zuni, who had grown up in one of the lumber towns on these slopes. Sheep used to graze in this valley, Zuni would tell her, and the hills were green with mint, and fruit trees covered the terraces like ornate stitchery. Teeg had always been surprised, the way the older woman's eyes would soften when she told about the Willamette Valley.

Can I tell her about Whale's Mouth Bay, about the settlement? Teeg wondered. No, no, she decided, it would be madness to confess this hunger for the wilds to the mother of the Enclosure.

Fly the shuttle, she reminded herself. There must be no mistakes on re-entry. Each time she returned from a mission she feared they would demand proof that all her time had been spent making repairs. But the insiders who staffed Security never dared go outside, so they grew more ignorant of the wilds each year. With no idea how long a repair job should take, they let the wildergoers alone.

At the junction of the Willamette and McKenzie Rivers she spotted the yellow beacon of the sanitation port. Come here, the beacon seemed to promise, come here all you who have wandered from the human system, come and we will purify you, bathe you in artificial light, admit you once again into the charmed circle of the city.

8 January 2028—*Vancouver, British Columbia*

From the platform where I supervise the dismantling of Vancouver, I can watch through binoculars as health patrollers search the ruins for wildergoers. When sonics drive the renegades out of hiding, gliders swoop down, stunners freeze them, and the patrollers bind them in nets. Rehabilitation centers are the next stop. I am told that many elect suicide. Most conform.

Every day my credentials are checked, and those of my crew, to make sure we are legally entitled to remain outside. They examine Teeg with grave suspicion. Why is a child outside? they demand. She is six, seven, is she not? She belongs inside, in school, in safety. They look at me as if I were a savage, to keep my child with me in the wilds.

Gregory throws me the same accusing looks from the vidphone. Zuni Franklin would look after Teeg as if the child were her own daughter, he promises. No doubt, no doubt, and suck the blood from her in the bargain.

FIVE

The image of Teeg squatting beside the map screen kept burning in Phoenix's mind. The geography of Oregon and the imagined geography of her body merged for him into one sensuous landscape. He tried calling her after the evening of maps, to apologize, to arrange a walk, anything to be near her. But her answering tapes informed him she was meditating, she was at the clinic, she was on a repair mission, always somewhere painfully out of reach. He could not have felt a greater craving for her if they had sparred through all twelve stages of the mating ritual.

When he finally did track her down, overtaking her at the bottom of the firestairs as she began her daily seventy-story climb, she told him she was about to leave for a two-week seminar in Alaska City. Something to do with thermionics.

"Look, can I go with you?"

"Phoenix—"

"I can arrange leave. We can talk after your classes. We can walk in the disney there. It's a fine one—famous—with mechanoes of beasts from all the continents—"

37

"Phoenix!"

He hushed. She let him chill for a few seconds. Then she calmly told him, "Another time. This trip I'm very busy. Understood?"

Breathless from the stairs, he halted at the next landing and let Teeg climb ahead by herself. Something about the determined swing of her hips, something in the angry strength of her climbing, so alien to everything he had been raised to believe about the body, convinced him she really would slip away from Oregon City one day, enter the chaos of the map, and never look back. That meant annihilation, first of the mind, cut off from civilization, then of the body, poisoned or broken or devoured by the wilds. Dizziness sat him down upon the landing. The metal felt cold through his gown. With eyes closed he listened to Teeg's bare feet slapping on the stairs above him, fainter and fainter as she climbed.

Yes, the work coordinator assured him, Teeg Passio was on a two-week leave. Yes, the Preservation Institute informed him, a Teeg Passio was signed up for the thermionics seminar. But when Phoenix reached Alaska City, driven there by his desire to see her, he found she had never registered with travel control, nor with the health board, nor with the Institute. The officials studied him cautiously. Do you need a psyche session? they inquired. No thanks, he assured them. Just unbalanced by the change of air. But our air is the same as yours, surely? Yes, of course, he explained, fatigue, nothing more.

His return to Oregon City was delayed by a leak in the seatube—one of his colleagues evidently had failed to warn about a hurricane or a shift in ocean current—and by the time his shuttle was on its way he felt crazed. The curved walls, the molded seats, the incessant loudspeaker babble: everything squeezed in upon him. Bottle, he kept thinking, glass bottle.

Back in Oregon City he could discover nothing more

about her going. Do you want us to list her as missing? the
health patrollers asked. Put a trace on her? No, Phoenix
answered, backing away. She'll turn up. Just a misunderstanding.

He even considered phoning Zuni Franklin, to see if she
knew where her protégé had gone. But no, Teeg had moved
away from Zuni years before. And besides, a person of Zuni
Franklin's august reputation probably would not answer his
call.

Nothing to do but wait, and turn over the possibilities
one-by-one like cards in a game of solitaire: She had lied to
him about going to Alaska City? She had been mangled by
some piece of machinery? She had gone outside to stay?
The maps, he thought: perhaps that was all she had ever
wanted from him. She might even have known he was a
geo-meteorologist, might have lured him with her walking
just to get hold of them. But no—that was nonsense. How
many people would have opened their doors to find her
outside walking, barefooted, and felt nothing but mild
alarm or loathing? She could never have predicted the fierce
hunger the sight of her triggered in him, this boiling-over of
restlessness. She could not have known he would envy her
for living in a space less entangled than his own, a space in
which voice, eyes, arms seemed to move in gentler gravity.

In those two weeks of fretting he discovered how little
presence of mind his ordinary life required. He traveled
through the city, performed the necessary bows and signals
in conversation, processed skeins of satellite photos, fed
himself at the cafeteria, even played mediocre chess, all
without diverting his thoughts from Teeg. He was convinced she had gone outside, into the chaotic world of the
map. At odd moments—while a lightshow played on the
screen or the eros couch worked at him with its electronic
charms—he would visualize that map in all its unruly
colors, and he would imagine her as a tiny laboring speck
lost in it, lost climbing through mountains, lost wading in
the blue hooked finger of water.

If she came back—when she came back—she *had* to come back—he would find some way to keep her from ever again putting him through this agony. Make her take him with her next time. But not outside. Somewhere human, safe, the inland cities, the spas. Anywhere but the wilds. And he would persuade her to change jobs, never go outside again. And if she insisted on going, then he would inform on her as a health risk, get her wilder-license revoked.

And then she'd be trapped in this bottle as surely as I am, Phoenix admitted. Trapped—but alive, insulated from the hostile disorder out there, shielded from disease, from weather, beasts, hunger, pain. It was simple nostalgia, he told himself, this yearning for the wilds, a mixture of childhood memories and antique books. Yet part of him was not persuaded, the part that trembled with ancient rhythms when he was in her presence.

His fingers shook as he punched the code for the health board. He explained his concern to the mechano face on the phonescreen, but without giving Teeg's name.

"Then you want Infection Division," the mechano said, its jaw slightly out of synchronization with the words. It was an old model, bearing the stylized markings for mouth, nose, eyes, like a child's drawing.

Soon Phoenix was talking to another mechano, which patiently recited the relevant portions of the code: Only licensed wildergoers are permitted to leave the human system, and only for authorized functions. Such personnel must be sanitized before re-entering the human system. Any persons breaking this code, either by leaving without authorization or by returning without decontamination, constitute an infection threat, and will be treated as beasts.

"Treated as beasts?" Phoenix echoed.

"One who deliberately endangers the human system becomes a part of Terra—a beast," the mechano explained.

"I see, of course."

Within seconds the lightsticks began glowing on his informat, printing a form headed INFECTION ALERT.

Fingering the slick polyfilm sheet, Phoenix asked the mechano, "And if the person is a licensed wildergoer?"

"First offense, revocation of license. Second offense, quarantine. Third, exile. Fourth, extermination." The mechano paused for what seemed to Phoenix a carefully measured space of time. Then it asked, "Do you wish to report name and circumstances?"

"No," Phoenix replied. "I am merely concerned. I have no evidence."

"Very well." Again the measured pause, the scrutiny by an eyeless face. "Infection from the outside is the gravest remaining threat to the human system. You do not wish to report?"

"Not at the present time."

Only when the mechano vanished from the screen did Phoenix realize that he had been addressing it in polite mode, with face turned at right angles, eyes lowered, body rigid, as if this machine, animated and sightless, were the most appealing of human strangers. Two weeks without Teeg, and already the web of inhibitions was tightening around him again.

The messages he left on her answering tape all made the same plea: *Call Phoenix Marshall immediately upon arriving. His sanity at stake.*

When she finally did appear it was not on the screen but at his door, hood thrown back to reveal an unkempt blaze of red hair, face bare of paint, yet reddened in a way he had never seen before. It was like having a bomb delivered. Phoenix hastened her inside before the neighbors caught sight of her.

"I hate those things," she explained, pointing a finger with a broken nail at his phone.

"How did you like the seminar?" he asked her carefully.

"I never went to Alaska City."

Watching her pad familiarly about his room, Phoenix looked for some taint of wilderness on her. Her wrists and ankles, escaping from the cuffs of her haphazard gown, seemed to be the same uncanny shade of red as her face. Did the sun do that? Her smell ran like a fire in his nostrils. He sensed a lightness in her movements, a thinning of gravity, as she sniffed at a bowl of protein pellets.

"Ugh." She grimaced.

"So where did you go?" he said.

She yielded him a faint smile. "Away."

"Outside? For two weeks?"

"Whale's Mouth Bay, to be precise. Look." From the pouch in her gown she tugged the map, now rumpled from many foldings. Squatting cross-legged on the floor, she spread the polyfilm across her lap and eagerly pointed where he expected her to point, at the blue finger of ocean that hooked into the Oregon coast about 44°.

"I guessed that was the place Mother and I used to go. And it was. The water's colder than I remembered, and the beach is narrower, but it's lovely."

"You were there all by yourself? With the beasts and poisons?"

"The only beasts are a few bedraggled sea lions and gulls."

A parade of childhood pictures began streaming through his mind. "You saw actual sea lions?"

"Not only saw them—smelled them. And the rock flowers! The spray! You've got to come see."

And so she went on for an hour, for two hours, in a delirium of talk, tracing her explorations on the map, pulling at his hands as if to lead him there that very moment, looking up occasionally to read his face. Unable to halt the parade of visions from his own childhood, Phoenix kept himself turned away. The desire he felt for her, and the dread, swelled to encompass the sea lions, the fossils, the slender ferns she told him of in her enraptured voice.

"Fossils!" she cried, as if this single word should convince him to share the delirium with her. "Leaves and ferns and even—once—a three-toed footprint between the layers of slate. And in the shallows of a great drowsy river I found some reedy things growing that Mother used to call cattails. Isn't that a name? And birds! Why doesn't video ever show any landscape with birds—or even with trees? Oh, just come look!" And she grasped both his hands in hers and tried to dance him round the room. But his legs would not bend, his whole body was rigid with the effort of containing his inner tumult. He wrenched his hands free.

"Teeg, you've got to promise never to go outside again."

She laughed once, harshly. "Dream on. Haven't you been listening to me?"

"You can't recreate that old world. You can't crawl back into your mother's lap. All that's finished."

"I don't need to create anything. It's all there, waiting. All I have to do is walk into it."

"To a brutal death."

Stretching her arms wide, she spun in a circle, gown and hair aswirl. "You see any wounds?" He shrugged, avoiding her stare. But she danced sideways until he was facing her again, looking into her inflamed eyes. "Hasn't your body taught you anything after all these months of walking? We were *made* to live out there, shaped to it. Look," she said, her voice softening, "just think about it. People've been inside—what? twenty-four, twenty-five years? Not even a generation. And before that humans lived outside for how long? Millions of years."

"In misery, sickness, and constant fear."

"Not always, not everywhere. Some people lived truly, handsomely."

"So tell me about Eden."

"Forget myths. I'm talking about real communities of people, living outside in harmony and simplicity. Listen, some of us want to try it, try making a place out there—"

"You can't go back."

"Who said anything about going back? I'm talking about going forward."

"No!" He clapped hands over ears, frightened by what she was offering.

"Phoenix, please listen—"

"No no no!"

When at last he looked up, she was gone, the door standing open. On the threshold rested a small gray parallelogram of stone. Stooping warily over it, he could see the faint imprint of a leaf in the surface—or perhaps it was a fern; it had been many years since he had looked at pictures of plants. With a tablemat he scooped up the stone, held it near his face. There was a faint smell of damp. The tiny veins of the leaf formed a riotous maze of intersecting lines that reminded him of the map's labyrinth of rivers. Had it been decontaminated? Where had she found it, in what mire out there? For a long time he hesitated, fingers poised a few centimeters above the stone. And then at last he touched the mazy indentation, gingerly, so as not to injure himself. The delicate lines of the fossil proved hard, harder than his cautious fingers.

The stone felt cold in his palm, slick with perspiration, as he shifted from foot to callused foot before her door. That was her doing, the calluses, the twitching in his legs, the lust for escape. Passengers streamed by on the pedbelts, slashing him with their glances as he debated what to do. But he ignored them, and that also was her doing. Should he report her, get her wilder-license revoked, then try coaxing her into sanity again? Could he betray her that way? Or should he let her make those journeys outside, each one longer, until, one day, she failed to return? Could he actually go out there with her?

His heart raced faster than it ever had from their walking or stair-climbing.

At last he rang, and the door clicked open. For the first time he entered her lair, smelling her, but unable to see anything in the dim light. He groped his way forward. "Teeg?"

"In here."

Her voice came from a second room, visible only as a vertical streak of blue light where the door stood ajar. With halting steps, hands raised to fend off obstacles, Phoenix picked his way through the darkness toward the blue slither of light. As he approached, the door eased open, forcing him to shield his eyes from the brightness. Swimming in the wash of blue was Teeg's silhouette, not naked, surely, but with arms and legs distinctly outlined. Was she in her working gear, a shimmersuit?

"I found this," he said, reaching the fossil toward her in his open palm.

"That was for you to keep," she snapped. "A gift for parting."

"I didn't come to return it. I came to have you read it for me—tell me what it means—tell me—I don't know." He halted in confusion. The hard edge of her voice, the blue glare, the inner turmoil made his eyes water. "You've got to be patient with me."

"So you'll have time enough to file that infection alert?"

"I didn't mean for you to see that."

"No, I'll bet you didn't."

"I won't file it. I can't."

She studied him. "Why did you get it in the first place?"

"I just wanted to keep you," he stammered.

"What do you mean, keep me?"

"Keep you safe, keep you inside."

"Well I won't be kept inside, you hear me? Not by you or the health board or *anybody*."

His eyes still watered, but he could make out her swift movements as she paced about the room gathering vials and cassettes and food capsules into a massive carrycase. It was a shimmersuit she wore, silvered to reflect sunlight, clinging to her like a second skin to allow for work on the outside. The disclosure of her body embarrassed him. Even in stage ten of the mating ritual he had never seen a woman so exposed.

"Where are you going?" he demanded.

"I'm not waiting here to be arrested."

"You're not going back outside?"

"Eventually. A few of us together, back to the wilds, home." She slammed the carrycase on the floor. "What do you think I've been wooing you for, you colossal idiot? We wanted a few more people, to build a little colony." A shove from her boot sent the case skidding across the floor. "So when you came out walking I thought maybe you wanted your body back. Maybe you wanted out of the bottle."

"You never told me."

"I didn't want to spell it out. I wanted you to hunger for the wilds the way I do." Her anger drove her prowling back and forth in front of him. Beyond her, directly under the hanging blue lamps, he could see a glass tank filled with a writhing mat of green. Plants? In the city? Her angry stalking drew his eyes away.

"But how can I want what I've never had?" he protested. "This is all I know." With outspread arms he gestured to indicate the floating city, the thousands of miles of travel tubes, and the dozen other cities he had lived in or visited, always inside, always insulated from the beast world.

She stopped her prowling in front of him. In the clinging shimmersuit her body trembled like quicksilver. Her stare no longer made him wince. And he noticed her eyes were almost the same gray-green color as the slate he still held stupidly in his hand. "All you know," she murmured, grasping him by a wrist. "Then come look at this."

She led him to the glass tank, drew him down to kneel with her and peer through the translucent wall. Inside was an explosion of tendrils, petals, stems, dangling frail seed pods, fierce blossoms like concentrations of fire, all of it in greens and browns and reds so vibrant they made Phoenix tremble. His eyes hunted for a leaf that would match the fossil she had given him, while his thumb searched out the delicate imprint in the stone. But there was too much activity in this amazing green stillness for him to see anything clearly.

"It's a terrarium," Teeg said. "A piece of the earth."

He ran his fingers along the glass wall, expecting to feel heat radiating from these intense creatures. But the tank was cool, sealed on all sides. "They're alive?"

She laughed at what she saw in his face. "Of course they're alive. That's dirt, the brown stuff."

"But how—closed in like that?"

"Wise little beasts, aren't they?" And she used the word *beasts* tenderly, as he had never heard it used before. "There's your chaos," she said. "That's what you're saving me from."

Phoenix started to protest that this was only a tiny fragment of the earth, without animals, without tornadoes or poisons or viruses, without winters. But his tongue felt heavy with astonishment. His eyes would not move from this miniature wilderness, at once so disorderly and so harmonious.

"Well," she said, her fingers tightening on his wrist, "will you go?"

"I might," he answered. And then, uncertainly, "I will."

1 July 2028—*Whale's Mouth Bay*
There is a humbleness in stones, a patience, a yielding to weather and to the restlessness of earth. Teeg gathers them by the bucketfuls, stooping low over the gravel bed so her little bottom rises like a peach. The sun turns her a warm sienna hue. When a stone amazes her, she brings it in her muddy palm for me to admire. Look, Mommy, another miracle!

Together we study fossils, cracking the slate with a hammer. She thumbs through my old ragged field guide for pictures that match what we find in the hearts of rocks. We walk around on so many thicknesses of history.

More and more I feel like a fossil myself, squeezed beneath the enormous burden of the future—at least what Gregory assures me is the inevitable future, the life shut up inside the antiseptic human system, life barricaded from what he calls the beast world. The Enclosure Act is not even two years old, and already the resistance movements are broken.

Soon there will be no one left outside except the sick and the vicious and the mad.

I only have Anchorage and Vancouver left to dismantle, and the small coastal cities in Oregon, and then my commission expires. "If you refuse to come in when the work is finished," Gregory warns, "if you insist on reverting to bestiality, you still must deliver my daughter to Oregon City." "Teeg stays with me," I insist. "The Enclosure Act, the health board—" he huffs at me, but I break contact and his voice withers away.

The stain on this page comes from Teeg's muddy paw, plumped down here to display a treasured fossil. I make no attempt to wipe it clean.

SIX

While friends and journalists speculated about her plans for the future, Zuni quietly went on severing the ties that bound her to the Enclosure. She delivered the last of her scheduled lectures (on the psychology of disembodied mind), speaking as usual for two hours, without notes, holding the audience spellbound, and then she declined all further engagements. She resigned from boards of directors, task forces, committees.

For the better part of a month she sorted through her files, assigning to the archives whatever she thought might be of use to future planners, piping the rest to recycle. There were sixty years' worth of blueprints here, beginning with plans for a ten-kilometer-square greenhouse she had designed at sixteen. Even so large a greenhouse, she had discovered, would not sustain a complex eco-system. Trees might thrive in it, but hawks could not. And if she altered the design to accommodate hawks, the ferns might die. Cyber simulations taught her that the smallest environment capable of sustaining a continent's menu of life would be the size of the continent itself.

Soon after age sixteen she had given up the notion of creating glass refuges for nature, and had begun designing human habitats. All the plans were there in her files, graduated in scale from single-person dwellings to planetary skeins of cities. Leafing through those early drawings—tents for backpackers, two-person space arks, bubble-villages for the ocean floor, flower-shaped colonies—Zuni was amused by their modesty. Between dreaming up tents for a single person and dreaming up a planetary Enclosure, her mind had gone on a long journey.

Not her mind alone, of course. Nature always unfolded in many persons at once. Beginning with the designs for villages, most of the blueprints listed Gregory Passio's name alongside hers. Zuni found it hard to recall, from this distance in time, which lines Gregory had drawn and which she had drawn herself. Others shared the confusion, for people soon began to treat the two of them as a composite creature, Franklin-Passio. He had been the greater technician, she the visionary. Most often she would conceive a structure, and Gregory—trained in the harsh conditions of Venus, where any miscalculation converted a habitat into a tomb—would reduce it to numbers and materials. When one of their structures was being assembled, he would oversee the building, while she rested content with the drawings. The transformation from numbers on a page to airy geodesic skeletons arching against the sky never ceased to amaze him. One of those building-site visits cost him his life, when storms capsized his floating rig off the Alaska coast.

"I'm a random element," that was how Gregory had always liked to describe himself. "I'm one of those little leaps nature takes every now and again. Most of us are flops."

Looking at him, Zuni had found the evolutionary leap easy to believe. Gregory was a tiny man with an oversized head, and even in those early days he was already bald. His vision as a child had been defective in such complicated ways that surgeons were forced to anneal multi-focal lenses to his eyes. Since he had no use for wigs or facepaint, his swollen dome and blue-veined face and faceted eyes were exposed for everyone to see, and made him look unearthly.

Zuni remembered most vividly their earliest collaborations, back in the first decade of the century, when she and Gregory and thousands of others had worked feverishly to devise a habitat that would preserve at least a remnant of humanity from the wreckage of the environment.

"What we need are a few billion self-sustaining modules," Gregory had maintained. "Like the exploration capsules we used on Venus. One per person."

At first Zuni had imagined he must be kidding. "Wouldn't that be a bit lonely, each of us in a separate box?"

"Oh, a man and woman could plug their modules together. Families could lock their units into a cluster."

"And when people grew tired of one another, they could just unplug?"

"Correct. Like our bodies, only better." There was no trace of a smile on Gregory's blue-veined face. "Doesn't that sound appealing?"

"It sounds awful. Like Brownian motion—dust particles bumping together and then careening off to some new collision."

"So what's your alternative?"

"Cities."

"You'd actually rather live in a city, jammed together with millions of other people, than in your own free-roaming capsule?"

"At least in the cities one could touch other people. And keep civilization alive."

Confronted by such evidence of mental aberration, Gregory would shrug, wrinkle his expansive forehead, then lapse into silence. And that was how their early debates about future habitats usually ended.

Gradually she chipped away at his notion of living-boxes with the tool he most respected—numbers. "Fabricating and supplying a few billion private modules would take many-powers-more energy and materials than my cities would."

"And where do we get enough materials even for your cities?"

"We mine the dumps and junkyards for metal. We dismantle the old cities, the burned-out factories, the abandoned machinery. We haul the rockets out of their silos and the wrecks out of the ocean, melt them down. There's plenty around to build a thousand cities or so, connect them with pipes, enclose them with domes. But not enough for your billions of hermit igloos."

Once Gregory had conceded the materials argument, Zuni challenged his enthusiasm for the free-ranging nomad. "You'd really trust all those billions of people, swarming anywhere they wanted to?"

"Why not?" he countered.

"Poking their noses into the nuclear graves? Tinkering with the weather-monitors? Snipping data lines?"

"We never had much problem with that on Venus."

"Because the population there is only a few thousand, and everybody's carefully selected."

Gregory had always found it difficult to understand ordinary people, and so Zuni's catalogue of possible mischief gave him pause. "Cut data lines? Scatter the plutonium? Would people actually *do* such things?"

"Listen, Gregory, if you turned seven billion people loose to go anywhere they wanted on this planet, each in her own capsule, there would always be a million people eager to work any sort of stupidity you could imagine. And a great many sorts you couldn't imagine."

Having been persuaded that Terra's population was less trustworthy than the elite population of space colonists, Gregory began adding to the catalogue of possible mischief. "Just think of the transformers, the deserts full of mirrors, the tide-generators. Somebody could block a laser avenue. And the whole electromagnetic spectrum is vulnerable to jamming."

"You see," said Zuni. "And suppose people keep dumping their wastes? Who's to stop them? And how much more will the eco-system absorb before the balance gives way completely?"

That brought a suspicious look from Gregory. His eyes reflected multiple chilly images of her. "Once we're sealed inside—capsules or cities—what does eco-balance matter? The planet's hostile already. We can cope with a little more hostility."

"Not really hostile, not when you think of Venus, say."

The wrinkles were plowing across his great forehead. "Zuni, you're not turning into some sappy nature-lover, are you?"

Here was unstable ground. At any moment a fissure might open, separating them forever. Zuni phrased her answer carefully. "It's not a matter of loving or hating. It's a simple question of survival. We're scrambling now to put a roof over our heads before the environment collapses. Why make matters worse?"

"True, in the short run. But in the long run, who cares? If the algae die, and carbon dioxide builds up, we can always get oxygen from rocks."

"Of course we can," Zuni soothed. "But the ocean's still doing a pretty good job with oxygen. Let's just help it keep working, and we'll be free to build the habitat."

"As soon as we're safe inside," Gregory insisted, "the eco-system can go smash, and we'll get by without it."

Gregory's yearning for liberation from the planet ran so deep in him that Zuni treated it as she would treat any religious impulse—with tolerance and silence.

Always a lover of solitude, whose idea of the perfect life was a one-man interstellar flight, Gregory had been reluctant to accept her scheme for a global network of cities. He was not even moved by her argument that no other plan

would preserve as many people from Terra's mounting
inhospitality.

"Humanity's the one item we have in surplus," he
commented sourly.

What had finally convinced him to work on the Enclosure
was a combination of esthetics and religion. He discovered
that it was far less challenging to design a one-person
capsule than to design an entire city. And he eventually
admitted that only the Enclosure was large enough to
sustain a civilization; only a sophisticated technical civilization could ever lift entire cities free of Terra. After a few
decades of operation on Terra, the system Zuni proposed
might be sufficiently perfected and powerful to venture off
into space, not merely to establish a colony elsewhere, but
to *be* a colony, a wholly human world free to drift forever
through the universe. Project Transcendence, Gregory had
named it. And that leap into space was the vector he had
been riding since childhood.

Zuni realized this was a vector that ran through the hearts
of many people, perhaps most people, on earth. Build a
shelter. Condition its air, its heat, its light. Put it on wheels,
on wings, on rockets, so you can move it wherever you
will. Scrub your hands, spray your armpits, paint your skin,
eradicate all the imperfections of flesh. Break free of Terra's
antique constraints, break free of gravity and frostbite,
banish infection, banish stink. This desire arrowed through
the hearts of billions of people, as potent and unfaltering as
gravity itself. It was a force Zuni could tap.

At the time she announced her retirement, in the early
months of 2051, Zuni had been tapping that force—that
human longing for escape from Terra—during more than
five decades. It made her regretful, now, in her spartan
office, to leaf through so many blueprints bearing the name
of Gregory Passio. But there was no use regretting those
years of falsehood. Gregory would never have understood
her deeper motives for advocating the Enclosure. Had she
tried to explain, he would have furrowed his brow more and

more deeply, would have glared at her with those unearthly eyes, and then dismissed her as a hopeless romantic, a throwback to the tooth-and-claw days.

Once, when Zuni hinted that saving the whales might be a pleasing side effect of the Enclosure, Gregory had flared at her, "Why all this moaning about stupid brutes that haven't even figured out how to hoist themselves out of the sea? Millions of years of evolution, and what have they got to show for it? Songs. Zuni, sometimes you remind me of my wife. Wilderness, wilderness, that's all she thinks about. She's out there in the wilds now, dismantling the old cities. Wriggling her toes in mud and smushing her face in green things. And she's infecting my daughter with the same wilderness disease."

That was the first time Zuni ever heard him mention Teeg, then four years old, and it was the last time she ever hinted at her own deeper motives.

No, it was no use regretting that her collaboration with Gregory had been woven of truths and lies. Surely he took some of his own secrets with him into the frigid Alaskan waters.

Eventually her files were sorted, and all but a few blueprints disposed of. These few she would take away with her, including plans for a twelve-person geodesic dome, a miniature tidal generator, and a fish pool. The other mementos she kept from her office were tools: drafting pens and rulers, pocket cyber, 4-D modeler, scrolls of plax, ink, everything small enough for hiding in a beltpack.

Her apprentices and her few remaining projects she assigned to other master architects. When one of those apprentices, a young woman named Marga, begged to remain with her, Zuni replied:

"Surely you will learn as much from Sventov as you would from me."

"But I have not modeled myself on Sventov," Marga protested. "I've modeled myself on you."

Zuni interrupted her sorting of blueprints to study this troubled visitor. The mask was a cinnamon-colored blur, the wig a swatch of black. Solemn and reproachful, another earnest child of the Enclosure. "And are you certain you know what I am?"

Marga seemed startled by the question. "You're the architect of humanity's liberation from Terra," she said, repeating a phrase Zuni had seen in print a dozen times.

"One of them, perhaps," Zuni conceded. "A very minor one. And you will carry on that liberation after I am gone?"

"Of course, of course. But why should you leave us, with your head still so full of visions?"

Zuni held a blueprint against the viewlight, squinting. "My eyes no longer serve me."

"I'll see for you, I'll draw your ideas." In her excited gesturing, Marga thumped the model of the Enclosure, and the fretted globe wobbled overhead.

The young woman's intensity reminded Zuni of Teeg. But Marga's intensity was directed inward, ever deeper into the Enclosure, while Teeg's—as Gregory had feared—was directed out into the wilds.

"That is kind of you," said Zuni, "but there are other things I must do now."

"What can be more important than Project Transcendence?"

"In China—" Zuni began patiently. Then, realizing that Marga would only know the domed cities on the Asian mainland or the float cities in the Japanese Sea, places scarcely distinguishable from Oregon City, she explained, "In old China, before the Enclosure, it was the custom for a person to devote her youth to learning, her adult years to community work. When she reached a certain age, however, she was free to withdraw from the world and pursue her quest for enlightenment."

Marga pondered this. "And you've reached such an age?"

"I have."

"Nothing will make you change your mind?"

"No, my dear." Zuni longed to tell this solemn young architect the truth, reveal to her the private self who had been kept secret during six decades of public work. But the habit of deceit was too old now to be broken. She would be freed from it soon enough.

"Enlightenment?" Marga repeated the word quizzically.

"Getting back in touch," Zuni translated.

"With what?"

"With the center, the origin of things."

"Isn't that where we're all headed?" Marga said. "Out of this stink of matter, back towards the state of pure energy?"

Zuni only smiled, knowing it was foolish to speak of spiritual things. "Sventov will teach you well."

"So you say."

When Zuni busied herself with the stack of blueprints again, Marga asked shyly, "Do you suppose I could have a little something of yours to keep?"

Zuni withdrew from her modest heap of mementos one of the drafting pens, and this she pressed into Marga's hand. The touch was obviously a shock to the young woman, but not so great a shock as the kiss Zuni brushed on her cheek. "Now go on, leave me alone," Zuni said, "and be sure you draw kindly cities with that pen."

After Marga left, Zuni sat for a long time at her desk, staring out over Oregon City, wondering how kindly a place it was. Nothing lived in it except people and experimental animals and the essential bacteria. Older citizens reminisced about the abundance of life in the wilds, about hickory trees and rutabagas and kangaroos, but they did not reminisce about typhoid or starvation, about mercury poisoning or radioactive dumps. At least within the Enclosure people were shielded from toxins and drug-resistant germs. The apartments were stacked a thousand meters high, nearly reaching the dome, but at least no one lacked a roof or bed. The algae-based food tasted like pap to anyone who could recollect dirt-grown vegetables, but it was abundant and pure. The young people, those born inside the Enclosure, had never seen dolphins or potatoes, had never seen anything except what human beings had made. The young did not reminisce. Their parents and grandparents had quit the wilds, as irrevocably as their remote ancestors had left the seas.

At least Zuni hoped the move inside was irrevocable. Have I betrayed them? she wondered fleetingly. But no, she had settled that doubt long ago. She had only to recall the decades before the Enclosure, when environmental burdens crushed down more heavily each year like snow swelling a glacier, to reassure herself that the move inside had been the sole path to survival. And how could it be a betrayal if it was what people had always longed for? Wasn't the Enclosure just a cave, a hut, a walled village, a shopping mall carried to its logical extreme, stretched out over the globe, hermetically sealed, perfected?

The few items she chose to keep from her years of professional work all fitted into a satchel. They were light, easily smuggled. Before closing her office for the last time she looked carefully about to make sure no trace of her was left behind. Satisfied, she gave the hanging model of the Enclosure one last swing and shut the door.

5 November 2029—*Seattle*

Gregory's bulbous head gleams like an ornament on the vidscreen. Teeg should be in school, he protests. Teeg must learn to socialize—that's the actual word he uses, socialize—*with other children. Teeg must be sheltered from filth and disease. I only glower at him, knowing he can't force me to deliver the child until she reaches breeding age.*

Suddenly a woman's face appears on the screen, and Gregory announces, "Zuni Franklin. She'll explain why the girl should be sent inside."

I have seen the face hundreds of times on video and

*newsfax, but always filtered to disguise its nakedness.
Now I see clearly the delicate features, nose and
cheeks finely molded, creases streaming out in rays
from each eye, mouth softened as if from patient
smiling at the world. I am prepared to find the woman
ugly, but find her beautiful. How old? Perhaps about
sixty. And this is the one he intends for Teeg's
Enclosure mother?*

*I expect to hate her, yet when she begins speaking—
about the child, about the Pacific Northwest where she
grew up, about my dismantling work—I find myself
drawn to her. And can this possibly be the visionary of
the Enclosure? The hater of flesh?*

*After fifteen minutes of talking about the Cascade
Mountains and the old timber industry, she has still not
mentioned sending Teeg inside. Fearing that she soon
will, I break contact.*

SEVEN

Is it the wilds he's hungry for—or is it only me? Teeg could not decide. His eyes would glaze over whenever she told him about the wilderness. But then, his eyes glazed over and his breathing quickened whenever she leaned close to tell him anything. He was so ensnarled in the mating rigmarole that she would probably be disentangling him for months before they could actually make love. In the meantime, whether or not he was hungering for the wilds, he was certainly hungering for her, and that appetite would have to do, until she could deliver him into the wilderness. Once he was outside, the sea and forest could work on him. If she had to be the bait that lured him out there, then bait she would be.

She had already reported to the other seekers, after her two weeks of prospecting, that Whale's Mouth Bay would make an ideal location for the settlement. Tonight, when the crew met for an ingathering, she must speak with them about Phoenix, before his passion cooled or his wilderdread returned.

61

Bits of gravel crunched between her boots and the city's metal floor as she made her way through the abandoned tank farm to the meeting place. A ghostly blue light filtered over from the neighboring gamepark. The whine of sirens and the high-pitched bleat of scoreboards rose above the city's perennial hum. Occasionally, when the air-current shifted, Teeg could hear the voices of revelers, giddy with desperate pleasures. Except for those noises she might have been creeping over a pockmarked asteroid, for the tank farm, useless now that the petroleum supplies had given out, was being demolished to make way for an expansion of the gamepark.

The city devours itself, Teeg reflected. Stalking among the ruins of the tank farm, she was reminded of her mother's handiwork in Portland and Seattle: buildings reduced to steel skeletons, skeletons reduced to lengths of girders, girders melted down into metal soup, congealed into ingots, shipped away for the building of the Enclosure.

Most of the pipes that had once led from this place to refineries on the mainland had already been carved up and recycled. Where oil tanks had stood there were now only circular black stains, like gigantic colonies of bacteria. Teeg avoided them, not wanting to leave oily tracks. In the vague blue light she found the tank where the crew always gathered. According to the numbers painted on its side, this would be the last one demolished. But how long before the wreckers would show up with their laser torches? How many more weeks to plan the escape?

She climbed the ladder, cranked the great spoked wheel of the valve. Quietly she lowered herself through the opening. After nearly two years of gathering here with the others each week to worship and to plan the settlement, she had grown accustomed to the way voices, footsteps, even breathing echoed and re-echoed within the cylindrical walls. But she had never overcome the feeling, as she crawled in through the valve, that she was entering the throat of a machine.

Inside, the others were already seated in a circle, meditating, four men and four women in silvery shimmer-suits. She peeled away her gown and streetmask, stepped out of her boots, bowed low to the unseen presence. No one looked up as she settled cross-legged onto her mat. Now the circle was complete. Teeg stilled herself, waiting for the power, waiting for the inward voice to rise.

From the center of the ring a flare cast rainbows on the oil-slick roof and curving walls. The crew formed a rainbow of flesh, Teeg thought. There were Arda's high-cheeked cinnamon, Jurgen's chocolate, Indy's olive, Sol's velvety purple-black, the sandy skin of Coyt and Marie, the pale blond of Josh and Hinta. A rainbow of flesh, and a rich genetic pool for starting a new society.

In shadows beyond reach of the flare she could make out the bulky shapes of crates waiting for transport out through a pipeline to the coast. These supplies were the last they needed for the settlement, and would soon be hidden away in the basalt caves at Whale's Mouth.

Her thoughts were still skipping about over the details of the escape when the first wave of power swept round the circle. It lifted her, let her fall again, as waves toyed with her when she bathed in the ocean. Center in, she urged her buzzing brain. Still yourself. Yet she found it hard to let herself go. With everyone anxious for departure, would they accept Phoenix? she kept wondering. And even if they did, would he be strong enough to survive outside?

The other faces around the circle were already on the threshold of trance, eyes lowered, jaws slack, and Teeg had to keep herself from rushing to catch up with them. Rushing never carried you inward to the still point. The only path to the center was through patient listening. Legs crossed, feet tucked up close, hands loosely clasped in her lap, she tensed all her muscles and then slowly relaxed them. After one last glimpse of Marie's serene weather-beaten face and Sol's stunning profile—white beard on black skin—she lowered her eyes. Sol and Marie, these were the two she liked to carry with her into the darkness, for they shone so brightly with the inner light.

The day slowly emptied from her: crowds shuttling through avenues, lightsigns commanding attention, gliders whizzing overhead, the blare of informats, the synthosmells, the petty abrasions of a day in the city. The buzz in her head thinned away until all she could hear was breathing. Then the echoes of breathing dwindled away and she was bathed in silence. There were no words, no images, only stillness.

Wave after wave of power poured through her.

Sometime later a voice spoke. Teeg did not bother to attach a name to the speaker. She contained the voice, and the voice contained her.

"Praise the Lord," it chanted, "praise the sun, praise the moon, praise the green world."

The words sifted down through layers of silence into her mind.

Then another voice: "Lift the stone and you will find me, cleave the wood and I am there."

And another: "One of the mystics said, 'Whether you like it or not, whether you know it or not, secretly Nature seeks and hunts and tries to ferret out the track in which God may be found.'"

And a voice rose up and sang greenness until all the world was green, and every last cell of Teeg's body was dancing. And she found words vibrating in her own throat, but what spoke was no more *her* voice than the others had been: "Another wishes to join us, a walker who is weary of the city. His heart longs for the wilds. Shall he become part of our circle?"

Silence for a time, then a whisper: "The flow unites all things, the living and the unliving. In the depths of me, within our circle, in every creature and gathering of creatures the river flows on."

And later: "The city is a dam across the river. The people of the city are deafened. They do not hear the waters."

More silence, an atmosphere of silence, and Teeg was

floating inward to the source, and there was a shining in the stillness, and she was the shining, and there was nothing but light.

After a time stillness gave way to movement, silence gave way to the sound of blood in her ears. She had eased back into the supple envelope of her skin. Now she saw again through eyes of the body. Where the shining had been there was an oil-smeared patch of floor.

At last Jurgen's baritone murmured, "Peace," and the circle began to stir, bodies stretching, faces lifting to gaze at one another. The indrawing had been accomplished once again, they had touched the center, and the seekers were refreshed for another bout of work together.

Teeg remained still for a few moments, relishing the inward peacefulness. She knew she would have to speak for Phoenix convincingly. Thoughts of his callused feet and skittery rabbit eyes made her smile.

A hand grasped her from the right. Turning, she found Hinta's depthless blue eyes fixed on her. "Tell us about your new recruit," Hinta said.

Suffused with the tranquillity of ingathering, the other faces were watching her. Better now than later, Teeg thought, and so she began telling them about Phoenix. He was a global weather man, she explained, a seer of patterns and reader of maps. He knew how the satellite spy-eyes worked, so he might help them avoid detection by Security. He was twenty-seven, a walker, in good physical condition but in need of yoga training. Not a meditator, out of touch with the flow, he was all tangled up in the tendrils of the Enclosure, but she would remedy that, would teach him yoga and the arts of contemplation and loving, if they were willing to accept him. Both his parents were dead, and he had no siblings, no close relations, so far as she could tell no eros mates or even goodbuddies to bind him to Oregon City. And she kept on without knowing why she told these things, about his milky pale skin showing through the face paint, his shuffling walk and cockeyed wigs and his frightened heart.

"You want him very much?" Hinta asked quietly.

Teeg was saved from having to answer this by Jurgen, who demanded gruffly, "And his record?"

"Clean," Teeg answered, grateful to him. Mountainous Jurgen, the rock. Depend on him to shrug eros aside and talk about nuts-and-bolts. "I scanned the net, and Security shows him a pure insider. Health board the same. He went to state nursery, school in New Mexico City, geo-meteorology institute at Baltic, then to work here in the big bottle."

"Sounds like another sleepwalker," Jurgen mused.

"But he's waking up, I know he is."

"Because of the attractions of one Teeg Passio?" Marie suggested in her grandmotherly way.

"Of course," Teeg admitted without hesitation. She had danced the dance of sex with enough men and women to recognize the softening in the gaze, the heat of nearness, as if Phoenix were melting in the retort of his own body. "Sure, that's part of it, the desire for me. Maybe at first that was all of it. But now I think he's smelled the outdoors on me, and that's drawing him on." She didn't know how true that was, but she wanted it to be true.

"It doesn't matter," said Marie. "Wilderness is wilderness, and you're territory enough to keep him busy a long while."

Coming from anyone but Marie, this remark would have embarrassed Teeg. But when this old woman—the veteran spirit-traveler, the keeper of songs—when she focused her gentleness on you and told you the truth, how could you be ashamed?

"We could use someone who knows maps and weather," Sol observed, the words shattering into coughs at the end.

"So we could," Jurgen agreed. He peered at her across the circle. Black curly bush of hair, then broad forehead crisscrossed with scars, then wide-set eyes and mashed-in nose. Battering ram, hammering a way forward. Lovely chocolate skin. He and Hinta were the nearest to being leaders of this leaderless crew. And now he was demanding, "You trust him?"

Teeg had settled that with herself the night Phoenix brought the fossil to her in his outstretched palm. "He won't betray us."

"He would submit to the test of our ingathering?"

"He would have to."

"And if he fails?"

"We leave him behind," Teeg whispered.

Hinta wrapped her long healing fingers more tightly around Teeg's hand. Sol grasped the other, with the uncertain grip of an ailing old man. All around the circle hands joined, a chain of flesh. There was a lull in the talk, then a deeper silence, as the questioning turned inward. Each person listened into the communal silence. Teeg's last thought before entering the stillness was that schools of fish veered that way, spontaneously turning, as if guided by an inner signal.

Sometime later Jurgen rumbled, "My sense is that we should accept this new one into our circle. But he is to learn no secrets until he dwells in the light with us."

"I agree," said Hinta.

"That speaks my mind," muttered Sol.

"And mine. And mine." The welcome carried from voice to voice around the circle until all had agreed, and so the decision was made.

Blueprints of the settlement soon appeared on the overhead screen, superimposed on a map of Whale's Mouth Bay. The oil tank hummed with technical discussions of heat-gain, amino-acid balance, heliostat orientation.

Amid that babble, Teeg heard someone mention the name of Zuni Franklin. Curious, she asked, "What about Zuni?"

"We're going to adapt some of her early dome-flower designs for the settlement," Sol explained.

"Does she know about that?"

Sol's eyebrows tilted upward, white strokes on his plum-dark forehead. He was aging, eaten up by the plutonium lungrot, and it pained her to see it. "You don't imagine we'd tell her, do you?"

"I've been tempted," she confessed.

All eight faces swiveled toward her then. The mixture of feelings was hard to sort out—alarm, regret, surprise. Hinta was the first to say what the others apparently felt, for heads nodded as she spoke:

"Teeg, we all have reason to be grateful to Zuni. She's done each of us favors. But in the end we all had to break away from her influence, because she's identified herself with the Enclosure."

"Yes, yes, I know."

"And now she's a danger to us. If she knew about our plans to move back outside she'd have Security down on us in ten minutes."

"And yet," Teeg objected, "she gave each of us a little shove that helped land us here in this grimy tank, plotting escape. Doesn't that seem a bit odd, for a woman as private as Zuni Franklin?"

"She's private, secretive, but she's influenced many thousands of people," said Jurgen.

"Influenced them to come inside, yes. But what about us? Here we are trying to get back in touch with earth—and what does that have to do with Zuni?"

Jurgen heaved his massive shoulders. "That's puzzled me for years."

"Well, it's too late now to do anything about it," Hinta insisted. "We'll do well to integrate your new recruit before we have to clear out of this place. We'd never be able to convert such a devout leader as Zuni in the time we have left."

"No, I suppose not," Teeg said reluctantly.

"Then it's settled?" Jurgen looked from person to person, seeking consensus. "Do we need to submit it to an ingathering?"

No, no, the heads gestured.

"Then the circle has decided," Jurgen announced. "After Teeg's recruit, we will take no new seekers."

Teeg unbent her legs. Shuffling across the oil-slick floor to record on the map the data from her last trip to the bay, she realized from the stiffness in her body how tense she had been during the silent gathering. She took a deep cleansing breath and allowed herself to smile. Zuni was lost to her. But at least they had agreed to risk opening the conspiracy to this gawky friend of hers, with his callused feet and visionary eyes. Now all she had to do was transform Phoenix into a true wildergoer and mystic.

17 January 2030—*Seattle*

Lonely. I can summon up books on the informat, music and theater and games on the video, data on the cybernet. What I can't summon up is an adult companion, let alone a mate. Wreckers are a hard lot, men and women both. For most of them, dismantling is the only work they can get. I find it hard to stand more than one night's mating with any of them.

Inside the Enclosure—as Gregory informs me, dried old prune that he is—there would be potential lovers in abundance. But they all prance about in costumes and masks, hiding that shameful thing, the body. And sex is fenced round by so many rules, even looking into someone else's eyes requires months of labor. I don't see how anyone has the patience to work through all the levels of loving. Hence the eros parlors, I suppose. They give the quick fix. Libido express. Just lie down, insert your credcard, and the orgiastic field embraces you.

I guess if you can't eradicate the flesh you can trivialize it, with eros parlors, or etherealize it, with mating rituals.

In our solar room Teeg and I go naked. She enjoys her body—the toes like kernels of corn, the seashell ears, the pouting nipples and the little silken purse between her legs. She has learned every yoga position I have to teach her, and she practices them with a gay seriousness. The pleasure in her body, like the limberness, is easy at age nine, out here in the wilds where no one has taught her that the flesh is something one must escape.

EIGHT

"*What* sort of test is it?" Phoenix asked nervously, licking the narco-flavored paint from his lips.

"It's called an ingathering." Teeg lay face-down, back arched so that her upper trunk was lifted off the floor. "It's a form of collective trance. Pioneered by the Quakers centuries ago."

They were in Teeg's apartment, where she was demonstrating yoga positions for him, and he was doing his best to avoid staring at her. She wore a body-colored shimmersuit—"The next best thing," as she had informed him one day, "to nakedness." Phoenix sat muffled in several meters of gown, feeling like a cheap present extravagantly wrapped. He had come to her place straight from work, so he was still bedaubed and bewigged and befrocked in the public manner. "All right, I fall into this trance. Then what happens?"

"*If* you achieve the trance," she corrected him, her back arching further, vertebrae popping, "you drift toward the center."

71

"Where's the center?"

"It's not a place. It's an experience. Kind of a stillness, a brightness. In the ingathering we all gravitate there. If everyone's perfectly clear, we merge together in the—well, the shining."

"Shining?"

"It's no good describing it. It's like loving. You've got to be there yourself to understand, and once you've really been there, you don't need to talk about it." The tension of her arched body put her voice under strain. "This one's called the cobra."

Phoenix drew a stick-figure to illustrate, omitting the red spill of hair, the enticing swell of her rump. Beside it he printed, COBRA. Talking about mysticism is to mysticism, he reasoned, as a stick-figure is to Teeg's body. That made eight drawings on his notepad, and beside them were eight queer names. Lotus, plough, crab—such mysterious titles for these shapes her body was passing through. She seemed liquid, pouring from shape to shape, like clouds on the time-lapse film of a storm. Her shimmersuit caught the overhead lights; as she moved she blazed incandescently. He was painfully self-conscious, watching her, because she was so little conscious of herself. Where did she learn that ease in her flesh?

He felt as rigid as a stick-figure when he tried to imitate the yoga positions. Cobra seemed the tamest so far. But when he lay belly-down and arched his back, alarms rang up and down his spine. He collapsed in a heap of cloth and sweaty wig and rocked moaning on the floor.

"Easy does it," Teeg cautioned. "You can't undo twenty-seven years of abuse overnight. You've got to coax your body along. It's like growing plants."

"It's like suicide, is what it's like."

"Poor Phoenix!" The room filled with her laughter. "But just keep at it and in two or three years you'll be something worth looking at."

"Three years!"

She eyed him, with the sort of look you would give an oversize console to see if it would fit through a doorway. "Maybe four, unless you work hard." She ignored his groans. "Look, here's what you do to get the kinks out." She lay on her back, legs flat, with finger-tips lightly resting on her diaphragm. "You breathe in deeply. Count to ten. Then bunch your fingers together and press them on your forehead. Like so. Then exhale slowly—slowly—and when you do, try to fill yourself with light." She rolled on her side and swatted his tail. "Now flop over and you try it."

"Haven't I had enough torture for one day?"

"How do you ever expect to learn anything?"

Obediently he lay on his back. The gown draped over him like a clammy blanket. With stiff fingers he prodded his chest.

"Lower down," she said, guiding his hands until they rested just below his ribcage. "And loosen up. You're not touching a corpse. Now breathe. Deep. Deep." She waited while he sucked air. "Now fingers to forehead and breathe out."

He obeyed, searching behind his shut eyes for the light she spoke of. "I don't see anything."

"You probably won't, not until you've been through the ingathering."

"How do you find the center?"

"Same way rainwater finds the sea."

"Translate."

"You quit clutching at things, and the curve of the universe guides you home."

"Forget I asked."

He tried to sit up, but she pushed him firmly down. "Do the breathing again," she ordered. While he ballooned with air, she told him, "You do this seven times after you finish the exercises." When he sighed the breath out again she stroked the cloth smooth over his belly. "Better. I almost feel a hint of muscle in there."

"Beneath this paunch lurks a man of titanium."

"Okay, man of titanium, when you do yoga at home, always go naked. The power flows more smoothly that way. Flesh to flesh."

Dizzy, he lay still, with the memory of her hand like a brand on his belly. Such touching would have placed them at level nine of the mating ritual—if she had ever acknowledged the ritual.

"So if I tie myself in yoga knots," he said, "and I do the meditations morning and night, and I change my diet, and I study all this nature stuff you've given me—eventually I'll be ready for the ingathering?"

"Eventually."

"And how do we know when I'm ready for this test? When I'm—how did you say it—clear?"

"We won't know ahead of time." Kneeling beside him, she drew his head into her lap. Fingers crept under the wig and toyed with his ears. "We won't know until we're all joined together in the circle. If everyone's clear, we reach the still point, the brightness. If there's any. anger, any hatred or dishonesty in the group, then we—then nothing happens. Darkness."

"The ingathering doesn't work?"

"It doesn't happen. That's the beauty of it. No spies allowed. No bitterness. If we have problems in the crew, we've got to work them out, or quit the whole business."

Phoenix was aware of her thighs against the back of his skull, the warm angle of her legs. He knew his facepaint would be streaked from sweat—a clown's mask cradled in her lap. "So it's a truth experiment?"

"Partly."

"Who invented it?"

"The apes, probably. The ingathering is ancient. All the old literatures talk about it."

"But where did you all find out about it?"

"When Jurgen and Hinta and Sol and Marie started the group a few years ago, they were all reading these journals by a mystic named George Fox, and he told about seeking the inner light." As she spoke, she trailed her fingers through the paint on his face, smearing the colors. "Marie came across the books and liked the name. Fox. Sly one, you know. Bushy-tailed animal sort of like a dog. Pointy muzzle, eyes very solemn and wise," she said, trying her best to resemble a fox. "You've seen the pictures?"

"I think so. When I was a child."

"Anyway, they started reading Fox's journal, meditating together, and hunting for God."

From where he lay he could see the blue veins under the span of her jaw, a pale tract of skin framed by the twin prominences of her breasts. "So you joined them?"

"About two years ago. We were all outside on a repair mission, and we began talking about how we felt more in touch with things, somehow, out there in the wilds, and wouldn't it be great to just stay outside. The talk went on, and pretty soon Marie was teaching me how to meditate. Water seeks its origin naturally, you know, but people have to be taught. And eventually they invited me to the ingathering. I made it to the central fire, met them there. It turned out everyone else in the work crew was already a seeker. I was number nine." She tilted her face down at him. Strands of red hair dangled to within a handsbreadth of his eyes. "You'd make ten."

"If I survive."

When she smiled, the brightness in her eyes grew more intense, a luminous green, as if she carried about with her sparks of that inner fire. "You'll survive." Her legs shifted beneath him. "Sit up now, while I go get you something else to study."

He sat there dazed, body aching. From the next room came the sounds of Teeg humming, drawers rolling out and in. Hunting for God—the phrase left him uneasy. God was the rind of an outmoded hypothesis, like phlogiston, like ether. Much of what she said made him uneasy. But his peace of mind had already been shattered by this woman, so he had no choice but to keep following her, in hopes she

would eventually put him together again. Humpty Dumpty.
Her God-talk seemed to him as whimsical as nursery
rhymes. Metaphors for the ungraspable.

"Home study," she told him, returning with a scroll of
microfilm. "The flora and fauna of the Oregon coast." She
tucked the scroll into a pocket of his moodgown. Tranquil
green eyes considered him a moment. She was all there in
her eyes, gathered up.

For parting, they touched palms as she had taught him.
Flesh to flesh. The power flows more smoothly that way,
she had said.

"Morning and night without fail," he promised. He
patted the lump in his gown where he had pocketed the
drawings, those stick-figure caricatures of Teeg doing yoga.

"And remember," was the last thing she told him,
"when you do them, take off that tent, scrub the muck off
your face and go naked."

He meditated. He coaxed his body into limberness. He
studied the microfilms of trees and rocks until his eyes grew
bleary. Twice a week he went to her apartment for coaching
and comfort.

"Don't try to make yourself into a noodle," she warned,
her fingers reading his stiff limbs like Braille. "The point is
to learn to dwell in your body, find your center."

Long after he had memorized the name of every plant in
the terrarium, she made him stay back there in the blue-lit
room, studying the miniature wilderness until each leaf and
curving stem stood out in his memory.

"Watch until you disappear," she urged him.

As usual, Phoenix did not understand what she meant.
Feeling like a child learning a new alphabet, he pressed his
nose against the glass terrarium and watched by the hour.
Gradually he perceived how the leaves unfolded, as if each
plant were a rivulet slowly seeping its trickle of green. He
saw white roots groping into the dirt. Dirt. He still could not
bring himself to touch it. Even the bits of shell and bark that

Teeg delighted in showing him made him uneasy. Poison and muck. If the healthers knew she had smuggled these bits of the wild inside, they would clap her in quarantine.

"Look," she would say, handing him a milkweed pod or a sea-smoothed pebble. And he would juggle the gift in his palm as if it were a hot coal.

Sometimes his fear made her laugh. More often it made her frown, and her frown could make him feel as if he had lost the outer layer of his skin. "Trust the earth," she scolded. "It's what we're made of."

But the earth was hostile; he could not get over feeling that. Why else did we scramble up out of the sea, down out of the trees? he reasoned. Shelter in caves, build thatch huts, wrap ourselves in animal hide against the cold. Cave to cabin to city. And building the space colonies, enclosing ourselves inside the domes—wasn't that the next logical step?

Yet here was the terrarium in front of him, a patch of wildness, and it was surpassingly lovely.

From time to time, when he was studying the plants in her blue-lit room, Teeg would look in at the doorway and say, "Have you disappeared yet?" He never knew what to answer.

She gave him other microfilms to read—on ecology, on wilderness skills, on what she called the technology of survival. Because he was adept at grasping patterns, he soon understood the basics of nutrition and superconductivity, thermal shielding and coastal eco-systems and dozens of other subjects he had never dreamed of before meeting Teeg.

She loaned him the holograms she had made during her stay at Whale's Mouth. "Project them at home," she explained, "so you can get the feel of wandering about in the wilds."

With the holos mounted in his projector he could explore one slice of the bay at a time. At first the ghostly shapes frightened him, the vibrant ferns and grasses, the rocks and water-birds, the disorder. They're only images, he kept reminding himself, mere concentrations of energy. But then what is anything in the universe, except a concentration of energy? Reaching out cautiously to stroke a fern, his hand merged with the plant's shadowy curve. His feet melted into the illusory sands underfoot. Where moisture seeped down over the black pockmarked face of the sea-cliff, there was a sumptuous green carpet. Moss, that was the name for it. But he could never touch that inviting softness. His outstretched hands found only air. Nor could he pick up the shells that glimmered iridescently on the beach.

One night he decided to leave the holos shining, to see if he could sleep amid these images of the wilds. He chose a beach segment and lay down well away from the water, beside a hummock of grass. Immobilized in the hologram, the grass blades were bent under the force of an onshore wind. The nearest wave was capped in a froth of white, frozen there at the peak of its curve. Overhead a gull hung motionless with parted beak.

Although he knew there was no danger in these phantoms, he wrestled for a long time on that imaginary beach before sleep came on. By morning the wave had not yet broken, the grasses had not unbent from the wind. No beast had pounced on him in the night.

After that he always slept among the phantom shapes of Whale's Mouth, advancing the projector each night, to display a new segment of the bay. While his body grew more limber from yoga and his mind grew clearer from meditation, the sweep of Oregon coastline was becoming as familiar to him as the miniature landscape in the terrarium.

Gradually he entrusted himself to the simulated wilds, he saw patterns in the ecology texts, and the planet came alive in his imagination. Studying global weather, he had always thought of Terra as a vast mechanism, a spaceship on which a single conscious species led a precarious existence. His teachers had spoken of the planet as an engineering challenge: how do you make it yield the materials and conditions necessary for support of the human system? Nature was a warehouse; you went there when you needed something. Otherwise, you stayed inside the network of cities. Life on Terra—so the teachers and books and videos had assured him—was no different in principle from life on Luna or the orbiting colonies or the asteroid settlements. The engineering problems differed, there were differences in the degree of environmental hostility, and that was all.

Except for the odd museum specimen—a lump of sterilized rock or an insect embalmed in plastic—before Teeg showed him the terrarium he had never seen anything that had not been made by humans. Looking at the satellite images of Terra, it was hard to believe these weren't just electronic mirages, no more real than the photomurals continually parading across his wall. Only when a seatube developed leaks, or quakes split a dome and exposed a whole city to weather and infections, or O_2 extractors failed and several thousand people suffocated (as had happened recently in Calcutta City), or the build-up of the anthrotoxins caused a massive die-off in a place like Brazil City— only then did nature seem tangible. Between catastrophes, nature could be safely forgotten.

Now when he closed his eyes he saw Terra whole, a sphere of green and brown and blue, a bubble afloat on the ocean of space, as Oregon City was afloat on an ocean of water.

"When are you going to quit pouring that junk into your body?" Teeg asked him one day, as he sat in his room with a steaming mug of narco beside him.

He dumped the brew down the sink. Within the next week he gave up all the rest of his chemmies: the wakers and dozers, the vim-pills, the breeze capsules. Bottle after bottle vanished down the recycling chute. For days his head threatened to split open, his brain clamored for the drugs.

At work he dozed over the monitors and at home he lay awake through the night, staring up at holographic stars. Revolts broke out in the nether regions of his body. Then gradually the pain subsided. He left off going to the gamepark or lightshows. He quit seeing his cronies from the office. There didn't seem much of anything to say to them. He wouldn't dare tell them about the wilderness that was sprouting inside him. He even gave up visiting the eros parlors, and desire backed up in him like a dammed river.

Now it was Teeg or nothing. She spoke with him and touched him, or refrained from touching him, according to her own rhythms. And Phoenix, who had never learned any other way of dealing with a woman except the mating rituals, struggled to read the meaning in her gestures.

Often when they meditated together, he seemed to feel a call from her, a reaching toward him, and he groped around clumsily in the spiritual darkness, but could not meet her. He imagined the two of them in that inward spirit-space like the halves of an arch leaning together, without quite joining.

Then one night he was peering into the terrarium, watching the snout of a fern break through the crust of soil. Teeg was humming one of her melodies in the next room. And suddenly the uncurling fern was his half of the arch, reaching out, reaching delicately out, far into the darkness, and it was met there, and the arch was joined and it spanned all the world.

When the moment passed he turned away from the terrarium and looked out through the doorway at Teeg. Only when he saw her face streaked with tears did he feel the tears on his own.

"So you disappeared?" she said gently.

Suddenly he understood. "Yes, yes I did."

"And it was good?"

He bit his lower lip and nodded sharply. "What does it mean?"

"It doesn't mean anything. It just is, like sunshine."

He considered that, trying to imagine sunshine, trying to imagine anything as potent as that delicate touching in the darkness. "Is the ingathering like that?"

"A little."

"Will I be ready for it soon?"

"You're ready now," she said.

12 June 2030—*Willamette Valley*

We have spent two days camped on Hardesty Mountain, waiting, because one of my glider-pilots swears he spied a deer grazing up here in a clearcut. Teeg and I hiked around the base of the mountain, searching for trails. At last we found the forked print of a deer hoof, only one print, as if the creature were not sufficiently alive to make a continuous trail.

So we camp beside the clearcut, binoculars aimed out over the field of stumps and blackberry vines and new-growth alder. At first Teeg won't be still, fidgets around and makes a racket. But on the second morning, as fog blankets the clearing, she sits quietly in my lap. "Will it come?" she whispers. "If it chooses," I say.

And then a four-legged shadow glides from the shelter of the woods. A yearling doe, ears pricked forward cautiously, great brown eyes staring at us through the fog. Teeg grows still in my lap. I cannot even feel her breathe. We are one flesh, waiting. The doe takes a few more hesitant steps, bends down, snatches a bite of grass, then lifts her head alertly. The narrow jaws work side-to-side, grass dripping from the prim lips.

Then I can see the withered hind leg, the tumor on the belly. As genetic damage goes, she has come off lightly. At least she has survived for a year, which is rare enough. And she might bear young.

As the sun burns away the fog, the doe retreats, a hobbling ghost, into the forest. Teeg sighs deeply, and stirs in my arms.

"A deer," she says. Her first, and I pray to God it is not her last.

NINE

Because Zuni replied to each absurd speculation about her future with vague smiles and crooked answers, the media soon decided she was not the proper stuff of news. Her face vanished from the video, her name from the newsfax. Before long only her colleagues at the Institute and her few friends still wondered what was going on beneath that meticulous bun of white hair.

Even those friends could not pry the secret from her. Zuni had clutched it for so long that her will had sealed over it, like the bark of a tree grown around a nail.

Left in peace at last, Zuni holed up in her apartment to meditate, to gather strength for the journey, whenever it might begin. She had set events in motion, but now they had run their own course. To be ready when the break came, if the break came, that was all she could hope. Only let it be soon, soon.

Meanwhile there were the records to keep. Instead of checking weekly on the movements of the conspirators—

the ones who called themselves seekers, such a quaint name—now she checked daily. On her info terminal she would punch the code for Jurgen or Teeg or one of the others, and within moments the Security cyber would inform her of the person's current work assignment, itinerary, health status, credit balance and the like. Writing with a pen, one of the anachronisms which gave her pleasure, she then noted on file cards whatever seemed like new information. Under Sol's name, for example, recent cards showed the increasing frequency of his visits to the C-clinic, and then his abrupt refusal to accept any more synthetic organs. Apparently his lung cancer was galloping out of control. He would be urgent to escape. Hinta and Jurgen must also have been feeling urgent, for their cards showed they had spent their credit balance nearly down to zero, mostly for tools. For the first time in several cycles, Arda had skipped the fetal implant. Pressures for escape were building up in several other members of the crew. This discovery was what had prompted Zuni to announce her retirement, to make herself ready.

Over the years she had kept such records for hundreds of people. In each of those lives she had scented a whiff of rebellion. One person might have been nostalgic for a youth spent blasting canals through the Amazon rainforest. Another, like Jurgen, might once have fought against the Enclosure as a wilderness guerrilla. Dozens of these restless ones merely suffered from urbophobia. Whenever she could, Zuni had nudged these rebels into contact with one another, while remaining careful to seem no more than a casual friend.

Now all but nine of those hundreds of names had been struck through with black ink. Beside many of the canceled names she had written, NATURAL DEATH. Many others bore the legend, SUICIDE. Beside most she had written, CON-FORMED TO SYSTEM or ISOLATED.

For each of the remaining names there was a stack of

cards. Zuni kept them hidden in the battered tin box she had used as a child, back in the 1980s, to carry her lunch to school. Hints of rocketships showed through scratches on the lid. The cards themselves, yellowed now with age, dated from the era when cybers were still referred to as computers and when computers still punched some of their findings onto flimsy cardboard. Brittle, multiply-knotted rubber bands held the cards in their nine bunches.

After withdrawing from the institute, Zuni would squat on the floor of her apartment with the cards circled about her like the rayflowers of a daisy. Stack by stack she thumbed through them. Her handwriting, always tidy, had grown larger over the years as her eyesight failed. She could no longer make out the earliest entries. But she did not need to, for she knew the details of those nine histories, knew about Arda's exhausting career as a host-mother, Hinta's work as a spiritual healer, Sol's exploits as a saboteur of Fourth World breeder reactors (hence the cancer?), and all the rest.

Teeg's history she recalled most vividly of all, for Zuni had known her since Gregory forced the thirteen-year-old girl to move inside the Enclosure.

"So you're helping Father shut everybody inside here?" the young Teeg had said at that first encounter.

"Helping build the Enclosure, yes," Zuni admitted.

"Then you're wicked," the girl announced. Tanned from traveling outside with her mother, lower lip thrust sullenly out, green eyes alight with anger, this girl would not be tamed easily to life inside the Enclosure. And Gregory never had tamed his daughter, in part because, whenever he traveled to building-sites, he left her with Zuni. And Zuni fed her wildness.

"Why does everybody inside here get costumed up?" the girl might ask.

"Perhaps they regard the body as a stubborn beast," Zuni would reply, "an ugly donkey in need of disguise."

"Do you agree with that?"

"Have you ever seen me paint my face or stuff my head into a wig?"

And that little heresy would be stored away inside the red-haired skull.

Often Teeg asked her what she remembered of life outdoors, particularly in Oregon, where Judith Passio still lived. And then Zuni would tell her about rafting on the McKenzie River, about the sheep scattered like furry cobblestones across the Willamette Valley, about the ocean gnawing holes through rocks at Cape Perpetua. The girl's eyes swelled with longing.

"Of course, as toxins built up and erosion grew worse," Zuni was careful to explain, "the sheep died out. And you wouldn't dare climb into a river without a suit."

"But earlier, when everything was green and growing, you loved the place, didn't you?"

"Oh," Zuni hedged, "it had its beauties."

"So if you loved it," Teeg once asked her, "how come you got yourself into this city-building business? Why didn't you just hide away out there somewhere, the way Mother did?"

"Someday I'll explain that to you," Zuni answered.

The time for explaining was put off from year to year, and Teeg eventually gave up asking. For a long time after Teeg moved inside, the mother kept sending messages: flee the city, come back to me. Gregory intercepted most of them, but not all, and every message reaching Teeg made her more sullen and aloof.

"If only the woman were erased," Gregory speculated, "the child would be content to stay inside."

Soon afterwards, he announced that his wife had died while trying to escape the health patrollers, and he begged Zuni to tell the girl.

"Has she been killed off for real, or for convenience?" Zuni asked.

Gregory blinked his faceted, otherworldly eyes at her and repeated the story, word-for-word, like a script.

Skeptical, Zuni postponed delivering the news. But when the messages stopped arriving, Teeg—then seventeen and shrewd—demanded of her:

"Something's happened to my mother, hasn't it?"

"They say she's killed herself," Zuni answered carefully.

"*Mother?*"

And then Zuni recounted the story: how the patrol glider swooped down over Judith Passio's wooden shack in the ruins of Portland, loudspeakers intoning directions, stunlight beamed at the hovel's doorway, until the woman burst through a back window, stumbled over the city's rubble, glider kiting overhead in pursuit, stun-light arcing charge after charge into her, slowing her down, dazing her, so she was clawing along on her belly when she wriggled over an embankment into the Columbia River.

"Drowned?"

"So they say. Officially, it was suicide." Zuni drew a cautious smile. "Resisting health arrest is generally suicide."

The girl looked as stunned as the mother in the tale was supposed to have been. Was it only a tale?

"And unofficially?" asked Teeg.

Zuni raised her eyebrows, but kept silent.

"Murder," the girl concluded bitterly. The green fire in her eyes burned more fiercely than ever.

Gregory did not have to suffer his child's bitterness for long. His own drowning occurred soon after. Zuni was left to inform Teeg of this death as well.

"What was he doing in Alaska?" Teeg asked without any show of emotion.

"Overseeing the construction of a new float city," Zuni explained.

Now Teeg smiled grimly. "Served him right. Frozen brain drowned in a frozen sea."

The cruelty of the ignorant, Zuni thought. And for one of the few times in her dealings with Teeg she let her impatience show. "That is a callous thing to say."

"He was a callous man."

"Your father helped save billions of people from eco-death."

"He murdered my mother!"

"The health patrol was on a routine sterilizing mission."

"Then his ideas murdered her! Him and his obsession with transcendence. He couldn't stand knowing she was out there. He was always terrified of germs and dirt, scared of clouds, bugs. His ideal was pure consciousness floating in a vacuum."

"Those yearnings are ancient, Teeg. Your father didn't invent them. Where do you think the dreams of angels come from, the creatures without flesh? And Nirvana? And all those visions of heavenly cities filled with spirit and light?"

By this point Teeg was not listening. She swept Zuni's words aside with a wave of her fist. This was a private grudge, and she would not have it diluted with talk of history. "No, he didn't invent them. He had lots of help—from people like you. You're just as much to blame for this"—sobbing, arms flung wide to smash the whole city with her grief—"this *bottle* as he is. And for Mother's death."

"If believing that makes it easier for you," Zuni answered with a forced calmness, "then go ahead and believe it."

"I do! I do!" Teeg cried. "And don't try to wrap it up in your cool reasons and sympathy and pretty memories. Keep that for someone else."

Zuni swallowed her grief that day. Living a masquerade, she had to remain silent when her sham identity was mistaken for her true one. It was many weeks before Teeg came back for a visit, and then it was only to ask, sullenly, that Zuni nominate her for a job as troubleshooter. Zuni was glad to help, because she had already directed many restless ones into the repair corps. Several years into this job, a svelte woman of twenty-three, Teeg came back once more to ask Zuni's help in applying for the status of master troubleshooter.

"Do you swear you mean no harm to anyone inside the Enclosure?" Zuni demanded. "You would never abuse the master security clearance?" She studied the young woman's rebellious eyes with an expert's knowledge of deceit.

"I swear," Teeg replied.

Zuni signed the form. On the application she wrote: "Judge this candidate by her father, one of our greatest shelterminds, not by her renegade mother."

The signature of Zuni Franklin evidently charmed Security, for they granted a master's pass to this daughter of a wildergoer.

On one of Teeg's rare visits in the following years, Zuni planted a last seed of cunning: "Your mother was foolish to stay in the wilds alone, without allies or equipment or medicine. She was a fool to live in the infected ruins of a city, right where the health patrol would stumble over her. If she'd chosen some clean, secret place, and some resourceful companions, she might still be alive out there."

"Still alive?"

To Zuni, the slender young woman, defiantly barefaced and free-haired, looked more intense than ever, more charged with the passion of revolt. "Who knows?" said Zuni.

Meanwhile a few of Zuni's rebels, the ones who smelled to her of discontent, had joined together in a repair crew. Into that same crew she nudged Teeg, and then stepped back to await the results.

The results were arrayed about her now on the floor of the apartment, in these stacks of cards. Teeg's stack was filled with brief references to those long-ago heretical conversations. The other eight records were less painful to Zuni.

Together they formed a constellation. Others might have acquired the same information about them, since most of it was available on the cybernet, but only Zuni knew what pattern to seek. They were a repair crew who did their job quickly and well. True, they kept their bodies fit, but that was a condition for survival in their work. They were fanatically committed to one another, and they shared some patched-together religion; but that was common among repair crews and health patrollers and security squads, among all those who faced the dangers of the wilds. No, there was nothing outwardly suspicious about these nine.

You had to know what questions to ask about their past, what patterns to look for in their present movements, before you could see the outlines of a conspiracy. You had to look even more shrewdly to detect the separate lives meshing together toward a crisis. Zuni prayed the conspiracy and crisis were real, and not simply her invention. She had already staked on that hunch what little future remained to her.

3 March 2031—*Anchorage*

Between the cold and poisons, my dismantling crew suffers terribly. We erect portadomes over each wrecking site, we pipe in air and water from the Enclosure, but still people fall ill every day. The buildings themselves, the rusting furniture, the pavements, everything is contaminated, and no filter yet devised will guard a person entirely. The medics report fevers, skin rashes, vomiting, breakdowns in the nervous system. Eight deaths so far, six of them men, who appear to succumb more readily than women.

Teeg remains healthy, except for an occasional worrying bout of dizziness. Three more years until she reaches breeding age—and then what?

On his vidcalls Gregory quizzes her about mathe-

matics, doubtless trying to prove that I am not teaching her adequately. When Zuni Franklin comes on the screen, she's likelier to ask the child what mosses she has found, or whether the Chinook salmon are still spawning in the Susitna River.

TEN

In boots and hoods and ankle-flapping capes, with masks drawn close to hide their faces, Teeg and Phoenix walked among the circular oil stains of the tank farm. Behind them, the gamepark flung its riotous colors toward the night-darkened dome, and farther behind, near the city center, buildings heaped up in pyramids and honeycombs· of light. Ahead of them loomed the dark knobby shapes of the few remaining oil tanks.

"What if I can't—" Phoenix began.

Teeg shushed him quickly. "You *can*. Now be still and keep your mind centered. No doubts. You've got to be clear."

They passed between two partly-demolished tanks. Where lasers had cut through the triple-hulled walls, cauterized edges gleamed with a dull luster. This might be the last ingathering here, Teeg realized, for the wreckers were gnawing their way each week nearer to the tank where the seekers met. The pipeline leading from here to the mountains near Whale's Mouth Bay had already been severed. Phoenix had to pass the test tonight, for there might not be another chance.

Teeg climbed the ladder first, feet quiet on the rungs, and when Phoenix joined her on the roof of the tank she motioned for him to slip off his gown and streetmask. They added their garments to the pile beside the entrance valve, pried off their boots. Turning, with Phoenix between her and the distant glow of the gamepark, she could see for the first time his actual shape, hugged in the fabric of his shimmersuit. The months of training had drawn his body tight. She touched him lightly on the chest, felt the quiver of muscle, then trailed her fingers downward over ribs to his waist.

"I'm afraid," he whispered.

"Of course."

Through her bare feet she sensed the hum of voices in the tank below. As she cranked the valve open the hum grew louder, then separated into distinct and familiar voices. Jurgen's gruff baritone, Hinta's soothing purr, Sol's gasping with the sound of blood in it. They were discussing Phoenix, wondering aloud if his light would merge with theirs.

"You follow me," she whispered to him. "And relax, keep yourself clear."

His silhouette blocked out a man-shaped chunk of inner-city lights. "But am I ready? Maybe I need more—"

"You're *ready*."

She lowered her feet through the cold jaws of the valve, swung down from handhold to handhold. Before her feet kissed the floor the voices hushed. She bowed deeply. Grave faces nodded at her: the lovely rainbow shades of skin, cinnamon and plum, olive and cornsilk—the colors of growing things. A moment later Phoenix swung down beside her, looking self-conscious in his silvery shimmer-suit and naked face. She had never before seen him scrubbed perfectly clean of paint. His cheeks were the color of peaches; descent through the valve had left one of them smudged with grease. As the conspirators stared at him, he shuffled his feet nervously, and that little stagger caught at her heart.

"Phoenix Marshall," she announced.

"Peace," murmured several voices. Each person raised the left hand, palm exposed. Although the backs of the hands were the color of salmon and copper and chocolate, a mixture of races, the palms were all yellowed with calluses. They carried this imprint of the outdoors with them always, this thickening of the skin from work.

After bowing, Phoenix licked his lips and carefully pronounced the formula she had taught him. "I am seeking the light. I ask to join your circle."

Hands waved him to the mat which had been made ready. Teeg lowered herself onto the mat next to his, and the circle was gathered. She noticed Sol and Marie staring across at Phoenix, sizing him up—curious, probably, to see what had attracted her to him. If asked, she would not have known what to say, except that something in her leapt up to answer the yearning she felt in him.

When at last the two old spirit-travelers lowered their eyes, Teeg did the same, and immediately power began to flow around the circle. There was a roaring like the joining of rivers inside her, and then stillness began trickling through her.

Open up to us, Phoenix, open up, she chanted over and over to herself.

After several moments she realized her back was tensed and her jaw was clamped tight. She was trying to *will* the coming together. Gradually she relaxed, let go, made herself into a gauzy sail that winds of the spirit could shove along. And the winds set her quivering, caught and spun her, leaf-light, across the waters. Presently she drifted up against some barrier, could not break through. She was conscious of her skull, an enclosure trapping her, and then the walls of bone evaporated like mist and she floated outward, nudging against the curved walls of the tank.

Those also gave way, and after them the walls of Oregon City, and then the vaporous envelope of the planet, and so on outward past solar system and galaxy, always adrift, until her frail craft burst through every last barrier and coasted into the center of light. Here all was a dazzle and a blazing stillness, a burning without movement, a chorus without sound. A fierce energy gripped her, spinning her round, and yet she felt calm.

Against the dazzle at the center shone fainter lights, like dim stars set off against the awesome fire. The lights formed a ring, and with her last shred of consciousness Teeg knew which light was her own and which Phoenix's. The ring drew inward, the ten lights merged into one and that light merged with the fire, and Teeg was Phoenix was Jurgen was Hinta, Teeg was all the other seekers, and she was God, and she was herself. There was no wind anymore, for she was at the source of all winds, and no time passing, no urge to go anywhere else; there was only abundance and peace.

After a while the breeze caught her, shoving her away from the center, back toward the two-legged packet of flesh called Teeg Passio. The walls thickened around her again, walls of galaxies, walls of bone, shutting her up once more within the confines of her own self. Yet as she roused from the trance she brought with her glimmers of that inner blaze. She held her fingers close to her face and bent each one in turn, feeling the joints mesh, the blood flow, the billion cells flame with their sparks of the infinite burning. Each time, coming back from the center, she was more amazed by life, by this flame leaping in the meshes of matter.

She reached out to left and right, found Marie's hand on one side and Phoenix's on the other. Hand joined to hand around the circle and the shudder of return passed through them, like the involuntary shudder after a bout of crying or lovemaking. Following a spell of quiet, to let the ecstasy settle in them all, Jurgen said, "Peace."

"Peace," said Teeg.

"Peace, peace, peace," Phoenix murmured. His cheeks were slick.

"Welcome, new one," the others said.

Phoenix gazed at them, letting the tears come. He sat there with a look of baffled joy on his face while the seekers approached him, each one in turn pressing palms to his palms and forehead to his forehead. Marie came last. Her shaved head glistened. She beamed down at Phoenix with all the intensity of her weathered and finely-wrinkled face. "Now you know where we truly are," she said, brushing her forehead against his, "and don't you ever forget."

"That's where we are," Phoenix echoed her. "And all this," he said, gesturing at the other people and the oil-smeared walls of the tank, "all this is illusion?"

Marie's gleaming head wagged side-to-side. "No, it's not illusion. It's performance. We're all performing the history of God, all of us, men and women and trees and pebbles, each one carrying bits of fire."

She withdrew to join the others at the far side of the tank, leaving only Teeg beside him. His lips parted as if he were going to thrust out his tongue and taste the air.

"That's Marie," Teeg said. "She and Sol have taken the longest spirit journeys, so we listen to them. Sol's the one over there with skin the color of ripe plums." Realizing Phoenix had never seen a plum, she pointed. "There, see, the one kneeling down and unrolling the map."

Phoenix nodded sleepily, but his eyes were not focused. It was no use telling him the names of the others tonight; he was too dazzled to see their faces. Their voices chattered on about dates, routes, meetings, about plans for escape from Oregon City. Contrive a water accident, make Security think the entire crew had drowned, then boat to Whale's Mouth—that was the gist of it. Teeg was not paying close attention to the talk, for she had this joy to share with Phoenix. She kept his fingers laced in her own, giving him time to come down, to come back. Let him giddy about on his own inner winds for a while longer. She remembered her own first ingathering, the sense of coming home at last to the place she had been seeking all her days. Rainwater rediscovering the sea. Sexual orgasm was delicious, but it could not rival the splendor of that homecoming.

At last his fingers came awake in her hand, and this time when he looked he really saw her. "Now I know why you gave up trying to describe it," he said.

Later, walking back with him through the ruins of the tank farm, after the crew had worked out all the details for escape, she asked, "Was it what you expected?"

"The test?"

"The journey inward."

He lifted both arms, hands cupped domeward. "How could I ever dream of a trip like that?"

"Of course you couldn't." She skipped gaily, boots scuffing on the metal floor. She felt like a gauzy sail again, blown along.

"Is it always like that?" he said.

"Is sex always spectacular?"

"Is sex—what?" he stammered.

"Spectacular. Like fireworks."

"Do you mean—"

"I mean sometimes loving is magnificent, sometimes it's okay, and sometimes it's just a sweaty thumping of bodies. And the sky's not always perfectly blue and the crocuses don't burst through the soil every day. There's rhythms to these things." She couldn't stop using the speech of natural things, even though she knew it meant little to him. Soon it would mean a great deal to him, once he was outside. "Things come clear in their own sweet time. We just prepare, open ourselves, and wait."

"So it was special?" he said.

"Rare, very rare. We'd never been that close to the center before. Some of the others might have, privately—Sol, maybe, or Marie, even Hinta. But as a group, that was a whole new . . . intensity. Maybe you were just the bit of chemistry, the trace element, we needed."

"And you think they accepted me?"

"You were there, weren't you, in the fire? What other proof do you need?"

He didn't need any other, for he seized her by the hands and danced her in circles, their gowns kiting outward, their boots clumping. Gravel skittered away over the gray metal floor. They were like two stars orbiting one another, drifting closer as their spinning slowed, until they danced to a stop with hips and breasts and lips pressed together. For once his body felt easy against hers, yielding, as if the glacier that had built up in him during years of emotional restraint were melting at last. This time, when his cock bulged against her, he did not turn away. He kept his lips on hers, his hands on the curve of her rump. They stayed that way for a spell, with the scraps of cut-up oil tanks heaped around them, with sirens and delirious shouts rising from the nearby game-park. Then Teeg felt the chill slowly coming over him again, the glacier accumulating, the cold spreading through his body like crystals of ice. And finally he pulled away.

"I lost control," he said with an abashed tone. She could see him ticking over in his mind the articles of the mating code.

"What you lost were those stupid shackles, for about half a minute." She kicked a chunk of gravel, sent it clattering. Patience, she reminded herself. He had already come a long way in a few months. He had become a walker, an inward exile from the Enclosure. Did she expect him also to become an uninhibited lover so quickly? "I'm sorry," she said. "I keep forgetting. And we'll have time, outside. We'll melt the polar icepack if we need to."

"Polar icepack?"

"Never mind. Let's go, before the healthers come sniffing after us."

She led the way cautiously through the outskirts of the tank farm, avoiding the rings of oil. The crew had decided not to meet again in the doomed tank, but still, it would not do to give the place away. Properly booted and hooded, with streetmasks over their faces, Teeg and Phoenix skirted the last heap of scrap and emerged into the many-colored illumination of the gamepark. The noise was deafening. People shuffled from one buzzing electronic box to another, climbed in and out of bump-cars, stood howling in the laughter booths. The loudest shouts came from the eros parlors, long anguished cries of pleasure, as if the customers were releasing in a single burst all the pent-up emotion of the day. Around the chemmie dispensers people hopped on one leg or flapped their arms, eyes rolling, or crowed with heads thrown back, or skittered about on all fours.

Teeg drew the gown tight at her throat, made sure the mask snugged down over her jaw. Beast time, she thought. A few minutes of licensed animalhood to relieve the dread they carry with them all day. She stopped short to let a man slither past on his belly; his painted face lunged at invisible targets in the air, jaws snapping. Before he left the park he would swallow a capsule of eraser, and never know he had played lizard.

"Hurry," Phoenix hissed over her shoulder. "I can't stand this."

No one paid any attention to them as they passed, quickly, through the park, their pace as frantic as the revelers'. At the gate, where pedbelts dumped the rigid bodies of new customers and carried away the limp exhausted ones, Teeg hesitated. She turned for a moment to look back the way they had come, across the riotous glow of the park toward the squat oil tank where so many ingatherings had taken place. She could not actually see the tank—which was just as well, since she would go there no more. The crew would remain scattered until the next call for emergency work, and that call, if the weather and the sea cooperated, would carry them outside the city for good.

Sometimes, even here inside the dome, she thought she could detect shifts in the weather, as if some antique portion of her mind had never fully submitted to life indoors. This was one of those times, standing there at the gateway of the amusement park with Phoenix. A stirring in her marrow-bones, a tingling along her spine, told her of storms brewing outside.

Turning back around, still holding onto Phoenix, she stepped on the slick black river of the pedbelt and let it carry her away.

27 August 2031—*Whale's Mouth Bay*
Salt-water. I keep coming back to it, like a reptile who has changed her mind and decided the sea is not so bad after all. I sit on the beach while Teeg explores the tidal pools, her small hands groping like cautious crabs among the rare starfish and sea anemones. Of all salty places on the Oregon coast, this one is my favorite. The ocean has scoured the basalt cliffs for thirty million years, gouging caves where moss drips down, carving holes through the softer parts of the rock. When the wind is strong and the tide is right, the incoming waves spout water through those holes. I guess that's why the place is named after whales, because of the spouts and because the black walls of the bay open like a mouth toward the sea. Once you could even see whales from here, perhaps as recently as the 1990s. Imagine the geyser rising, the hump breaking water, and even, if you were lucky, the broad flukes lifting skyward and then crashing down!

Driftwood lodges in the caves, and smooth round stones as large as ostrich eggs nest in the driftwood. South of here along the coast sea lions haunt the caves. When the water is calm, their barks can be heard all the way up here. I wonder if anyone has studied them to see why they have survived the poisons so much more successfully than the other mammals.

When I first brought Teeg here—it must have been

six years ago, when she was four—the name frightened her. I had shown her pictures of whales, and she was afraid the bay would swallow her. Even when I told her that the magnificent great beasts were extinct she was not reassured. But once she saw the place, she soon grew to trust it. And now she splashes about in the shallows as boldly as any seal.

ELEVEN

Zuni set the battered lunch box on the table. The lid was decorated with a 1980s artist's notion of rockets—long phallic spikes like sharpened pencils with fire gushing out the tail. Nothing at all like today's ships, which were floating conglomerations of struts and screens and bulging chambers. Whatever had possessed her mother to buy that rocket-covered pail, way back there in an Oregon lumber town, a thousand miles from any launch pad? Was it because the world was closing in, and she wanted her daughter to dream of escape? Now, seventy years later, Zuni was still dreaming of escape.

She lifted the lid, plucked out the nine topmost bundles of cards, then shut the box for the last time. Dangling by its plastic handle, it felt heavy as she carried it to the vaporizer, heavy with hundreds of file cards, all those records of failed rebellion. After placing the box inside the vaporizer she studied it through the glass door. The flame-spewing rockets and pockmarked planets appeared to her with luminous clarity, even though the actual decals were so scuffed that she could barely make them out with her dim eyesight. Silly, she realized, to feel so attached to a little box of stamped tin. She set the timer for a minute, then peered in through the glass door to watch the vaporizer work its swirling molecular dance. After thirty seconds a congealed lump of metal still rested on the shelf, but after half a minute more nothing remained except a spiral of mist, which the recycling vents quickly sucked away.

Back at the table she riffled through the surviving bundles of cards. Where on earth did the conspirators mean to settle? She had been retired now for nearly five months, strenuous months of calisthenics in the bedroom and meditation in the mindroom, and at last she felt gathered and ready, yet Teeg and her crew seemed to be going about their business very much as usual, biding their time, waiting for the right moment. If that moment came before she guessed their destination, she would lose track of them altogether.

She dealt the cards on the view-table, with the most recent entries uppermost, the ones written in her large block lettering as in a child's primer, and for the hundredth time she hunted for some clue to the location of the settlement. Jurgen and Hinta had been working almost exclusively on the aquafarms in recent months, out here in the ocean near Oregon City. Arda, Marie, and Coyt had also spent most of their time at sea, changing turbines in the geo-thermal installations far up north over the Aleutian Trench. Josh and Indy were at work cleaning membranes in the salinity gradient systems. Sol had apparently been too sick in recent months to venture outside at all. That left only Teeg to do scouting on the mainland, and for the last eight months solo repair missions had taken her all over the Pacific Northwest. Squinting through a magnifier, Zuni had carefully plotted each of those repair sites on a map, an antique paper map with holes worn through at the folds. There were place names for all the vanished towns, for the rivers and mountains and bays. At the location of each repair mission she daubed a spot of purple ink. The resulting rash of dots looked wholly random, like the bullet-perforated roadsigns she used to see as a child. Zuni stared at that map until the purple flecks seemed to crawl about; yet no pattern emerged.

What if, she wondered at last, the key is not space, but time? How long did each of those trips last, and where else might Teeg have gone besides the repair sites?

She typed her question to the Info cyber. The lightsticks soon printed time-elapse figures for each of Teeg's missions. Zuni glanced at the numbers, heart skipping. They seemed high, very high. How long should each of these repairs take? she asked the cyber. ESTIMATES VARY, the cyber replied. THERE ARE NO HARD FIGURES FOR REPAIR RATES. WORK RATE FOR T. PASSIO FALLS WITHIN SLOW-NORMAL RANGE.

Zuni had observed Teeg during her troubleshooter apprenticeship, watched those brisk hands flying deftly over tools and machines, and she knew there was nothing slow about her work. No, Teeg was staying out longer than necessary on her repair missions. But how much longer? Zuni estimated the time each repair should take, often drawing on her own experience as a builder, sometimes guessing from what troubleshooters had told her. The difference between this number and the actual elapse-figure was the amount of time Teeg would have to play with. To avoid the spy-eyes in her shuttle, she would have to hug the contours of the land, probably average no more than sixty or seventy kilometers per hour.

Excited now, sniffing a solution, Zuni drew around each of the purple dots a circle whose radius was equal to the distance Teeg could have traveled in her surplus time on each trip. Before half the circles were drawn, already the pattern was emerging, arc after arc intersecting on the southern Oregon coast. Each additional circle narrowed the region of overlap. By the time the last one was inscribed, Zuni was staring at a tiny portion of the map, a few miles of coastline bordered on the south by the Oregon dunes and on the north by Mount Wind. She squinted through the magnifying glass to make out the smaller print. Square in the middle was a yawning blue inlet called Whale's Mouth Bay. When had she heard that name before? As a child in Oregon? Perhaps, but the memory seemed fresher than that. She repeated the words to herself. In a moment she recollected hearing Teeg speak fondly of the place:

"Whale's Mouth Bay. My mother and I used to go there whenever she could slip away from work. It was our favorite place. It's the last place I saw her."

Only when the map lifted and fluttered on the slick table did Zuni realize she was panting. Steady, she thought. But she felt like heading for the coast straightaway. After a moment's hesitation the desire lifted her off the chair and sent her pacing from room to room.

6 September 2031—*Whale's Mouth Bay*

Back in the jaws of Leviathan. Every workbreak, Teeg begs me to bring her here in the glider. The burned-out towns we pass on the way make my heart ache.

If the earth didn't curve, I could see Oregon City away out over the water. Gregory will be tinkering with it, perfecting his gigantic machine. "At last we've built a safe home for humanity," he scolds me, "and you refuse to come inside."

If he and the other architects of the Enclosure hadn't been trained on the space colonies, they would never have dreamed of shutting people inside domes. (I suppose Zuni Franklin is an exception. I think she actually trained in the wildcities of the Northwest, the very ones I'm dismantling.) I can hear Gregory object: "You're swimming against the current of human history. Enclosure is the next logical step in our emancipation from Terra. It is the necessary future."

I cannot refute him. I can only say no. Every message he beams to me carries the same refrain: "If you don't care about poisoning yourself, at least think of Teeg."

I do think of Teeg, all the time, and of the shrunken world she will inherit. Tonight I must scrub her with special care.

She prances up to me, palm thrust forward, to show me how the whorls in a shell resemble those on her thumb. "We're made the same," she cries with pleasure.

"So you are," I answer.

TWELVE

Phoenix tossed notebooks, microfilms, bits of bark and stone into the vaporizer. Footprints of rebellion. He listened with regret to the hiss as each tell-tale item withered to a memory of molecules. Down in the guts of Oregon City devices would sort the vapors and reuse them for making plastic kidneys or glowrods or spoons. He searched the apartment for other incriminating evidence. Guides to meditation, maps of the coast, stick-figure illustrations of Teeg's yoga positions—all went into the shaft. Hiss, hiss. Soon the only remaining clues were the holos of Whale's Mouth Bay, tiny cubes intricate with the shapes of beach and cliff and grasses. He squeezed them until the points dug into his palm. Once he destroyed them he would have no way of bringing the wilds to life. And what if the city spun its webs of comforts around him again, lulled him in the hammock of its pleasures, until he grew to dread the outside?

Why not just leave the holos in the projector until the last moment? It was early in the year for typhoons. But you never knew about weather. Cantankerous, the weather. Any day, a storm could roar across the Pacific, tearing at the Enclosure's skin, and the crew might be called out to mend a float or weld a cracked tube, and if the call arrived while he was away from the apartment, there would be no time for returning home to vaporize the cubes. And he must leave no tracks. If the crew simply vanished, apparently gobbled up by the sea, the health patrollers would lose no sleep. There were always too many bodies crowding the Enclosure. Security would simply recruit new troubleshooters. But if the H.P. came along, found the holos, and recognized the Oregon coast, they would have gliders waiting in Whale's Mouth Bay when the crew arrived. Welcome to quarantine, ladies and gentlemen.

Better to be safe. Phoenix quickly opened his fist and brushed the miniature cubes into the shaft. With a sizzle his phantom bay was gone—the black cliffs and pebbled beach, the windbent trees, the waves frozen as they broke into foam, the glittering shells, the sky.

He surveyed the apartment one last time to make sure nothing looked amiss. Wigs dangled on their racks like trophies from a scalping expedition. Moodgowns of various cuts, bereft of bodies, hung neutral gray in the closet. Paint bottles stood in parade formation before the mirror. Photo-murals slathered pattern after abstract pattern across the wall. There was nothing in his library of tapes that a contented citizen of Oregon City would not read. The video and food vendor and info terminals were all standard, their sterilized surfaces gleaming like new teeth, their control knobs and keyboards waiting for commands. Nothing anywhere marked him as a renegade. After he vanished, a team would come here to inspect things, to wind up his affairs, to unravel the ties between the late Phoenix Marshall and the human system.

There would be precious few ties to unravel. As Phoenix moped around the apartment he was struck by how little imprint he had left on the place. The furniture, of mirror-surfaced pipe and curved polyglass, was for sale in every city in the network. The posters and prints that hung on his wall also hung in the windows of half the decorating stores of Oregon City. The mood synthesizer, chemmie-dispenser, eros couch and other appliances had come as a set from Teledyne, and the whole outfit could be plugged into any apartment in the city. In fact, the entire apartment could be unplugged from Portland Complex and reinserted in any one of several hundred housing towers.

"You aren't what you own," Teeg had scolded him one day.

"On my salary, that's lucky."

"Then why do you cling to all this stuff?" The sweep of her arm dismissed everything he had worked for years to buy. "Remember what Thoreau said: 'A person is rich in proportion to the number of things she can live without.'"

By that measure, Phoenix was growing richer all the time. In the seven months since he had first come upon her in the corridor, her feet bare and her armpits sweaty from walking, he had let most of his possessions go. Between yoga and meditation and study there was little time outside working hours to use the gadgets. Now he wandered through his own apartment with a sense of detachment, as if this were a museum exhibit of some remote and dim-witted culture.

In a belt-pack, thin enough so that when it was strapped to his stomach no bulge showed through the gown, he stowed the few things he cared about: the fossil Teeg had given him; microfiche texts of poetry, philosophy, meteorology, and the history of science; photographs of his parents from the time before their divorce, before his mother's accident, before his father's drug coma; a bone-handled pocket-knife (bone of *what*? he often wondered); emergency food and medicine to see him through the water-borne trip to Whale's Mouth Bay.

Whenever he tried to imagine what it would be like, out there bobbing around on the waves like a bit of flotsam, with actual wind in his face and the naked sky overhead and the awesome continent unrolling before him, he felt a rising sense of panic. The early astronauts must have felt the same queasiness, just before launching for the first time to Luna or Venus or one of the countless inhospitable rocks afloat in the solar system.

When the fear grew too strong he shut his eyes and meditated upon the fire, and the other seekers rose within him: Teeg with her hair like flame; bald-domed Marie, whose face seemed to concentrate emotion the way a magnifying glass concentrated light; plum-faced Sol with the lacerated voice; massive Jurgen, with a dark stare like the mouth of a cave; and all the rest of them, face after face. They flamed in him, licked him into their single fire, until he felt at peace.

At work he studied the monitors with extra care. Give us a nasty storm off the northwest coast, he thought, crack a seatube or drown an algae farm, and outside we go. Data on air pressure, wind velocity, and ocean currents oozed from the teleprinters. The measurements came from floating buoys and moored balloons, from satellites and seabed stations. Cybers turned the numbers into images on his console, abstract designs like Persian carpets, like shattered glass, and his job was to read meanings in them. He thought of the old shamans, hunting for omens in the entrails of pigs.

On the screens the North American cities and interconnecting tubes showed a pale green. Across this human web the cyber traced movements of air masses, high-pressure and low-pressure zones, temperature gradients, the scudding ballet of wind. Kindly weather appeared on the screens as arabesques of blue. The more menacing the weather, the more its color shaded toward the far end of the spectrum, through yellow and orange to incendiary red. The color of Teeg's hair, Phoenix had decided. Which was appropriate, since she had burst into his life like a typhoon. He had read about foul weather—gales whipping up whitecaps on the ocean, snow smothering the mountains, rain drenching or sun scorching the plains, hail hammering the dandelions—but he had never felt the weather on his own skin. He had only watched it glide soundlessly across the ovoid screens, a dance of abstract forms.

After glancing stealthily at the workers who occupied desks to his right and left, to make sure they were studying their own consoles, Phoenix dialed the scanner to highest resolution and set the coordinates for Whale's Mouth. The satellite took half a minute to respond, since an auto-program was necessary before it could fix upon an area outside the surveillance net. On visual, all that showed were clouds, so he switched over to infrared, then to the radiation display bands, then to magnetic and gravitational field scans. Nothing suspicious appeared on any of those channels. Just another deserted patch of earth. Once the settlement was built, however, and once solar collectors and wind dynamoes and domes began trapping heat, a keen eye would be able to detect aberrations in the infrared scan. But it was unlikely that such an eye would ever direct the sensors upon Whale's Mouth, unless some dramatic sign gave the settlement away. Teeg had chosen the spot shrewdly. No artery of the human network passed anywhere near the place. The renegades who had once lurked in the Oregon forests had long since been rehabilitated or exterminated. The bay and its encircling mountains had dropped through the meshes of history.

Phoenix switched back to visual mode. At last through a gap in the clouds he spied the hooked finger of blue where the bay clawed into the cliffs. The boulders in the shallows were ringed with lacy collars of foam as the waves broke over them. The black cliffs were pockmarked with even blacker caves, like the sunken eyes of very old men who have seen much sadness. Tides had scrubbed away all evidence that Jurgen and the others had stashed several tons of materials in those caves. The path leading away from the beach to the oil pipeline in the foothills was invisible except where it passed over dunes. There Phoenix could see faint wheelmarks. A few days of wind would scatter those signs as well.

Returning the satellite to routine surveillance, Phoenix erased from the cyber all evidence of his visit to Whale's Mouth. Leave no tracks for the H.P. He leaned forward and gazed along the ranks of observers, each painted face tilted upward, each wigged head clasped by earphones, eyes turned glassily upon the screens, intently watching the ballet of clouds. Mesmerized. You could not follow that dance of white and blue for longer than forty minutes without the mind going blank, the self dissolving into mist and air.

So rest breaks came every half hour. Phoenix's relief—a slump-shouldered woman whose last name he had learned after two years of working with her and whose first name he had never been told—now stood beside his chair.

"Break," she said. And that was about all she ever said. She kept her face averted while he unclasped the earphones and stood up.

"All quiet," he reported, wondering idly what she looked like beneath the facepaint, beneath the wig (chartreuse and mauve today, like the mistress-of-ceremonies on *Win a Planet*), beneath the muffling clothes.

Without answering she placed her cushion in the chair, wiped a sani-cloth over the desk wherever his arms might have rested, then took his seat at the console.

Touch me not, he thought, riding the belt to his rest cubicle. Other workers rode away to their own cubicles or rode back to the monitoring room with eyes lowered and voices still. Some he recognized from the way a paunch humped beneath a gown, or the way a head seemed to perch like a bulb atop a scrawny neck. But most were costumed and painted into anonymity. Their eyes, when you could glimpse them, were rarely the same color two days running. You never saw the person; you saw the current persona.

Hiding behind a disguise had once seemed reasonable to Phoenix, since he had been raised to believe that contact with other people was the chief source of disorder and sorrow. How else will we ever liberate ourselves from the slavery of flesh? his teachers had asked. How will we survive the friction of life in the city unless we insulate ourselves?

Inside the cubicle he closed his eyes. He counted breaths, rode in and out with the air, until the stillness of meditation began to wash over him. Husk after husk fell away, leaving him naked, waiting to be touched.

When the alarm buzzed after fifteen minutes, he opened his eyes onto the grid of holes in the acoustical tile overhead. His limbs felt sluggish, unwilling to resume the stiff pose of a citizen. Back to cloud-watching.

The slump-shouldered woman made way for him, sweeping her cushion from the chair, scouring her handprints from the desk.

"Quiet?" he asked.

"Nothing," she conceded in a monotone. And then she was gone—only to return half an hour later. And so they would alternate through his shift, like two lepers locked in a dance in which touching was forbidden.

A week had passed since the last ingathering, then three weeks, four. It was March, a month Teeg assured him made a difference in the wilds. Everything would be greening up, she told him. Ferns would be uncurling their new fronds like question marks through the loam. Birds would be singing with amorous intent, little feathered balls of lust. March was also dandy for stirring up foul weather over the Pacific. Tropical seas heated up, cloud clusters straggled into shape, and occasionally one of those clusters would begin to swirl, sucking heat and moisture from the ocean. It would look on the satellite monitors like a great spiral galaxy, graceful arms of cloud curving outward, with a deceptively peaceful eye in its middle, and this typhoon would then play hell over the ocean.

So far in March three typhoons had formed in the Pacific, but each had surged westward, cracking travel tubes and battering aquafarms near the float-cities of Japan and the Philippines. Near Oregon City the weather remained gentle. No violent storms, no gales, no hint of typhoons. The lights on Phoenix's monitors hovered safely in shades of indigo and blue.

Most of those March days the crew spent working repairs on the city, replacing photoelectric cells or mending flotation collars. It made Phoenix uneasy to think of Teeg laboring away shoulder-to-shoulder with some sweating companion. "Who're you working with these days?" he asked her by vidphone.

"Does it matter?"

"Just curious."

"Depends on the assignment. Sometimes Jurgen and Hinta, sometimes Marie or Rand." She gave him a sharp look—or rather, her image on the vidphone, flat and odorless, untouchable, gave him a sharp look. "Phoenix, I despise jealousy. There's no room for it in the ingathering."

"Jealousy?" He forced a laugh. She could read him even through all the electronics that separated them. "I ask a simple question and you decide I'm jealous?"

"Forget it." She looked away from the camera, off to one side, as if she were bored with him, as if some more interesting spectacle—a chemmie-tripper or disney-bird—had suddenly materialized in her apartment. "The waiting's getting us all down." Now she faced him again, playful. "What good is a weatherman if he can't deliver us a hurricane?"

"Typhoon," he corrected her. "They're called typhoons in the Pacific. Hurricanes in the Atlantic."

"Typhoon, then."

"There's a vicious one south of here. But it's tracking westward, like all the earlier ones."

"Why don't you steer it our way?"

"They gave up on that idea. Typhoons don't obey."

"I'm only kidding," she said.

"Last time they tried it was in '39, when the thing backed up on them and drowned four-hundred-some people on the Alaska City crew."

"Yes," she replied soberly. "That was the one that killed my father."

"I'm sorry."

"Don't be. I'm not."

Teeg was gazing off to one side again, moody, unreachable.

"When can I see you?" he pleaded.

"You're looking at me now."

"Touch you, I mean."

This won a smile. "Listen to the man talk! I'll free you yet." Soft green glow of her eyes. "Brew us up a little tempest, just enough to crack the bottle somewhere nearby, then you and I can go outside and do all the touching your heart desires."

Heart, he thought, desires. Teeg would not let him visit her, for fear the H.P. might grow curious about their weatherman's friendship. She even rationed their vidcalls. Now a week had passed since he had last talked with her, and he was on his hour-long break, riding pedbelts around the hem of Marconi Plaza. At each angle of the belt's hexagonal route other passengers stepped aboard or stepped off, but Phoenix kept on riding, round and round the plaza, trying to unsnarl himself from the web of the city. He was afraid to go back to his rest cubicle. Its emptiness terrified him. In meditation that morning he had been unable to summon up more than a flicker of the inner light. If he did not gather with the crew again soon, he was afraid the light would fade away entirely and dread of the wilds would paralyze him.

The air smelled vaguely of bodies and lemons. The

bodies were a constant background flavor, despite the
universal application of deodes. The lemon meant it was the
last week of the month, time for a change of fragrance in
Oregon City. What had it been before lemons? Coffee?
Burnt candles? He could not remember.

The last week of March. Back at the office another
typhoon was skidding across his monitor, but again it was
far to the south and heading westward. Zuni Franklin and
the others had known what they were doing when they
chose the location for Oregon City, at the warm junction of
the California and Japanese Currents, away from the paths
of most foul weather. Most, but not all. One of these storms
would eventually leap its tracks and come howling toward
the city.

Phoenix gazed up past the spiky summits of office towers
and apartment complexes, up to the frosted surface of the
dome. The sky ballet for the day was a swirl of russets and
golds, probably meant to harken back to some racial
memory of autumn. From this far below you could not
distinguish the struts that bound the dome together. As he
rose in thought to that arched ceiling, his inner space
swelled to include the million-windowed towers, the hur-
tling gliders, the citizens meandering through the city like
molecules in a blaze of light, the display boards where ads
bedazzled noontime onlookers—swelled to encompass the
whole of Oregon City. It was a mighty place, technology's
cathedral, the visible architecture of a dozen centuries of
thought. How could he leave it? The city fed him, kept him
warm, sheltered him from beasts. The city was the climax
of evolution on the planet. How could he dream of leaving it
to go live like a savage in the wilds?

He tried to summon up the inner light, even to recollect
Teeg's face, but the dome pressed around him like the plates
of his own skull. There was no seeing through the walls of
glass or bone.

The buzz of his wristphone broke the spell ₍of the city.
Back to the desk, he thought. Then he noticed his lunch-

break was only half over, and the phone was blinking on the emergency circuit. "Marshall," he whispered into the tiny microphone.

"E-class alert in sectors 44 through 46," came the mechano voice of the shift-coordinator. "All monitors report immediately. Repeat—"

Quenching the synthetic voice in mid-sentence, Phoenix leapt from the belt and raced across Marconi Plaza to the entrance of the Surveillance Tower. Faces swiveled toward him in alarm, then swiveled quickly away before he could return their frightened stares. Madman, they would think. Chemmie-crazed. A victim of the resurgent beast.

Phoenix had no time to care what they thought as he let himself through barrier after barrier with palm flattened against the identi-plates. E-class alert might only mean a severe ocean spill or volcanic activity in the Aleutian Trench, but it could also mean the typhoon had swerved and was now heading for Oregon City.

He kept poking the elevator button until the doors wheezed open. Rising the one hundred forty-three stories, he felt more than his usual vertigo.

Back at his desk he did not give his relief woman time enough to wipe her fingerprints away. He flounced into his seat, grabbed the headset from her. She backed away with her painted features barely under control.

"Tracking north-northeast at eleven degrees, speed thirty-two knots," the voice of the cyber was droning through the earphones.

The satellite monitor showed the spiral typhoon edging into his sector. He replayed the ninety-minute elapse record, tracking the storm's movement back over the Pacific. He soon identified the point, far south of the city, where the typhoon had suddenly veered from its westward path. Oregon City lay squarely in its way. Why hadn't the sector-thirty people caught this two hours ago? A glance down the ranks of mesmerized faces reminded him of how many times he also had stopped believing in the significance of these gauzy cloud patterns. Storms raging outside? What outside? Weren't these just images on a screen?

"Notify controller of seatubes, aquafarms, and generators, segment Astoria through Seattle," he murmured into his headset, keeping his voice to a monotone.

The cyber tinted the satellite images a vicious red, to register the gravity of the storm. On the screen the typhoon looked like a huge scarlet spiral of blood, drawing yet more blood from the sky. He knew the extremely low pressure beneath the cyclone would suck the waters upward and drive a storm surge before it. And that was what would slam into the outflung domes and tubes of the Enclosure, that raised fist of water. Unless it changed course, it would soon intercept the frail north-south line of the Alaska seatube.

On a private channel he dialed Teeg. The call was transferred from her apartment to her belt-phone, so she must have been out somewhere, perhaps on another job. "Passio," she replied. Faceless, her voice withered by electronics, she might have been a mechano speaking to him.

"Teeg, are you outside?" he said anxiously.

"No, we're down in level K, overhauling a desalinator."

"Is everybody down there?"

"Yes," she answered. "It's a big job."

"Who's on sea-alert?"

"We are."

"Good. Get the crew together and be ready for a call. This could be our storm."

"How long?"

"Forty-five, fifty minutes. Unless the thing changes direction again."

"Is it big enough?"

He glanced at the screen. The snarl of red thickened, sucking all the sky's energy into a fist of wind. "Plenty big."

"We hadn't figured on your being at work when the storm came," she said impatiently.

"I don't run the weather."

There was a pause. He could sense the wheels spinning in her quick brain. Then she asked, "How long until your next rest break?"

He checked the clock. "Twenty-four minutes."

"Okay. No questions now. Just do exactly what I say. When your relief comes, take off as usual. Go to your cubicle, strip down, grease your body all over. Then put on the shimmersuit and belly-pack, and get back into that traveling tent of yours."

Listening to her, he plucked nervously at the folds of his gown. He stroked the mood-seam, to shut off the fireworks of color the garment was flashing. "What do they think when I don't show up at work again?"

"They think you're a statistic. Another body they lost track of."

"But people don't just—"

"People *do* disappear," she interrupted, "all the time. Pressure of work. Despair. They'll just think you couldn't stand the ugliness of another hurricane—"

"Typhoon."

"Whatever. Couldn't stand knowing all the damage it would do. So maybe you crawled into the nearest vaporizer."

"But they—"

"What do they know? What do they care? Look, Phoenix, we've been through all this. Your apartment's clean, your record's clean. You simply vanish. Another breakdown. A statistic. Poof."

The puff of air seemed to ease through the speaker into his ear. "All right. I change clothes, grease up. Then where do I go?"

"You go as fast as you can to the hovercraft terminal, number seventeen. That's where we ship from, if something gives way outside."

"How do I get through the sanitation barriers?"

"Hinta will meet you outside the port. Her palm will open any health gate."

"If the mechano asks me for a voice-ID?"

"Hinta knows the override code."

"And what if the storm misses us? What if nothing breaks?"

"Just come. Shut up that rattling brain and follow the light."

A metallic click broke the connection. Her excitement rang on in his ears. When the relief woman sidled up to his chair, waiting mutely for him to leave, he stood up with a tremor in his legs. "Grade C typhoon in sector 45," he told her simply, "tracking on visual."

In his cubicle he smeared himself with grease, for protection against salt water. But as he rode belts across Oregon City to the hovercraft terminal, his sweat kept trickling through the grease, as if his body's own salt were seeping out to meet the salt of the ocean.

22 January 2032—*Vancouver*

The last pieces of Vancouver left by tube this morning for the ocean building site of Alaska City. Gregory, who hates the wilds in any weather, travels up there in the midst of winter to make sure his blueprints are followed to the letter. The Franklin woman stays in Oregon City. Will he see my handprint on any of those chunks of Vancouver, copper and aluminum and steel, before they melt and take on the shapes of his vision?

When we were studying architecture at Houston I never dreamed he would one day build new cities while I tore old ones down. He calls me the destructive one, because I oversee the salvaging of empty shells. He doesn't understand my need to touch the old materials, smell dirt and trees in the parks, wander through the antique buildings with their windows and doors that open onto the actual air.

If people can't live in the outside cities, I tell him, at least we can incorporate some of the old materials in the enclosed cities. Urban reincarnation, I tell him. He looks at me blankly through the telescreen. Spirit-words leave him cold.

I can tell from the fish-slide of his eyes he has given me up. Let the wild woman rot in her filthy paradise. But everytime we talk, in words or silences, the same command seeps through: Send Teeg inside.

THIRTEEN

On the hovercraft instrument panel an amber light kept flashing. More data on the seatube rupture, Teeg guessed. But she dared not answer the call, for it might also be Transport Control, demanding to know why the crew still hadn't left the hangar.

Come on, Phoenix. If he didn't show up in about two shakes they would have to leave him behind. Could they smuggle him from the city later? That would be risky, might give the colony away. But waiting for another seatube emergency would be even more risky. Since losing their meeting place in the oil tank they had gone over a month without ingathering, and the forcefield of spirit that bound them together was weakening.

The thought of leaving Phoenix behind swung a weight in her heart.

"Any sign?" Marie asked from the cabin.

No, Teeg was going to answer, when she glimpsed Hinta jogging down the ramp from the sanitation port. Behind her loped a clown-painted figure in billowing gown. Tassels and sleeves fluttered about him as he ran, and the green tresses of his wig trailed behind like seaweed. Even through this bizarre get-up, Teeg recognized him by the way he bit down on his tongue and by the shape of his ears.

"Yes," she answered Marie gaily, "here he comes in all his finery."

Hinta soon ducked through the hatch, straw-colored hair lolling across her cheeks. A moment later Phoenix lurched through behind her, fringes flying, skirts clutched in each hand. Cheers greeted him.

"Made it," he panted. "Long way—crowds—stupid belts."

Hands disentangled him from his outlandish costume. The facepaint (green forehead and chin, purple cheeks, orange nose, vermilion lips) would have to wait for soap or saltwater. Lightfooted in his shimmersuit, he danced a little jig, and then collapsed into a seat.

"Buckle in," Teeg called, "and put blinders on that giddy clown."

With chest still heaving from his run, Phoenix submitted to the black eye-patches.

As soon as the hatch sealed tight with a kiss of gaskets, Teeg thumbed the lift button. The hangar doors swung open and the hovercraft coasted into the sky. There was a smash of sunlight, a shudder as wind caught the craft, and they were out over the sea.

"Goodbye, city!" Marie cried, and she sang a few words for departure.

Silence followed her song as the crew turned inward to celebrate their deliverance. Teeg had to keep her eyes open to watch the instruments and the waves, yet she could feel the strength of the ingathering. It was a little bit like the heavy g-force you felt when accelerating in a rocket, only pleasanter, a gravity of the spirit.

After a while easy talk fluttered through the cabin. Oregon City dwindled behind them, humped and glittering, like a cold glassy sun perishing in the water, and the satellite domes surrounding it were so much froth.

Once the hovercraft escaped the city's turbulence, Teeg set the autopilot and went back to sit with Phoenix. His knuckles were pressed white on the armrest. "You all right?" she asked.

"The light," he answered through clenched teeth. Tears seeped below his eye patches.

"But you can't see a thing," she objected.

"I feel it on my face, my hands."

She peeled one of his hands from the armrest, laid it in her lap. The hand was a many-boned wonder, with slivers of paint in the crosshatched grain of the skin. She began tracing figure-eights around his knuckles. "You'll get used to it."

"Sure, I know, I know." His head tilted back against the seat cushion, Adam's apple prominent, showing the border along his jaw where the purple mask gave way to the tawny color of his own skin. He seemed to doze while she traced the symbol of infinity around his knuckles. When the hovercraft suddenly bucked in a crosswind he jerked his hand free and seized the armrest. "What's that?"

"Wind."

"It felt so sudden. Like a fist." He drew his legs up as if to make ready for a jump. "It always looked so deliberate and slow on the monitors."

"This is only the trailing edge of the storm."

His body coiled even more tightly. "You mean it gets worse?"

"Look, why don't you let me take those blinders off, put the smoked glasses on?"

"It gets *worse*?"

"The raft will be much rougher. So you've got to get used to it. Now let me take those blinders off."

"No, no, not yet." He flattened a hand over each eye.

"You'd rather fly blind?"

After a moment's hesitation the hands lowered. "Go ahead."

She quickly replaced his blindfold with sun-goggles, glimpsing the puckered skin around the shut eyes, like two purses laced tight. "Now open them slowly."

Through the somber lenses his eyes appeared as black slits, winced shut, then slitted open again. He slowly craned about, squinting through the hovercraft windows. "So that's sunlight?"

"It's what your goggles don't filter out."

"It's bluer than I thought."

"That's from the rain clouds." Near Oregon City the clouds had been silver fishscales, each flake catching the light. Out here in the storm, clouds sloped away in great slabs toward the horizon, ranging from violet to deep purple to black. It was like an incline in the mind, tilting away toward sorrow.

Phoenix pressed his face to the window, nose and lips smushed against the glass, drinking in the spectacle. "All these colors. Are they always there? And the ocean! Video never showed it so . . . *huge*."

"You can't squeeze all that onto a wall screen."

"The satellite images make it look far away, like another planet. Tame somehow."

"Tame it's not," she said. Though the typhoon had already left these waters, the hovercraft still bucked and sawed in the wind. Occasionally a high wave slapping the belly sent a shudder through the frame. Just a little reminder—a cat toying with a bird. "You sit tight," she told him. "We've got to get ready for work."

Tool packs slumped around the hatch at the rear of the craft. Some of the conspirators were wriggling into wet-suits. Marie was helping Sol, who seemed too weak to dress himself. The ones already dressed were checking the waterproof bundles, the uninflated raft, the tanks of compressed air. So many membranes had to hold—skin of boat and skin of body—or they would not survive this savage dunking long enough to reach Whale's Mouth.

"Everything set?" Teeg asked Jurgen.

He had both legs in a wetsuit and was shoving his arms through the sleeves. "Set as we're going to be. You just keep this bubble aloft and keep it handy. Doesn't look very friendly out there."

In the wetsuit he seemed like a bulky merman, green-skinned, heavily muscled. When you wanted to lean on someone who would not give under your weight, someone sturdy and rooted, you leaned on Jurgen.

"I'll be up here," Teeg promised him. "Signal when you want the raft."

On her way back to the cockpit she stopped beside Phoenix. He had changed the first window, smudged with his facepaint, for another one. "The streak down there—looks like an icicle—that's the seatube," she said. "You see where two orange balloons are whipping and bobbing? Those mark the break."

"We're that close?" Behind the goggles his eyes widened.

"Just a couple of minutes. Get your wetsuit on."

In the cockpit she returned the controls to manual, easing the hovercraft alongside the floating tube, heading for the tethered balloons. Waves still licked over the pontoons onto the seatube. A vicious one—or a few hundred vicious ones—had cracked the polyglass outer wall, releasing the balloons and triggering alarms in Transport Control. *Emergency, emergency, the human skin is broken, the beast world is invading.*

"Going down," Jurgen shouted.

Teeg heard the sucking noise as the hatch opened, the slither of the exit chute unfurling. Half a minute later there were eight heads bobbing in the rough water beneath the seatube, then eight bodies clambering onto the pontoons. Several arms waved assurance to her, legs staggering to keep their balance. "Hang some zeroes," Sol's words came crackling through the speakers, "and be ready to come get us." His voice was labored.

"You okay, Sol?" Wordless static in her earphones. "Sol?"

He grunted yes. His plum-dark face, fringed white with beard, hung like a troublesome weight in Teeg's mind as she tilted the hovercraft into a lazy circular glide. She knew the screens tracking her from Oregon City would show her path in glowing loops.

"Time for me to play fish," she told Phoenix.

He was taking great sticky steps about the cabin, trying out his wetsuit. "This thing will really keep me dry in that chaos down there?"

"Wet isn't what will hurt you. It's the cold. And these outfits keep you warm." Sliding on, the wetsuit always felt clammy and stubborn, like the skin of some slow-witted beast. A shark, maybe. Soon all of her, except the oval window at her face, was sheathed in this rubbery hide.

While she and Phoenix lugged raft, survival bundles, and air tanks to the hatch, she calculated how much longer the repair would take: flotation collars to stabilize the broken segment, torches cutting away the weakened polyglass, patches shaped to the curve of the tube and fastened with epoxy, then torches fusing the edges. Healed scar. The skin of the human network intact once more.

"Another dozen circles," she told Phoenix, "and they should be ready. Into the float vest with you."

It took fifteen circles before Sol's voice crackled through, panting between each word: "All—done—notify—Control —and—bring—us—up."

No one would ever be hoisted into this hovercraft again, but messages beamed over the radio and monitored back in Transport Control had to pretend the mission was an ordinary one. (Would they detect the pain in Sol's voice, the wheeze of cancerous lungs?) Teeg sent word to Oregon City that the break was sealed, the crew was recovered, the craft was headed home. And that lie would probably be her last exchange with the Enclosure.

As the hovercraft glided past the seatube, eight slick

bodies again balancing on pontoons, she opened the hatch and the raft tumbled out. She kept the hovercraft steady while the torpedo-shaped raft smacked the waters. Aerators quickly pumped the yellow skin tight, swelling the small package to nine meters of cushiony boat, roofed and windowed like a toy hovercraft, flimsy, wallowing on the waves. Most of the seekers had to lurch two or three times before wriggling onto the yellow bobbing ark.

"Now you," she told Phoenix, shoving him down the escape chute. He resisted her with a slight back-leaning weight of his body, and then he was gone, reappearing a moment later amidst a flurry of spray and flailing arms beside the raft. The others soon tugged him aboard.

That left Teeg alone in this doomed machine. She set the pilot for a skimming flight-path back toward Oregon City, a path that would take the hovercraft thirty-five or forty kilometers before it nipped the waves. It would skip a few times like a flat rock, then smash into the unyielding water. Screens tracking the flight would glow with urgent sparks where the ship went down. Rescue teams would find the wreck, its raft and survival gear jettisoned. Satellites could spy nothing through the storm, so shuttle planes would scout the area of the crash. Verdict after seventy-two hours: all hands drowned.

Long before that, if all went well, the raft and its ten passengers would be safely snugged away in Whale's Mouth.

Teeg cinched the flotation vest tight around her chest. Another artificial skin, to keep the saltwater in her cells from mixing with the saltwater of the ocean. She glanced around the cabin, alert for any sign of their conspiracy. The place looked innocent, except for a splotch of Phoenix's facepaint on the window. With licked palm she smeared it away. His gown and wig had already been vaporized—and good riddance, she thought. Shed all the old skins.

She gave one last hasty look, like a traveler careful not to leave anything behind in a hotel room. The hovercraft was already nosing away on its ill-fated trajectory. The raft swayed farther and farther astern. Finally she yanked the facemask into place, skidded over the lip of the escape hatch. For a fraction of a second the chute brushed against her sides, feathery, then she fell through open air, the ocean spread its corrugations beneath her like a vast and rumpled bedspread, and then water crashed around her.

Before she could gain her bearings a wave dragged her sputtering through its guts. The vest bobbed her to the surface, but she could not spy the raft. Away off to one side the seatube floated, endless frosty stripe, too far to swim in such rough water. Nothing else visible in any direction except furious green. Another wave gobbled her, spat her out. If she couldn't see that wallowing yellow ark, they'd never see her. Easy, she thought. Don't panic.

Another wave jammed brine down her throat. Shutting her eyes, she listened inward for the stillness. Dwell in the light, the light, the light. With tons of water thrashing all round her, heaving her about like a chip of wood, she grew calm. Once she quit fighting the waves there was pleasure in the muscular heft and sway. She rode with mind gone blank, a toy on the ocean, until a crest lifted her high enough to make out the yellow blob.

Fifteen minutes of swimming landed her, belly up and exhausted, on the floor of the raft.

"We'd about given you up for lost," Hinta told her. The long healing fingers smoothed water from Teeg's forehead.

When she tried to answer, all that emerged was a salty sputter. The faces bent over her were tinged yellow by light suffusing through the roof and walls of the raft. One of them was a clown's cockeyed mug, with makeup smeared by the sea into a pie of colors.

"Hello, fish," said Phoenix.

"Hello there, clown-face."

The way she reached up to stroke a finger across his cheek must have convinced the others that she was in no danger of dying from her swim, for they sang her a brief welcoming song, a song of resurrection, and then they scattered to their stations in the raft, to map-screen and compass and wheel. Phoenix stayed beside her, on hands and knees for balance, and still the bucking of the raft made him scuttle to keep from rolling over.

"The green in my face isn't all from paint," he said.

"Pretty rough here," she agreed. Through the portholes she saw canyons and mountains of waves. "Everybody all right?"

"Arda wrenched a knee. Sol's hacking up blood."

Teeg propped herself onto elbows, searching for the plum-dark face.

"Don't worry," Phoenix soothed. "Hinta's with him. You rest."

She slumped down again. The raft bucked wildly. "Are we making any headway?"

"Jurgen swears we are. But it looks to me like the same old water over and over."

She listened to the seethe of bubbles at the stern, where the air jets were shoving against the ocean. It seemed uncanny, to be driven by these little bags of nothingness, these bubbles, all the way to land.

A heavy surge threw her on the floor and made Phoenix scramble crabwise. Before she could laugh, an even more violent wave tossed them both into a heap and piled four others on top of them. There was a sharp pain in her side where an elbow landed, and as the others unpiled she only had to rub the spot once to know it was more than a bruise. She remembered this knife-point of pain from earlier accidents.

"Fasten down!" Jurgen roared from the wheel.

Everyone climbed into a seat and buckled harnesses across chest and lap. Teeg had to loosen the straps to keep from squeezing her rib. Phoenix plumped down beside her.

"We caught up with the storm," he observed. For the first time she noticed he no longer wore goggles. His eyes seemed swollen from a steady diet of surprise. "It must have run into a cold air mass over the coast. That means we'll be hitting rain soon."

Here was the weatherman suffering his first weather. Teeg didn't blame him for being scared.

"These tubs are indestructible," she said, just as the first patter of rain sounded overhead. Soon the roof was thundering and the ocean, smoky with rain, looked as if it were afire. Phoenix called something to her, but she could not hear it above the drumming of the rain. She lifted her eyebrows.

"I said you look pale!" he shouted.

She made a megaphone of her hands and spoke into his ear. "I think I cracked something in that pile-up." His hair, brushing her nose, smelled of sweat. She nuzzled into it and kissed his ear, that whorl of cartilage and skin she would know from any other's.

Something—the news or the kiss—brought his face around to her and opened wide his eyes. His brown irises madly compensated for the sudden increase in light. "Cracked what?"

"A rib, I think. We'll patch it up when we get to shore."

"I'll tell Hinta!" he yelled.

Before she could stop him he was scrambling on all fours down the row of seats, legs and arms unsteady from the pitching of the raft. He spoke something close to Hinta's ear, then scrambled back, Hinta following with the first-aid satchel.

Like the others, Hinta had skinned back the hood of her wetsuit. Her long hair, knotted behind, was the lemony color of the raft. "Where is it?" she asked.

Teeg pointed to the rib three rungs from the bottom on her left side. Hinta's touch felt dull and distant through twin thicknesses of shimmersuit and wetsuit, until she reached the point where the knife pain was, and then Teeg winced. Lips pursed, Hinta focused an ortho-scanner over the rib. Teeg imagined what she would see—the creamy curving bone, the inky slash of the break. Phoenix wavered behind

Hinta's shoulder, peeking at the scanner, and Teeg could read the injury in his eyes.

"Can't it wait?" Teeg mouthed at her, unwilling to shout because of the pain.

"It'll have to," Hinta yelled. The tendons in her neck stood out. "Can't wrestle you out of these suits with it rough like this." Her hands moved gently around Teeg's waist. "Just hold very still, no sudden movements. If the rib snaps, you could puncture a lung."

"Can't you give her narco?" Phoenix pleaded.

"No chemmies. Her head has to be in working order in case we smash up."

Watching Hinta stagger back to her own seat, Teeg thought: If we smash up I'm finished anyway. Could never swim with this knife in my side.

"Anything I can do?" Phoenix said. Hunched beside her, his face a pie of colors, he looked in worse pain than she was.

"Smooth out the ocean!" Her attempt at laughter broke down into a cough, dredging up the taste of brine in her throat, and the pain of it blacked her out for a few seconds. Phoenix looked more distraught than before. She curled a hand around his neck and pulled him close, his ear to her lips. "Be still and don't worry. I'm going into trance and dive under this pain."

His crazy-quilt face swung out of sight and she closed her eyes. Wash of yellow light through her lids, gullying lift and fall of the raft, thunder overhead, fire in her rib. She kept her breath shallow, riding the air in and out. Then the yellow began to fade and there was only brightness. Stars, flung like salt through the brightness, congealed into one great sun, and the sun was still, and there was no bucking motion, no raft, no rough sea. The fire in her rib was a slender jet of flame from the sun, and there was no pain, there was only fire.

When she swam up out of the trance the pain swam back with her, but she ignored it, for the sea felt gentle and the roof was silent and the molten columns of sunlight streaming in through the portholes had turned a mellow rose. At the portholes across from her Phoenix and several others were shouldering for a view. Between their heads Teeg saw a ragged strip of brown, draped across the horizon like a scrap of cloth. Land.

She dipped in and out of the trance, shallower each time, thankful. When at last she surfaced for good, Jurgen was saying, "We hauled the supplies overland, from those hills back there. I never saw the place from the sea."

Arda, who was tracking the raft on an overhead projection of the Oregon coast, said, "We've got to be within a few hundred meters. I can't map it any closer than that."

"Hey, everybody move out of my way," Teeg said. "Let me have a look."

Her voice turned their worried faces around.

"How's the pain?"

"Does it hurt when you breathe?"

"Keep still until we land."

This last came from Hinta, who shook her head sharply *no* when Teeg reached for the buckles of her harness. She had to answer all their questions about the rib before they would shuffle aside to give her a view through the portholes. Teeg surveyed the rumpled strip of coast from left to right, a circular chunk at a time where the portholes opened, and in the next-to-last circle she found what she was looking for.

"There," she said, pointing, "you see that headland, the one with the nub on top? Isn't that the base of a lighthouse up there? Cement, flaking white paint?" Whale's Head, and beneath it Whale's Mouth, the gaping jaws of volcanic stone that had frightened her once when she was a child. Mother's place. Mother. Home.

Marie, with the binoculars, confirmed her vision, and Jurgen set the wheel accordingly.

The surf thickened near the shore, but the sea had spent its rage and only rocked the yellow ark enough to remind them all who was master. The bay accepted them like any other sea-offering, like driftwood, like a tangle of weeds. A few gulls carved the last dying colors of the day, skating across the sky with the ease of experts.

Phoenix knelt on the cushion beside her and watched this lazy flight. "Birds," he said wonderingly.

Of course, Teeg reminded herself, all this is new for him, like landing on some alien planet. "Herring gulls and kittiwakes and terns," she told him. The names tasted good on her lips. "If we're lucky, there might be cormorants and sandpipers."

"How can they just hang up there like that?"

"They ride the wind."

To the left waves shattered against a blunt cliff, and to the right against a fractured wall of rock that seemed to be sloughing into the sea. As a child she had thought of them as the whale's upper and lower jaws. Jurgen guided the raft skillfully between, until the prow, hesitating on a breaker, touched shore.

Teeg could not hear her own voice amidst the cheering. The whole raft trembled with shouts and the stamp of feet. Even Sol, who held a wad of gauze against his mouth, cried out in triumph. Phoenix hugged Teeg and pawed her hair and she nearly passed out from the wrenching in her rib. When she undid his hands she realized from the way they shook that he was clinging to her as much from fear as from joy.

"We're home," she said.

"I guess so."

"Aren't you glad?"

"Oh, sure, sure."

Sol was unloaded first, on a makeshift litter. Jurgen and Coyt set him down gently on a patch of sand. When they returned with the litter to fetch Teeg, she waved them away and walked from the raft on her own. Phoenix escorted her as far as the hatch, and there he balked, his hands raised as if to fend off the feeble strokes of the sun.

"Aren't you coming?" she said.

"In a minute."

Teeg watched the unpacking from a barnacle-encrusted rock on the beach, waiting for Phoenix to emerge. She kept her distance from Sol, for she sensed that he wanted to be left alone. Hinta was bending over him, touching his chest, murmuring. After a few moments she withdrew, and approached Teeg with the medicine satchel thumping against her leg.

"How is it with Sol?" Teeg asked.

"The artificial lung's okay," Hinta said. "But the other one's hemorrhaging."

"Why didn't he let them change the bad one?"

"The cancer's spread pretty much everywhere now. After the lung it would have been the liver, kidney, and on and on. He said he didn't want to die in pieces."

"Plutonium." Teeg spat out the word.

"Memo from the twentieth century," said Hinta, without any trace of irony.

Teeg glanced over at Sol, who sat with knees drawn up, holding himself together, while the other seekers carried equipment from the raft. "How long's he got?"

Hinta was peeling the wetsuit and shimmersuit down to Teeg's waist, uncovering the troublesome rib. "He's alive now, isn't he? And now's the only time we have."

"But wouldn't he have lasted longer inside?"

"More hours probably." Hinta gently touched the reddened skin above the fractured rib. Her fingers seemed to draw pain out of the injury. "But living isn't measured in hours, is it?"

"No, of course not." The late March evening, the mist from breakers, and the onshore breeze chilled Teeg's back and chest. The analgesic spray Hinta applied to the rib felt colder still. Her skin was a rash of tiny welts. Goosebumps, her mother used to call them, back when there were geese.

"Let me get some tape around here to keep that rib from wandering," Hinta said. She grazed one of the taut nipples, and Teeg was surprised by the sexual alarms running through her body. "After I get this on," Hinta explained, "all you have to do is loaf for about two weeks. No lifting, no pushing."

"No heavy breathing."

"Suit yourself in that department." Hinta smoothed the tape with birdsoft strokes. "But if you make love," she said, glancing toward the raft, "be sure you ride on top."

"Don't worry." Teeg grimaced. She knew the broken-rib routine from two earlier falls. She held the other woman's hand against the ache for a moment, imagining Hinta's spirit-power knitting the bone together. Hinta knew medicine the way a million people knew medicine; but it was because of her healing touch that she had become the crew's physician.

"Do you want Marie to go talk with him?" Hinta said. "She could help him deal with his wilderfear."

"No, let me see what I can do," Teeg said.

"Just take it easy. And don't worry about Sol. He's where he wants to be."

Hinta scrunched away over the sand until she reached Sol. He struggled up, wrapped an arm over her shoulders, and together they hobbled to the caves where the others were sorting out food and sleeping bags and cook gear. Tomorrow they would all begin erecting domes farther inshore, in the meadow beside the creek, where an arena of hills would shelter them from storms and from orbiting spy-eyes. For tonight, they would sleep in the caves, playing like savages. Everyone was there except Phoenix, whose silhouette paced back and forth inside the translucent skin of the raft, like some rebellious meal in the guts of a beached leviathan.

Teeg stuffed her arms in the shimmersuit, zipped it up, then peeled the wetsuit away. Amphibian shedding skin. Her mother had shown her frogs doing it, the glistening new bodies emerging from worn-out husks. Except for missing her mother and Zuni Franklin, she felt newborn, exultant.

The tape encircled her ribs like a ring of bone. She kicked off her boots, shed her socks. The stone was lingeringly warm underfoot. Walking to the raft she was aware of the black scoop of cliffs, the hill slopes feathered with hemlock and fir, the sea unfurling its endless blankets of froth. Home, this was home now; no more nights in Bottle City.

Through the hatch she could see Phoenix pacing, hands balled into fists next to his cheeks.

"You aren't coming out?"

He gave a quick shake of his head. The eyes had retreated into slits.

"Food's ready," she said.

Again the nervous head-shake, quick, like a spring-wound doll.

"Is it too much for you all at once?" she said. "Is that it?"

His face, suddenly lifted to her, was stretched taut with a panic she recognized, the same she had felt for a moment while bobbing in the furious unlandmarked ocean. Lost, alone, adrift in the wilds. "I know," she soothed him; "that's all right. I'll bring some food and sleeping bags in here." As she spoke she drew the shades down, until the interior of the raft was a bath of honey-colored light. "We'll sleep here. We'll take it slow. The land's patient."

When she made to duck out through the hatch, thinking to fetch the food and sleep gear before dark, he tugged at her arm and said, "Don't go."

The urgency in his voice spoke to the restlessness, the frenzy of celebration she had been feeling since the raft had touched shore. At his throat she found the cool tab of the zipper and drew it down. As he shrugged free of the wetsuit and kicked the clinging rubbery hide from his feet, she unzipped both shimmersuits, his and hers. His body emerged pale, sunless, a brand-new creature. There was a whirlpool of brown hair around each of his nipples and a mop of brown where his cock rose, strung with veins, stiff.

It was a spring creature, his shy cock, and all of him was newborn.

"Help me," he begged.

"It's all right, it's all right," she said, wiping the last smudges of paint from his cheeks, stroking his lovely backside. "Just pretend you're flying. Ride the wind." One hand found the dip at his waist between hipbone and ribs, the other pressed the small of his back, drawing him to her. His chest smelled of the grease he had smeared on it to protect him from the sea. Her breasts were slick against him. The hollow at the base of his throat tasted of salt.

"But your rib . . ."

"What rib?"

After clinging fearfully to her for a moment, his hands at last came alive, two shy animals exploring her slopes and crevices. Wherever they brushed her skin tremors ran outward, like ripples on wind-kissed water. She pressed against him, their bodies tilting, until he lay beneath her on the floor of the raft. Her breast in his mouth was a delectable fruit, his cock was like an insistent root between her legs.

"Fly," she murmured, settling her weight onto him. "Let the current carry us."

The raft, though firmly grounded on the beach, rocked with the rhythm of the sea.

FOURTEEN

Terra's occasional rampages put the newscasters in a quandary. Reports of earthquakes and volcanoes and pestilence in the wilds made life within the Enclosure seem all the more desirable. But if the wilds actually broke through the skin of the human system? And if Terra, on one of these violent sprees, actually killed a few people, swallowed an Arctic research team down a sudden throat of ice, or drowned a repair crew in the ocean outside Oregon City? That sort of news would be disquieting. The trick was to remind people of Terra's brutality without making them brood too much about the Enclosure's fragility.

So the first half meter of newsfax unscrolling on Zuni's desk brought her word of the typhoon, without mentioning damage or casualties. FREAK STORM LASHES OREGON CITY, the headline proclaimed. DOME UNHARMED. At least my architecture is sound, she reflected wryly. How had the travel-tubes fared? No mention of that in the lead story. Curious, she skimmed over the week's fashion news, skimmed rhetoric tournament results and summaries of

143

World Council debates, skimmed the daily geometries and mating announcements, until she found, eight meters from the beginning of the scroll, a brief notice of damage to the Oregon-Alaska seatube. Typhoon generates high waves, the article stated. Seatube cracks—vacuum partially destroyed —commuter traffic disrupted—protective systems activated—wildergoers quickly repair damage.

Who worked those repairs? With a heart-pounding premonition of what she might find, Zuni spun the newsfax rapidly, eyes skidding over the headlines, until she reached the fine print at the twenty-three meter mark. There were legal notices and production quotas and, scattered among them like somber floor tiles, the black-edged obituaries. With a magnifying glass she studied these death reports, and eventually discovered the tiny caption she had been seeking and dreading: WILDERGOERS DROWN AT SEA. Beneath the heading she found the nine names: Jurgen Marberg, Hinta Wood, Sol Musada, Marie O'Brien, Teeg Passio, Arda Ling, Indy Chavez, Josh Swenson, Coyt Russell. The words strung out below them were painfully small and blurred. She squinted, tilted the magnifier, struggling for sharper focus. At last she made out the words: shuttle demolished—no bodies recovered—died protecting the Enclosure. And so on through a few more perfunctory sentences.

The projector cast a new mural onto the wall in front of her. She glanced up at it, unseeing, then stared again at the black-edged box. *No bodies recovered.* Zuni shut off the newsfax, but remained seated there, hunched over the blank scroll, thinking. *No bodies recovered.* Had they used the storm as a cover for their escape? Or had they really drowned?

Another mural slathered onto the wall, and she irritably threw the projector switch. All the machines bothered her now. She hurried around the apartment, turning everything off—the food vendor and fragrancer and ion-generator and all the rest. Soon the place was quiet, dark, with only the lamp at her desk to break the gloom. She sat there absorbing the silence for a few minutes. Her hands lay in the lamp's glow, palms up, cupping the light.

Could they actually have drowned? After all these years of planning, living a double life, with every detail of her journey plotted out—could it all come to an end in the blind smash of a wave?

Very easily, she admitted after a while. Very easily. The world was not set up to coddle us. It took no reckoning of our plans. Yes, they could very well have drowned. Or they could have survived the storm and slipped through Security's fingers. The only way to be certain was by carrying through her plan. And if the gamble failed, if the crew had died, well, she would go through with the plan anyway. She was too old to plant new seeds of conspiracy.

She rose from the desk, stretched her arms toward the ceiling. An old woman, she thought, with half my organs manufactured. But the spine is still pretty good, the legs will carry me, and the brain keeps ticking pretty well.

There were many things to do. Vanishing was a harder business than being born. Uncertainty rode heavily upon her as she moved about the apartment, yet it did not slow her down. She had lived with uncertainty too many years to let it bother her now. She had danced with shadows, with hints of conspiracy and fading green memories of Oregon, with architectural visions and the ghosts of hope. She would not quit dancing now.

For the next few days Zuni went about erasing herself from the city's records. She could have settled her accounts at the bank, the housing bureau, the clinic and elsewhere by vidphone, of course, but she chose instead to go in person. More often than not, when she arrived at an office she had to deal with mechanoes rather than people. She didn't mind. The mechanoes were fun to fool with crooked answers, and they had no feelings to hurt. The glittering bulbous heads, like chromium balloons, purred ritual greetings at her. Was she absolutely certain she wanted to close her accounts, terminate her insurance, cancel her lease? the mechanoes wanted to know. Yes, Zuni declared. Was she perhaps dead? No, she did not think so. Was she planning on dying? In a fashion, yes; in a fashion, no. That answer never failed to silence the chromium heads for a moment. Evidently the mechanoes possessed no polite formulas for responding to news of quasi-suicides.

"I am perfectly clear about what I'm doing," Zuni would assure them at last. "Now kindly settle this matter as I have instructed."

At that the glittering balloon head (or occasionally a human head, modishly wigged and painted) would nod in obedience and carry out her orders. From one tape after another her name was erased. Her lease, her insurance, her allotment of food and energy were set to expire in a week. In a week her vidphone would go dead, the lock on her apartment would cease to open at the touch of her palm. For seven days more she would remain a citizen, secured to the Enclosure by a chain of numbers—the numbers of policies, licenses, bank balances. Then at week's end all the numbers would rush to zero, and, so far as the Enclosure was concerned, Zuni Franklin would cease to be.

She spent much of those seven days riding pedbelts and gliders, tracing French curves high in the air above Oregon City. She had drawn those curves, once upon a time. And this was what kept her running errands in person, back and forth through the city, this fascination with the glass and alloy shapes her blueprints had taken on. Many others had worked on the design of Oregon City, to be sure, but she had always been given the final say. Her pen had moved the armies of builders. So each tower soaring domeward, each fountain, each plaza encircled by arcades, each sculptured facade echoed the shapes that had lived inside her since childhood. The entire city bore the familiarity of an obsessive dreamscape.

The simulated weather during that last week was halcyon

blue. Yet Zuni felt certain the weather outside the float city was stormy. When water trembled in drinking glasses, authorities might blame the extraction pumps, but she knew the shudder came from the ocean. As a young woman she had stood on the Oregon coast watching storms and had felt the cliffs tremble beneath her. Waters that could shake the basalt margins of a continent could easily shake a glass city.

Outside it would be early April, a time of green explosions, a time for bursting out of shells. Through all her years inside, where the seasons did not matter, where weather had been reduced to an electronic ballet played out on the dome, she had kept track of the turning year. And now it was spring.

She went about saying goodbye to friends beneath this illusory sky of blue, knowing that the real sky, far above, was dark and heavy with rain. Her friends had never been numerous, because she was a difficult woman to draw near, at once passionate and aloof. "Like fire inside an icicle," was how one of the draftsmen had described her.

Richard, the draftsman, could remember seeing icicles, for he had grown up with Zuni in one of the Oregon lumber towns, back in the 1970s and 1980s, when the last of the old growth forests were being cut down. He had studied forestry with her, and when she switched to the study of architecture he tried to switch as well. But exponential calculus baffled him, so he had to settle for becoming a draftsman in order to stay near her. During the sixty-odd years since childhood he had trailed her from project to project, a timid shadow. Once he even worked up the nerve to ask her to mate with him, and she agreed. Much of her remained hidden, however, a cold inaccessible depth, and when they separated peaceably after two years he felt relieved. Living with her had been like walking in limestone cave country, where any step might plunge you through the earth's riddled crust. Indeed, three mates had vanished after spells of living with her, and she had merely noted each disappearance with a hazy smile. All in all she was a woman to admire from a cautious distance, and that was where Richard lingered.

If he did not guess the truth about her plans, Zuni calculated, no one would. So he was the last person she called on to wish goodbye. She found him at his apartment studying plans for a space habitat. Even though the details were blurry, she recognized the drawings at once: Project Transcendence, a space-going version of the Enclosure.

His palms kissed her in greeting. "You go tomorrow?"

"Yes." Zuni sat across from him at the glass viewing table. While they spoke, blueprints of the space habitat glowed up at them through the surface.

"And you won't tell me where?"

"Do you really want to know?"

Images of the colossal orb of cities hovered in the glass. Fitted with sails and great looming scoops, the gauzy sphere was designed to voyage through space without being anchored to any planet or sun. It would glean what energy and materials it needed from the interstellar dust. The entire population of the Enclosure could be housed inside. *Transcendence.* Zuni repeated the word to herself as she waited for Richard to answer.

At length he said, "I've always respected your secrets."

"Then indulge me this one last time."

"At least tell me if it's suicide."

"Many people would think of it that way, yes."

"Would I?"

She studied him, lips pursed, recalling their talks of Oregon. "No, I don't think so."

"Then I can see you again?" Richard asked hopefully.

"Time will tell." Her fingers traced the frail outlines of the space habitat. His hands skated toward hers across the glass tabletop, then shyly retreated.

"You're like a squirrel with acorns about this," he said in exasperation.

That was one of the things that had endeared him to her, the way he still spoke in the archaic language of nature.

Squirrels and acorns. She nearly asked him what else he remembered from those years of growing up in the Oregon forests. But no, those were the wilds, taboo. "Promise," she said, "you won't sniff around when I'm gone and dig up the secret?"

"I can't believe you'd quit now, with Transcendence on the drawing board."

"Promise?"

"Yes," he answered glumly. Then he stammered, "I just don't understand. You've never given up before."

If he wanted to believe she had been defeated by the complexities of the new space architecture, then let him. That might be the kindest illusion she could leave with him. "So that's the future?" she said, pointing at a diagram of the gossamer habitat.

He looked puzzled. "What other future is there?"

"Yes, what other future?" she echoed. The gauzy construction of interlacing filaments brought back childhood memories of spider webs, dew-soaked, each strand beaded with water diamonds.

"That's where we're bound to go next," he said passionately. "It's where you've been pointing all these years."

She nodded. "Transcendence."

"Cut free of Terra."

"Free," she said.

"Flow with the cosmic energy."

"Energy," she echoed.

He clapped with pleasure. "That sounds like my old Zuni. Never lost your vision."

"No, I haven't," she assured him.

Packing her few remaining things in the apartment that night, Zuni thought regretfully of Richard. Once she had imagined he might go with her. But gradually she had realized his mind was too brittle. It would have snapped if he had tried to follow her. So she must go alone.

She selected from her library two of the rare paper volumes, Woolman's *Journal* and Noncinno's *Whalecall*. The other paper books she tagged as gifts for the Incunabulary. The remaining volumes, all fiches and tapes, she heaved by the armload down the recycle chute. Her visual and audio libraries soon followed. My little boost to entropy, she thought. The appliances were all standard issue, food dispensers and videowalls, and so were the furnishings. She ran the sanitizer over them and left them in place.

Alongside the two books in her beltpack she loaded the drafting materials from her office. That left just room enough for a first-aid kit, lighter, insul-blanket, knife, some high-cal food, a compass and the much-folded map. The health-security pass would pin to her traveling gown. After much hesitation she tucked Richard's gift into the beltpack as well. It was a model of the Enclosure, small enough to fit in the palm, with threads of silver to represent the transport tubes, silver beads for cities, and, inside, a blue-green sphere of glass to represent Terra.

As she strapped the pack to her waist, with its tiny cargo of mementos, she recalled how the ancients had loaded graves with tokens for the journey to the other world. Instead of miniature boats, grains of wheat, god dolls, she carried fragments of her own days.

With a thick moodgown slung from her shoulders and draping to the floor, the beltpack did not show. She set that gown aside and then dumped the rest of her clothes down the recycle. From vacuum storage she recovered the cotton shirt, wool trousers and leather boots. The boots were cracked but serviceable. Although the colors seemed to have faded on the shirt (or perhaps her stubborn eyes would no longer perceive colors as brightly as her mind recalled them), the cotton still felt soft against her neck.

From the top shelf of her closet she retrieved a scarlet wig and a face mask meant to resemble an Aztec sungoddess. They had been given to her as a joke some years earlier by fellow architects, who knew she would never paint her face or tint her hair, let alone wear such a frightful get-up.

When the closets were empty, the cupboards bare, every surface in the apartment gleaming, Zuni lay down on the airbed to wait for dawn.

Next morning the screen of her vidphone refused to glow when she tapped the keys. The food spout yielded nothing but a faint sucking noise. Bank, clinic, every agency replied with zeroes when she signaled them to see if they remembered her.

She felt a fool, tugging the wig over her neat bun, strapping the mask onto her face, hanging the moodgown over her shoulders. On her way out she paused at the hallway mirror to see if she recognized herself. A grotesque stranger gazed curiously back at her.

Outside the apartment she pressed her palm against the lockplate, to make sure it had erased her from its memory. The door refused to budge.

The pedbelt was jammed with people. Towering head-dresses, wigs of every hue, phosphorescent robes, sequined bodysuits—the normal office-going crowd. When Zuni stepped onto the belt (scarlet tresses wagging, gown flapping over the cracked tops of her boots) no one looked up from newsfax or chemmiedream to notice her. No one paid her any attention as she rode across Oregon City to the shuttle terminal, past the honeycombed towers, beneath the curving gliderways. With sadness, and with an almost giddy joy, she watched the city pass.

The ticket machine flashed questions at her when she requested passage to shuttle stop 012. Was customer aware 012 was repair terminus? Yes, Zuni replied. Was customer authorized to enter vulnerable zone? For answer, Zuni slipped her health pass into the machine, and a ticket wheezed out.

Today the ocean was not stormy, for the shuttle raced through the seatube without so much as a tremor. As Zuni rode toward the mainland she tried not to think of all she was leaving behind. Medicine, for example. Her least reliable implant—a kidney—was probably good for another twenty-five years or so, time enough for her to reach 100, if none of her original organs failed first. That was ample time. To dream of living longer would be greedy.

When the shuttle began decelerating for 012, the regular commuters looked up in mild puzzlement. There should have been no stops until Cascade Mountain Nexus, another twelve minutes away. Zuni soothed them by calling, "Just routine repairs," as she ducked out of the car onto the platform. The doors clapped shut behind her and the shuttle sighed away down the tube.

The emergency repair station was deserted. At each turn locks scanned her health pass before they would let her through. Near the last checkpoint she tossed her mask and wig and gown into a vaporizer. Then she entered the sanitation chamber, a gleaming white sphere that was the Enclosure's outermost defense against the wilds. Her last act as a citizen was to punch into the cybernet a code, known only to masters of health and security and design, which erased all record of her movement from the Enclosure's memory. After she satisfied another series of locks, finally a round hatch swung open and she stepped outside into the blinding green jumble of an Oregon forest.

She stood for a long time with eyes lowered, sniffing the mosses and ferns, listening to wind sizzle through the needles of new-growth firs, feeling the sponginess of soil beneath her feet. She ached.

At length she unfolded the map and blinked at it. Tears made her vision even more hazy than usual, blurring the lines, so she tucked the map into her beltpack and set off through the woods along a pathway of memory.

5 March 2034—*Vancouver*

If I do not let Teeg go inside for a visit, Gregory threatens to send the HP after her, as he certainly can now that she's reached breeding age. Unlucky thirteen. All he wants is a visit, just two weeks with his daughter, he swears solemnly on the vidscreen.

"And will they breed her up like a prize cow?" I ask him.

He clears his throat. His gleaming bulbous head wobbles on the screen. "I rather doubt it. Her—how shall I say it?—her middle section—"

"Pelvis?"

"Well, yes. It's narrow, they tell me. Other women are better suited for bearing her children. The eugenics board will simply preserve her"—he tiptoes gingerly around the word—"eggs, and match them with suitable"—again the hesitation—"male seed."

"Are you sorry we made Teeg in the old-fashioned way?" I ask him.

His eyebrows lift and lift, rippling the vast forehead, his multi-lensed eyes soften, and for a moment I think he is going to smile, an event as remarkable and rare as the northern lights.

FIFTEEN

In the morning Teeg padded about naked through the chill air to unshutter the portholes. Cylinders of daylight bored through the openings, playing on her flesh like searchlights as she walked the length of the raft. At the seaward end she paused, studying the bay, arms lifted to tie her red swish of hair into a knot. She had the body of a gymnast or runner, lean and taut, with narrow hips and small upward-tilted breasts and the flex of long muscles down her back and legs. The tape encircling her ribcage was a pale brushmark against her ruddy skin, which seemed to glow from inside, as if incandescent.

Phoenix admired her through barely-parted eyes, pretending to sleep. He still lay in their joined sleepsacks, where the lovemaking had deposited him. This was the way he imagined a drift log would feel, if it could feel, heaved and bulled by the waves, flung at last upon the shore, there to lie stunned and humble until caught again by the next high sea.

When she crawled back into the sleepsack, her leg

155

slithered against him and her finger began inscribing circles on his belly.

"You're not a very convincing sleeper," she said.

He snored loudly, imitating a mechanical bear he had seen once in a disney.

"I saw you watching," she said. "Brown eyes like saucers of chocolate."

He snored even more loudly.

With an exaggerated sigh she drew away. "So much for romance."

He clutched at her then, crying, "I'm awake, hey, I'm awake!" Need for her filled him. His hand, shying to avoid her tender ribs, came to rest between her thighs. Her own hand settled on top of his, a confirmation, and so he caressed her there—pad of hair over bone, moist lips parted—while they kissed. Heat gathered between them like morning light. Presently she straddled his hips, anchored herself to him, and began slowly rocking. The sleepsack fell away from her shoulders and haloed about their joined hips. Stroking her throat, her breasts, her belly, Phoenix thought how alive she was in her temporary skin, and she moved on him in slow circles, meditatively, like a woman on a pilgrimage.

Afterwards she drew pictures on his chest with her finger. Eyes closed, he was supposed to guess their meaning. The only one of half a dozen he guessed correctly was a seashell. The beach outside would be littered with them, purple as royalty. When his own turn came to draw pictures, his hand kept straying onto her breast. The nipple was a warm knot between his fingers.

"Unfair distractions," he complained.

"The wilderness of the body," she murmured.

He was not yet ready to face real wilderness. "Won't they be looking for you outside?"

With a groan, Teeg lifted her weight from him and began stuffing legs and arms into her shimmersuit. "Nobody expects lovers to use clocks."

He crawled to a porthole and looked toward the caves, where the other colonists were stirring, tiny silver figures toddling beneath immense black cliffs. "They *know*?" he said with dismay. The rumpled sleepsacks curled at his feet like an accusation.

She zipped the suit up the front, crotch to throat. Where there had been radiant flesh a moment earlier, now there was a metallic sheath. "What are we having here," she said, hands on hips, "a few withdrawal symptoms? The child of the city retreating into his don't-touch-me bottle?"

"No," he protested.

"Then don't look so hang-dog. We all came out here to get back in touch, didn't we?" She combed her fingers through his hair, bent down with a grunt to kiss him. "Back in a minute."

Touch. For the first time since clinging to her last night, when he had begged her not to abandon him in the raft, alone on the dark beach under that impossibly distant sky, he was overcome by the dread of the wilds. He mumbled *yes* when Teeg, ducking out through the hatch, told him to get some clothes on his bones.

As he finished dressing she returned with a plate of steaming gray mush. "Don't examine it too closely," she advised. "Just eat. We'll have to live on synthetics until our fish and veggies start flourishing."

He ate. Every time his eyes rose to the level of the portholes, they flinched away, stung by the blaze and hustle of the wilds. Last evening in the gloom the bay had seemed like a drift of huge, menacing shapes. This morning in full light he could see that these awesome shapes, the beach and encircling mountains, were a swarm of smaller things, ragged trees and rocks and driftwood and an infinity of grass. The world was drenched in detail, filled up with a bewildering intricacy of things.

"Still a little queasy?" Teeg asked, studying his eyes.

Phoenix tried to sound reasonable. "The fear goes pretty far back. Dad used to tell me how people got the outside

madness in the old days. Too much disorder, you know.
Reduced them to gibbering idiots." His father's drug-
blasted face, reduced to idiocy by chemicals, ballooned in
his memory.

"Coyt and Hinta and some of the others went through the
same fear, learning to be wildergoers," Teeg said. "My
problem was always the opposite, learning to be a citizen.
Mother taught me the madness was *inside*. Too much
order."

Even now, in the nervous flexing of her body, he sensed
she was eager to be out there, working on the settlement. "I
thought maybe I'd just watch things from the raft today," he
said. "Kind of get my bearings."

"Fine. I'll drop in later with lunch. Then tonight, when
the world gets dark and simple, maybe you'll feel like going
out."

He nodded doubtfully. She brushed her lips over his ear
before slipping away through the hatch. Stepping confident-
ly like some beast native to the place, she crossed the beach
to where Sol huddled on a driftlog. The sick man tilted his
face to greet her, black skin lustrous with ocean spray or
sweat. Phoenix felt a pang of jealousy. Sol reached out and
Teeg grasped his hand in both of hers. They might have
been lovers once, might still be, for all Phoenix knew, Teeg
and this old plum-dark man with his matted white beard, his
calm stories of commando raids on breeder reactors, his
lung full of plutonium.

Presently Hinta joined Sol and Teeg on the driftlog. For a
while the two women hugged the old man between them.
Seeing their embrace, Phoenix understood for the first time
why the crew could not think of leaving this dying man
behind when they made their escape from the Enclosure.
The whole crew was a marriage of spirit. Would he ever
truly feel a part of it? Before Hinta left the driftlog, she
placed something on Sol's tongue and stroked his forehead.
Over Teeg's rib she smoothed her healing palm. Later on,
Jurgen came to hulk down next to Sol, wrapping his arms

about the frail man. Teeg withdrew toward the caves, where the pieces of the settlement were stored.

Throughout the morning the other conspirators sidled up to the dying man, one by one, and sat with him to watch the sea. Phoenix defended himself from the dizzying assault of the wilds by watching these visits. Indy brought a clutch of wildflowers that shone on the foggy beach like distant lights. Coyt brought his violin, and Phoenix could hear, in the lull between waves, the high notes pirouetting. Marie was the last to come, hobbling across the sand. Her bald head bobbed side-to-side, as if overfull of thoughts. Sol lifted his hands to her, and she bent down, pressed her palms against his, her forehead against his forehead. They held so still, with so much quiet passion, that Phoenix looked guiltily away. Imagine, being loved so fully by these people, even in your weakness.

At noon Teeg brought food, drink, and the smell of outside into the raft. In one hand she dangled a long-tailed bulbous plant. "Here, meet a bull kelp." It felt slimy in his palm, undersea, one of the planet's secret organs. In her other hand she carried a bucketful of shells. "Get the feel of things," she urged. He fondled them, fascinated by their whorling grain, their microscopic perfection.

"You doing all right?" she asked, cocking her head at him.

He shrugged. "I've been watching clouds. I can't get used to seeing them from underneath, up close, after so many years of watching by satellite."

She nodded absently, shifting from one foot to the other just inside the hatch, impatient to escape the closed space of the raft.

"How's the work coming?" he asked.

"Slowly. Everybody's so drunk with being out here, it's hard to keep our minds on the job."

"I want to go help build. But every time I get to the hatch and try to walk through, there's this terrific pressure."

"Think how I felt when my father tricked me into visiting

him in Oregon City. And then he told me I had to *stay* there. Huge mountains of buildings and swarms of people. More people on one belt than I'd seen in my whole life. Talk about *pressure*. I thought my head would explode." Recollecting, she grabbed a fistful of red hair at each of her temples. The hard-tipped breasts rose with the motion of her arms, a reminder of the geography that had lured him out here.

"You go on back. I'm all right," he reassured her.

With a smile of relief she backed through the hatch, into that frightening immensity. Studying holos back in his apartment had not prepared him for the vast scale of the wilds. They just went on and on, first the turbulent ocean, and now the land with its frenzy of vegetation. The terrarium in Teeg's blue-lighted room had been a box of wildness engulfed by the city, a speck on a chessboard. Now wildness was everywhere, and the raft, with its manufactured walls and filtered light and symmetries, was the only assurance of human order. Space did not curve to a halt at the dome's edge, as it had in Oregon City, but kept on soaring into the watery distance. Overhead, beyond the skin of the raft, a haze of vapor was all that separated him from the empty infinities.

All afternoon he watched the colonists lugging gear from the cave, across the beach to the creek mouth, then through a gap in the hills to a meadow where the settlement would rise. Teeg was ambling back and forth between cave and building site along with the others, but carrying smaller loads. Whenever she disappeared into a cave, blotted out by darkness, some citified part of him feared she would never return. Grass hung down over the opening, water drooled from the upper lip, as if the cave were a slobbering, bearded mouth. Yet she emerged each time unscathed and made her way along the beach to the building site. By late afternoon the struts of a windmill jutted above the hill's flank, and the crescent of a solar dish gleamed nearby.

When Teeg ducked inside the raft with his supper there

was an excitement about her. While he ate, she kept pacing, halting only to gaze out through a porthole at the settlement.

"The meeting dome will be up before midnight," she said. "Look, you can just make out the white bulge there, above those old stumps."

"I found a spider," he told her, wanting to show her he had crept at least this far out of his shell. "It's already built a web in the life preservers. So quick!"

"Good, good," she said vaguely. "Of course it's only the outer skin so far, on the big dome. But it'll keep off rain. The heat-void and photoelectric hulls can wait." She prowled the length of the raft, thumping the yellow walls. "Coyt says we'll have electricity in two days. The footings for the veggie tank and the fish pools are all marked out. The digester's already working on a load of seaweed." She grabbed him by the ears, gently, as if they were two fragile handles, and pulling his face down she kissed him on each eye. "Wait till you see it."

He glanced outside. Lateness and rainclouds had thinned the light, simplifying the world, merging the dizzy details into great slabs of land and sea. Offshore rocks thrust up like fists through leaden water. He took a deep breath. "Let's go see it now."

He stepped quickly through the hatch, before dread could shove him back. There was a sickening looseness underfoot. Sand. Beach in front of him tilting up, then gravel, boulders, deserts of rock scoured smooth as tongues, then a green terrace speared down by huge trees, and next the misty outlines of hills, and then gray sky lifting away forever and ever into darkness. He leaned back, panting and terrified. The tremendous size of the world oppressed him. The mountains crushed down with a pulverizing weight. Behind him the surf breathed its mammoth breath.

It took him a minute to notice the tug at his arm, to hear Teeg saying, "Look at something close by, one single thing. That's the way to fight it. Here—get some sand."

He extended his palm and she scooped it full of grit.

"Now stare at it," she said. "Put everything else out of your mind."

He lifted his hand close to his face. Flecks of stone, rasped from mountains, dust of a continent. He stirred the specks with a finger. Some were dark with moisture, others tawny, and the driest grains were pale flecks of light, like sparks of some icy fire.

Teeg's voice reached him from the colossal world he had momentarily forgotten. "That's the secret. Look at one thing at a time. Everything's gathered there anyway."

Stumbling up the beach with his weight on Teeg, he obediently looked at a seagull's feather, a driftlog bleached white as bone, a moss-covered stone, the thorny arc of a blackberry vine, examining each with a mixture of caution and wonder, as he might have examined the alien debris of Mars. The shapes of these things were familiar to him from the holos; but now they were substantial, resisted the hand, like the furniture of dreams suddenly encountered in daylight.

Teeg reminded him of the names—barnacle and sea-lettuce and bearded moss. She steadied him while they scrambled along a creek bank to the meadow where the settlement was rising. Here the breathing of the surf was not so menacing. He felt more at ease, surrounded by crates, half-finished towers, sun-catching boxes, the hemispherical skeletons of domes. The sky, broken up by trees, was less daunting. With dusk coming on the air grew thick and intimate.

"Almost time for ingathering," Teeg said. "Do you want to go straight inside?"

Horror brushed him, yet now that he was finally out of doors the vastness was intoxicating. "Can't we look around a little?"

Her look measured him. "Maybe you can stand a few minutes."

She led him to a great circular swath of tilled ground. "This is where the outdoor garden will be." Marie was at work there, feet planted far apart for balance, stooping over to pick out roots and stones. She was a bulky woman, powerful in her old age. Mud caked her fingers and wrists. There was a smear of mud on her bald pate. When she inclined her face to look at him, the creases converging like pathways around each eye, it was easy to believe she was a spirit-traveler.

"So how do you like the wilds?" said the old woman, extending her dirty palms toward him.

Phoenix gingerly pressed his palms against hers. "I'm still a little shaky," he admitted.

"Good. Don't ever quit shaking. The world's an awesome place." Marie bent to work again, nabbing a rock and tossing it onto a pile beside the garden plot.

Phoenix closed his eyes and sniffed. There was a musty smell, distinct from the odor of brine or hemlocks or rotting wood. Dirt? He remembered pale roots lacing down into the soil of the terrarium, the probe of white tendrils. Now I'm walking in the terrarium, he thought. Grass underfoot, creek slipping through its channel, feathery trees gathered on all sides. Yet he still sensed danger stealing along behind him, tramping silently in his footsteps.

And so Teeg led him around the site, through lengthening shadows. Two sides of the meadow were rimmed by spruce-covered hills, one sinuous boundary was formed by a blunt escarpment, with Salt Creek Falls tumbling from its crest and the creek undulating along its base. The fourth side of the meadow opened across Whale's Mouth Bay to the sea. Throughout the site, blueprints were materializing. Some projects were announced as yet only by jumbles of unopened crates; others, like the fish pools, by forms bolted together around freshly-poured liquistone. Still others were set up and functioning, like the water purifier with its coil of pipe, the composting toilet, the faceted solar oven. Stakes driven into the turf marked where greenhouses and hydroponics tanks would go. Eighteen smaller domes, for meditation and privacy, were laid out in a necklace around the large central dome.

"Why so many?" Phoenix asked.

"For the other exiles who will come," said Teeg.

"You really believe there'll be others?"

Her eyes scanned the meadow, then came to focus on him. "I hope so. If we're the only ones, the last ones, it all seems like a dead end."

"But we have one another."

"Ten of us. Soon to be nine, when Sol dies. And in a few years, perhaps, Marie. Or someone else might die sooner from poison or accident. No, no," she insisted, "there have to be others. It has to go on."

A sudden yearning came over him. "We could have children."

She turned her back to him and said in a careful voice, "Arda is the only one of us who still carries her eggs."

He looked at her stiff shoulders, feeling the shock of tenderness. "It doesn't matter."

She swung angrily round and shouted, "It *matters*! Don't tell me being sterile doesn't matter!"

The depth of her feeling appalled him. He could only stare in silence as she walked away over the grass. Not yet inflated, the spare domes meant for future exiles lay in puckered folds at his feet.

In the thickening darkness he shuffled after Teeg. His fear of the wilds seemed selfish, an indulgence, when compared to the grief of her barrenness. As he trailed after her toward the dark verge of the meadow, he met other colonists, who had quit work for the day and were trooping domeward. Coyt stumped out of a half-roofed dome just as Phoenix caught up with Teeg. He was hunchbacked, with a badly twisted face, the chin far out of line from forehead and nose, as if before birth a mocking hand had yanked him out of shape. His brain had saved him from exile to the mutant wards. He was a particle physicist, his head full of matrices, according to Teeg, but his hands were the wise-fingered hands of a tinker.

"What pains you?" he asked Teeg, looking at her with concern. When she did not answer he paused tactfully, then addressed Phoenix. "Now that you've had a look outside, firebird, can we ever lure you back in?" He gestured with a misshapen arm toward the luminous bubble of the dome.

"In a minute," Phoenix replied.

Coyt stared round at the gloomy hills. "Mind the dark," he said, then went stubbing away on his uneven legs.

Marie also passed them on her way to the dome, her head visible only as a paleness, a hole hammered in the dark. "Don't let him stay out too long, child," she murmured.

"I know the danger," Teeg replied. Each word was balanced, like water in a brim-filled cup. "We're just waiting for the sunset."

But there was no sunset. Rainclouds shut down on the ocean, gray on darker gray. Darkness oozed from trees and stones and soil, weighting everything with longer shadows. The speed of the transition from day to night astonished him. In Oregon City there was no real night, only an artificial gloom when lamps dimmed for the hours of sleep, and even then one could look out the window to find the avenue as brightly lit as ever. Here the darkness seemed ponderous and final, heaving the mountains up like volcanoes of ink, swamping the meadow with liquid shadows. Darkness lapped menacingly at his feet.

"Let's go inside now," he said. Could she hear the tremble?

"Come," Teeg said gently, taking his hand.

He hastened along beside her over the treacherous ground. Lighted from within by flares, the dome swelled before them like a molten globe half-risen from the soil. As day cooled into evening, the fabric turned opaque, to conserve heat inside. At the threshold he did as Teeg did, kicking off his boots, hanging his soiled clothes on a hook in the entrance chamber. He spun naked beside her in the air-shower, brush of elbow against rump, shoulder against her fiery hair. Then he dressed in a clean shimmersuit, pure white for the ingathering, and followed her through a corridor into the meeting room, which was a canopy of brightness at the center of the dome.

Ten cushions formed a circle around a glowing flare. Eight of them were already occupied. As Phoenix took his place, the water-filled cushion swaying beneath him, he noticed the slumped shoulders, the exhausted faces. For all their rugged training these people were showing the effects of the ocean passage and the day of hard labor. Sol was propped in an air-harness, eyes sunken and bloodshot, with a cloth pressed to his mouth. And Marie was no longer young, must have been near ninety, for she had worked as a graduate student on the earliest synthetic proteins, back before the turn of the century. Even the younger colonists, Indy and Josh and Coyt, gave an impression of utter fatigue.

Rocking slightly on his cushion, with eyes shut and breath measured, Phoenix waited for the stillness to wash over him. It was always hard, the sinking down into stillness. Tonight he found himself growing more tense with each passing minute. The meeting space kept rustling with breath and the stir of bodies. Stealing a glance, he saw that no one else had settled into the posture of deep trance. All round the circle fists clenched on knees, backs hunched wearily, jaws worked with unconscious speech. Next to him, Teeg's breath came raggedly. The air wheezed through his own pressured lungs in tatters. What was wrong? Was he some poison that had murdered their closeness? That must be it, his city spirit poisoning the ingathering. He was about to rise and go from them, go somewhere, even outside into the annihilating blackness, when Jurgen's huge head lifted.

"We'll have to work ourselves clear again before we can draw together," Jurgen said. The struggle had left his great body trembling.

Phoenix stiffened on his cushion, waiting to be accused. A look from Teeg kept him silent. You do not understand these things, said her eyes.

"Let us eat," Hinta pronounced in a tone of profound weariness.

The warm bowls passed from hand to hand, and the grainy loaves followed them around the circle. Marie fed Sol, tilting the bowl to his lips while he lay propped against the cushions. Everyone kept a solemn hush, eyes lowered over the food.

Phoenix sipped the broth without hunger, nibbled at the loaf. After a while Coyt stood in front of him with a kettle. Steam plumed from the spout, obscuring the mutant's skewed features. Phoenix held out his empty bowl, let Coyt pour some hot water in, then swished it around and drank it off. If only we could cleanse ourselves like that, he thought, purge all the residues of our old lives and start out clean.

The meal was followed by subdued talk concerning the next day's work. Phoenix agreed to help Indy run assays on air and water and dirt, so the colonists would know for sure which toxins to dose themselves against. "That will keep you safe inside," Jurgen said bluntly.

Once the tasks were divvied up, people began retiring in pairs and triplets into the private cells surrounding the meditation chamber. Curious about the joining, Phoenix noted each departure. Hinta and Jurgen—that union he could have predicted, for the two always seemed to work in tandem, Hinta picking up vibrations as if she were a delicate antenna, and Jurgen hammering the world into a shape to fit her intuitions. Coyt, Josh, and Indy ambled away together, a surprising threesome. Marie and Arda were more of a surprise as they departed with arms round one another, the old woman and the young, intense Marie with the lovely, sleep-walking host-mother, Arda. That left Sol, slumped against his cushion, and Teeg and himself. "Ready?" Teeg said. When Phoenix glanced at Sol, she explained, "He asked to be left alone. He has a spirit-journey to make."

Sol opened his eyes, two points of gleaming blackness, and they reminded Phoenix of the night outside. Death was coming for the old man, yet the eyes showed no fear. The head nodded faintly, agreeing to something, perhaps to what Teeg had said. She kissed the old man's forehead on her way to the sleep-chamber. Phoenix padded after her, conscious of Sol's calm dark gaze upon him.

Two sleepsacks, zippered together to make one great pouch, took up the entire floor of their private chamber. A flare hung from the ceiling, and twin portholes opened onto the night. Phoenix quickly shuttered the windows, but when Teeg reached up to douse the flare he grabbed her hand. "Not yet," he pleaded, searching for a reason.* "Let's . . . talk a minute."

"You can't talk in the dark?"

"I want . . . to see you . . . see your eyes." She stared at him unblinking, two pools of calm green. He could find no hint of accusation there, could read nothing but desire. "Maybe I caused it," he stammered. "You know, ruined the ingathering."

"So that's why the donkeyface," she said with apparent relief. "I thought you were still brooding on my little fertility melodrama."

He despaired of ever predicting the swing of her emotions. By comparison, weather prediction had been easy. "I didn't ruin it?" he asked hesitantly.

"Of course not. It fizzled this morning, and last night, too, when you were out there playing fishbait in the raft."

"But doesn't the ingathering always work?"

"Usually, in the city. It was easy to dream up utopias

back there, easy to trust one another. Out here"—she collapsed in a boneless heap—"it's harder."

"So what's blocking us?"

"It could be a million things. Maybe somebody's a spy, maybe somebody's jealous."

"Spy?" He was alarmed by this talk. The spiritual magic was like electronics: if it quit working, what could you do?

"Or mistrust," she added, "or chemmies hanging around in the body."

"Could it be Sol's illness?"

She looked thoughtful. "Yes, it could be that. Or someone wanting a little power or hungering after a new mate."

"But I thought you'd worked through all those things."

"Nobody but saints ever worked through them once and for all. We just keep working." Teeg drew down the zipper of her shimmersuit and shrugged free of the clinging fabric. Her nakedness was still so new it astonished him. He looked at her flat belly with acute awareness of the vacuum inside, the zero where there should have been the seeds of children. "Well," she said, "are you going to hold up the roof like that all night?"

Then Phoenix realized he had backed away from her until his spine curved against the dome's outer wall. Through the flimsy hide he sensed the patter of rain. He undressed awkwardly, ashamed for her to see that all the while they had been talking, his cock had pursued its own designs.

"Will you get the light?" she asked. "My rib doesn't appreciate the stretching."

He touched the flare and darkness slapped tight around him. Inside the sleepsack his fingers soon found the cool paired globes of her ass. She rolled silkily toward him and nipped his nose. "Now is the dark really so bad?" she whispered.

For the half hour of their lovemaking there was neither dark nor light, only the river hurling them down its powerful current. Afterwards he was flung again onto shore, onto this Oregon beach with its encircling hills and ponderous surf and immense night.

"Tell me," he whispered, "which is real—the crowded daylight, with its billion dazzling pieces, or that great black vacancy out there?"

7 March 2034—*Portland/Whale's Mouth*

On our way from Vancouver to the sanitation port, where Teeg is to be purified for admission to the Enclosure, we stop over in Portland. I wanted to see what nature had made of the place in the seven years since we finished the dismantling. The scoured hills are covered with fireweed, huckleberry, salal, red alder, and great hedge nettles, the same plants that always reclaim this land after forest fires and clear-cuts. Vines lace up through the brick shells of buildings. Grass buckles the pavement. My cache of tools has stayed dry in the old slate-roofed mansion in the park. Many of the wooden houses have caved in, but a few could be salvaged. Now that Vancouver is demolished and shipped north to become pieces of Alaska City, and my commission has expired, and my wilder-license is running out, I think I will begin work on a sanctuary here. Perhaps I could have something underway when Teeg comes back outside in two weeks.

In the afternoon she begs me to stop at Whale's Mouth Bay, so I land the glider on the beach. Teeg skips across the sand with a show of lightheartedness, but I suspect she feels as heavy as I do. She opens her arms wide to the surf, licks the spray from her lips, as if to swell herself up with the sea. All you can carry with you into Oregon City, I want to tell her, are the shadows of this place and other places you love, traces in the mind like tracks of particles through the fog of a bubble chamber. Instead of speaking, however, I write these lines in my journal. When I finish, I will tuck the little notebook into her pack, let her carry along a piece of me, too, when she goes inside. Will she ever carry it back out?

SIXTEEN

As she toiled up into the foothills Zuni kept turning back to locate the repair station, making sure of her direction. When she had last walked these slopes, sixty years before, they had just been clearcut. Bulldozers had gouged the shallow topsoil right down to bedrock. Between stumps the hillsides had been a hideous mire of oil cans and sawdust and bonewhite slash. Dirt which had taken millennia to accumulate sloughed off the mountains in a season of rain, burying the valleys below in mud. Even though brush had partially reclaimed the slopes since then, and conifers crept skyward from ravines, Zuni still recognized the devastated contours of the land.

Just beyond this stony ridge she would enter the watershed of Wolf Creek. Downstream, where the Wolf joined Salt Creek, she would come to the site of her childhood village. What could be left there but the rotting sawmill and a few shriveled cabins, perhaps an overgrown orchard? It was an old woman's foolishness to try going back. But I might as well get some advantage out of growing old, Zuni

thought, something other than sore knees. She had to pass
that way anyhow, for Salt Creek would lead her, after one or
at most two days of walking, to Whale's Mouth Bay. By that
time over a week would have passed since Teeg and her
crew had disappeared at sea. If they weren't at Whale's
Mouth when she arrived? Can't waste energy fretting about
that.

On that windswept ridge, where lichens were patiently
rebuilding the soil, she sat down to let her body recover
from the climb. Far below the station squatted, unnaturally
white and spherical, like a ship that had just landed. The
travel tube glistened away beyond sight to east and west.
Presently a flicker of purple sparks announced a shuttle
approaching, lights shot through the tube, past the station,
past her, and away into the interior of America. Gregory
had been right, the Enclosure was beautiful, with its globe-
encircling filaments, its cities like stunning jewels. When
the skycities were finished, in another twenty or thirty
years, humanity could float free of Terra, free of the sun,
free of every star except the one glowing in our foreheads.
The mind was building itself a perfect house. Hadn't the
earliest molecules done the same, weaving membranes
about themselves, forming cells? However long Zuni lived,
out here in the wilds, part of her would always ache for that
jeweled perfection.

With a sigh she turned her back on the station and travel
tube, and headed laboriously downhill toward the gray
slither of Wolf Creek. Halfway down, while she rested in a
clearing, a shadow glided past her feet and she flinched her
gaze skyward, expecting a health patrol glider to descend on
her. But the shape cruising overhead was that of a large
bird, and Zuni was so astonished that she cried aloud,
"Come down! Come, I won't harm you!"

The great wings beat languidly and the bird sailed away,
magisterial, untouchable. Zuni stood there with heart
knocking. But she saw no more of it, and so she picked her
way downhill through ferns and brush, over fallen trees,
wondering what the huge bird found to eat. Rats, surely, for

no toxins ever invented could discourage rats. And if rats, why not rabbits and moles, a few at least, perhaps even foxes, black-tailed deer, elk? The mountain streams would most likely still breed fish, which meant black bears might have survived. As she hobbled toward Wolf Creek, parting the breast-high ferns, she filled the woods with dragonflies and scarlet tanagers, bobcats and loons, mountain lions and mosquitoes, all the creatures she had known from childhood. And why not wolves along Wolf Creek?

But she reached the stream through a tangle of blackberries and maple saplings without spying another beast. Swollen with spring rains and snowmelt from the mountains, the creek surged ponderously seaward. At least this much had not changed. It smelled the same, sounded the same. She remembered this springtime urgency of water, remembered how the uprooted trees used to hurtle past her down the current while she searched the banks with her father for mushrooms.

"Wolf Creek," she said rapturously, as if by naming it she would become again the mushroom-picking child.

She knelt down and lowered her face to within a few centimeters of the rushing water. The cool breath against her cheeks had arrived here from frozen mountains. The taste of creekwater, even sucked through a detox filter, was so familiar it made her cry. There was the taste of rock in that water, and lichen, wood, and earth. The flavor of canyons and pine mountains was dissolved in it. She knew it was absurd, after so many decades of masquerading as the inventor of cities, to kneel here now on a creekbank weeping over the taste of water. It was as if the flavor of the entire abused and abandoned planet had burst suddenly into her mouth after long fasting.

Where ferns grew thickest she unfurled her sleepsack, which quickly swelled with air until it assumed a mummy-shape. She wriggled inside and the inflated walls snugged tight against her. The pungent smell of broken ferns and the lingering taste of melted snow made her eyes water.

Listening to the creek distracted her for a while from the pain in her joints and muscles. When she could no longer ignore the ache she thought back over the day—the apartment treating her as a stranger, the cybernet answering zeroes to all her questions, the costumed monstrosity gazing back at her from the mirror, the last ride across Oregon City, the cautious locks of the repair station, the overwhelming green dazzle of the wilds.

What tale would they finally believe about her, back there? That she had crawled into a vaporizer? Shipped out to the asteroid colonies? Allowed her brain to be transplanted into a cyberfield? Changed her identity so she might hide among them under a new name?

It pleased her, lying there snug in a sleepsack beside Wolf Creek, to imagine them spinning modest little legends about her. The pleasure could not keep her body's pain at bay, however. Even in Oregon City she had rarely used chemmies. Out here, it was unthinkable. Instead she chewed a foodstrip slowly, grimacing at the harsh synthetic taste, waiting for sleep.

She woke into the gray light of predawn. Stars might have pricked through the gloom overhead, but her bleary eyes would never be able to make them out. She was reluctant to try moving, for fear some of her bones or sinews would refuse to obey. In that stillness, against the background purr of the creek, she heard a few hesitant twitters, as if a bird were testing the air. Then came delicate, flutelike notes. She had not heard that song for sixty years, but the bird's name sprang to mind. Varied thrush. Orange breast and black eye-stripes. After a spell the raucous cry of a jay interrupted the fragile melody, and suddenly the boughs overhanging the creek were filled with the chatter and whistle of many birds.

Zuni lay gratefully listening as the sky grew light. Wind sluiced through the blue-green branches, water sluiced through the rocky channel of the creek, blood sluiced through her veins. She felt intensely happy. But the moment passed over her like a breath and was gone, as her legs ached and her stomach grumbled and memory recalled that she might die out here alone. Was there even a settlement to find?

At least there was a remedy for hunger. Those infernal foodsticks. She reached out to dig some from the beltpack, but her hand found nothing except ferns. Thinking she had perhaps rolled about in her sleep, she sat up and peered around. There were her boots, tongues hanging out as if from fatigue, and there was her jacket, but no pack. She scrambled out of the sleep-sack, crawled anxiously over the bitter-smelling ferns, calculating how long she could live without food, filters, or anti-toxins.

Just as she was trying to imagine how death would come—slowly by thirst and hunger or quickly by poison— her outstretched fingers touched a strap. She tugged, and the beltpack emerged from under a heap of brush. Whatever had dragged it away in the night and hidden it there had slashed a hole through the fabric. Checking quickly, she found the filters and medicines and tools safe inside. Several of the foodstrips in their foil wrappers had been tentatively gnawed—the teethmarks were as sharp as compass points—but none had been eaten.

She rocked on her heels and shook with laughter. Wise beast, to be wary of city food! Raccoon, she guessed, or weasel. There might not be many beasts left, but one had managed to sniff her out in the enormous night. Were these the last of the old beasts, or the first of the new ones? The doomed survivors that would soon perish, or the genetically resistant ones that would eventually fill the forests?

So she would not die just yet. The beltpack was soon mended with glue, the sleepsack was deflated and tucked away. Only when she bent over the creek and splashed her face with the frigid water did she recollect her stubborn joints and muscles. In her excitement over the missing pack she had tricked them into motion. Now that she was up and packed and ready for the journey, her old bones would damn well cooperate. The face wavering up at her from the water was a little hollow about the eyes and cheeks, red as a poppy from the unfamiliar sun, but still merry.

Heading downstream, she chewed a foodstrip thoughtfully, her tongue playing over the beast's finicky toothmarks. The going was difficult. In most places the vegetation crowded down to the water, so she had to force her way through. Elsewhere the bank rose in a sheer cliff and she had either to pick her way precariously over stones in the creek, or else climb the steep ridge. Tributary streams cut through the bank, often plunging over waterfalls into Wolf Creek. When she came to one of these she had to follow it upstream until the water was narrow or shallow enough for wading.

Twice before sunset she stumbled onto game trails and followed them so long as they kept within earshot of the creek. She only let herself believe that deer had gouged these trails when she saw the sharp cloven hoofprints in a muddy stretch. She had to squat down and actually place her fingers in the tracks to make sure, because to her dim eyes the hoofprints might have been flakes of bark. For the rest of the afternoon she toiled along with the image of deer inside her.

With the pack tucked securely beneath her head, and the awning pulled over her sleepsack to keep off rain, Zuni abandoned herself for a second night to the growl of Wolf Creek.

In the morning she discovered that one of her boots had been chewed about the toe. Her own stockinged toes showed through when she put it on, and she gazed down at them with dismay.

She scolded the indifferent woods. "Do you start on my legs tonight, you impertinent beasts?"

Nothing actually bit her legs that following night, but she woke in blackness to find something nosing at her sleepsack. A wolf after all? Inside the inflated walls it sounded as if a child were clumsily pawing at a drum. When Zuni reached out, flare in hand, to see what manner of beast it was, all she glimpsed was the humped retreating back of something large and furry and quick. Two green eyes swung momentarily round to catch the flare-light, then disappeared. She felt as she had felt once, as a child, upon discovering that a bear watched her from a thicket of willows—not threatened, but observed, measured, the way any intruder is examined by those who belong in a place. "Come let me have a look at you!" she called foolishly into the blackness.

By noon of the third day she could sense the nearness of home. Wolf Creek was narrowing down between rock cliffs for its ten-meter leap into Salt Creek. The gullies and bogs atop the cliffs were so familiar that she thought to look for mushrooms, and there they were, in the leafmold and rotted logs, pale mushrooms as thin as fingers, mottled brown ones larger than two clasped hands, creamy fists. A pity she dare not eat them. Even swallowed with detox they were likely to make her sick, for mushrooms, like whales, had a way of concentrating poisons. Her father used to amaze city visitors by popping unfamiliar mushrooms into his mouth. "I know the few lethal ones," he had explained to her, "so everything else I can trust." From this man who had left home each morning with a chainsaw tilted over his shoulder, she had learned to trust the earth.

Her excitement mounted along with the rising tempo of the current. A dozen meters ahead the creek vanished over a ledge, leaving only a fume of mist in the air, as if it darted into a fourth dimension. Zuni made her way cautiously over the slick rocks, relishing the spray that soaked her face and hair, until she neared the falls. On hands and knees she crept to the very brim and peered down through the crash of water at the meadow. A gust of wind blew the mist aside, exposing the valley, and at last she was able to see— nothing. Where the village had been there was only a smear of black, no hint of decaying houses, no green ferment of returning forest. Perhaps her miserable eyes were playing tricks on her. She waited for another clearing of the mist, and then another, but each time the valley appeared as a blackened scar.

Trembling, she lowered herself down the cliff trail, careful to keep her back toward the charred vacancy that had been her home. The climb down the rockface beside the falls had seemed a lark to her as a child, when muscles were young and death was an impossibility; now she picked her way down over the slick ledges with breath trapped in her throat. Her flannel shirt and trousers were soon wet through from the spray. Hair fell in damp white strands over her eyes. Purple irises bloomed on these ledges, their delicate petals furling outward like tiny fountains, and every niche was awash in the yellow blooms of gorse. Zuni kept her eyes on these vibrant flowers, while the desolate valley yawned below.

At last she reached the base of the cliff and faced around to survey the landscape of her childhood. The falls boomed to her right. To her left Salt Creek curled away toward the sea. All before her was a desert of rock and blackened soil, across the valley floor and as far as she could see upstream or down.

She slumped against the cliff and shut her eyes. Orchards had carpeted the near bank, and vineyards, and tidy gardens which the lumberjacks used to fuss over in the evenings. The sawmill had loomed on the far bank, and around it the village had sprawled with crooked alleys and wooden houses. While she kept her eyes closed it was all as plain as a blueprint, but once she opened them again there was only this charred landscape. She might have been gazing from the porthole of a colony on the moon. On earth she had seen nothing so barren except the lava fields of eastern Oregon.

She scuffed her boot against the rock. It was very like lava, bubbled and swirled and intricately fissured, as if something had melted the valley. She remembered being told how the health patrollers went about in their laser ships sterilizing the old gathering places, flushing the last wildergoers from the forests. So this was what a sterilized town looked like. She picked up a chunk of the bubble stone and hurled it furiously over the water. It clattered against rock on the far side. There was no use crossing, only to see more cinders. In any case the bridge was gone. The HP had done a thorough job. No least sprig of green showed anywhere in the ashen valley.

Oblivious, Salt Creek purled along seaward past her feet. She was almost afraid to follow the stream to Whale's Mouth Bay, for if she did not find Teeg and the others there she would not have the strength or desire to search much farther. She wanted to sag down here and quit the pointless struggling. She had escaped into the wilds, had found her way home. Let this charred desolation be the end of it.

Yet the creek surged on, abiding and momentary. It had not changed in all her years of knowing; yet it changed constantly. You never quit, old one, the creek was saying. You live in this moment, and this moment only. After a while the sound of it lifted her up and forced her to hobble along the bank, over fissured stone. As if blind, she stumbled on for most of an hour, left hand fumbling against the cliff, through pain, past what she imagined must be the outer limits of exhaustion, until the lavalike stone gave way to cinders, the cinders to moss. She fell down there in her wet clothes and slept, with the valley of ashes gaping behind her.

SEVENTEEN

During most of that first week after the landing at Whale's Mouth Bay it rained. The meadow squished underfoot as the colonists went about erecting domes and laying pathways of glass. The needles of spruce and hemlock, glistening with rain, looked like fine green jets squirting from branches. Grass stems bent under the weight of water. Marie had to cover her garden with polyfilm to keep it from turning into a quagmire. Coyt grumbled because unbroken clouds reduced the power from his photoelectric cells. There was methane enough from the seaweed digester, however, and enough hydrogen from the vats of blue-green algae to fuel stoves and generators, so the colony enjoyed electricity and warm food.

Rain pipped the surface of the fishpools, which were stocked with fingerlings of bluegill and rainbow trout and bullhead catfish, all carefully smuggled from Oregon City. The smuggled crayfish had died in their barrels, so Josh and Jurgen went off hunting some wild ones. Rain pattered on the greenhouse, where Phoenix helped sow vegetables.

Teeg was delighted to see him poking his fingers into the sterilized dirt.

Rain drumming overhead soothed Teeg's heart at the nightly ingatherings. The still point, the luminous center where they all fused with the spirit, kept eluding them. "We must be patient," Marie counseled. "This is our time of wandering." But how long could they wander before losing touch with one another? Each night Teeg studied the haggard faces, wondering who had muddied the mystical waters. Could one of them really be a spy, willing to betray the colony? Or was it merely anger, jealousy, even Sol's dying?

One night Marie's voice rose above the rain's drumming to suggest naming the settlement Jonah. "Because we have all sojourned in the .guts of the Enclosure," she explained, "and now we have been cast up on dry land."

"Not so very dry!" Indy quipped.

Sol gathered himself to speak, and everyone hushed. "Out of Leviathan into Whale's Mouth," he whispered. His face shone with a many-wrinkled smile, even though, inside, his body was a shambles, one membrane after another yielding its fluid to the rising waters of death. "Yes," he whispered. "That is good. Let us call this place Jonah."

During that rainy first week Sol kept inside his meditation dome. The others went in to him by turns, stroking his face or talking quietly or merely sitting for a time in utter stillness. Even Hinta's touch could not bring healing now. Sol would swallow no chemmies, saying he wanted to be alert for his death. When pain tugged his white beard he was forced to cover his sagging mouth with a hand. Marie spent the most time with him, since the two of them had journeyed together on many spirit-quests. She was the one who stayed with him now through the nights, when desperate cries bubbled up out of the depths of his sleep.

Phoenix would only visit Sol in Teeg's company, and then he would stay no longer than a minute before hastening back to the shelter of greenhouse or lab, away from the old man's decaying flesh.

Teeg knew the fugitive look in Phoenix's eyes. He was suffering from a bad case of wilder-shock. Several times she discovered him at a porthole staring out, appalled, at the forest or sea. Or she found him with his ear pressed against the inner wall of the dome, listening.

Since first glimpsing Phoenix in the corridor all those months ago, in his ridiculous blue wig and video-actor's mask and luminescent gown, Teeg had assumed he would love the coast once he saw the rocky headlands and breathed the salty air. But the dread went deep, back into his childhood and perhaps further back, into the twisted messages of the genes. People had been walling themselves off from nature for a very long time.

Marie said Phoenix would have to break through the fear from inside; there was no coming at it, by words or touches, from without. So Teeg let him stay indoors, let him keep his aching distance from her in the sleepsack, let him dwell in his numbed silence.

There was still a great deal of work to do in the settlement. When she had finished helping Coyt rig the photoelectric cells and the methane generator, and had seen the first flicker of electricity illuminate a test lamp, she went on to help Jurgen pour the glass walkways. The black sand on the beach was ideal for the job. Trenches were cut into the meadow, wires and pipes were laid in, and molten glass was spread into them. While it was still warm Teeg etched the surface with a trowel, to keep it from being slippery underfoot. By week's end all the domes were linked by glass pathways. Sinuous black tentacles spread out from Jonah Colony to the beach and up Salt Creek and away into the coastal hills.

Whenever she felt tired of work or the thought of losing Sol became too heavy in her, she went in to sit with the dying man. Marie was usually there, giving him sips of water or simply holding one of his black hands between her two callused white ones.

Once, when Sol was alone, Teeg brought a cluster of the tiny bell-shaped flowers from the salal bush and laid it in his outstretched palm.

"The beauty goes on and on!" he whispered to her, drawing the flowers up close to his eyes. He made an effort to smile.

There was a silence. Teeg sat cross-legged beside him and fixed her gaze on the flare glowing at the center of the dome. Sol clutched the salal blossoms in one hand and in the other a blood-soaked gauze which he pressed from time to time against his lips.

"The rhodies should be blooming," he murmured. "It's May, and they should be glimmering on the cliffs. And the gorse should be burning their yellow flame."

"Yes, my love, they are, they are."

His eyes seemed completely black and sightless, as if they were gateways inward to some nether universe. The flare was mirrored in each one like a star. "And the gray whales are swimming up the coast," he whispered. "Mothers and calves and young bulls. North along the coast to the Arctic."

"They're not . . ." Teeg began, and then she held her tongue. Why remind him they had all died long ago? His eyes were extinguished and his cancerous body was forgotten. He was a young man in memory, and in that memory the ocean still heaved with whales.

"The cranes should be flying north," he said in a rhapsodic voice. "And petrels and ospreys. Look outside, dear, and see if there isn't an osprey overhead."

Teeg stared obediently through a porthole at the blank sky. Not even the ragged herring gulls, the only birds they had spied so far, were visible in the empty air.

"Here's one now," she lied. "All creamy below, and a brown head, and bands across the tail, and the wings nearly two meters across."

"Is it fishing?" There was a rising note of eagerness in his broken voice.

"Yes, there, it's just plunged down and caught a great squirming fish, and now it's flying up to the cliffs for its meal."

His eyes filled slowly with tears, like two ragged holes dug down past the water-line. Teeg watched the saltwater rise in them. The tears caught in the folds of his plum-dark face and dripped into his lap. He made no attempt to wipe them away. Propped against cushions, a star gleaming in each pitchblack eye, he held very still. Teeg could not move. His passion struck her dumb.

At last he dabbed the gauze to his mouth, drew it away bright with blood, and murmured, "Tell Marie I am ready for the journey."

"And where will we take you?"

"Up onto the headland, where the lighthouse used to be."

Teeg thought uneasily of that exposed place, where the most casual sky-eyes might spot them. "Everyone?" she said.

He nodded. Speech was a heavy labor. "I must have my whole family with me. Now go; Marie knows what to do." He waved the handful of flowers weakly.

Marie was in the garden, taking advantage of the rare rainless afternoon to plant seeds. She laid rows from the hub of the circular garden to the outer rim, like spokes in a wheel. She pressed a long tube into the soil, dropped in a seed, then withdrew the tube and shuffled dirt over the hole with her bare feet.

Teeg halted at the border of the tilled earth, heavy with her news. When Marie at last noticed her and looked up, her face seemed drowsy from the labor of planting.

"Sol's ready," Teeg announced.

At once Marie's lovely, rumpled face came alert. "Is he conscious?"

"Yes, but a little delirious."

"Talking of whales? He began seeing them last night, dear old visionary." Marie scraped the seeds from her palm into a pouch. "Here, child, help me cover the garden," she said, and the two women dragged fluttering sheets of polyfilm over the naked soil. Even with death coming—especially with death coming—the living must be provided for.

On the way back to Sol's dome Marie instructed her to gather the others at the lighthouse path, have Jurgen rig a stretcher, have Indy provide enough pure water for an all-night vigil.

The sun was falling through the roof of clouds, its lower edge brilliant against a ribbon of blue sky, as Teeg went in search of Phoenix. She found him in their private dome, enveloped in his sleepsack.

"I can't, I can't. I'm afraid." Muffled by the sack, his words sounded as though they had been spoken underwater.

"Sol needs you."

The tousled brown head emerged from the pouch, like a sea lion surfacing. "Aren't you and the others enough?"

"No, love. Once you join the ingathering you draw part of his spirit into you, and he draws part of yours into him. He needs everyone's power to carry him through."

Phoenix sat up and turned his harried eyes on her. The week-old beard stubbling his cheeks made him look even more fugitive. "He really *needs* me?"

"Yes; we all do. That's what it means to belong to one another."

His breath came quickly. He looked so frantic and displaced, like a merman flung gasping on the beach. "Is it raining?" he asked.

"Not just now."

"Should I . . . should I bring a poncho?"

Teeg smiled, knowing he would go. She hugged him against her sore ribs. "Yes, and a blanket, too. We'll be staying up there all night."

"All *night*?"

"As long as he needs for his spirit-journey."

Phoenix rose on unsteady legs and collected his poncho and blanket. She led him into the slanting sunlight, his hand in hers, tremors passing between them.

"Pick one thing and look at it," she reminded him.

His gaze skirted warily, until something on the forest's edge caught his attention. "What are those pinkish flowers up there?"

"Rhododendrons."

His head swiveled to take in the sweep of hills. "They're everywhere! Who planted them?"

Planted them! She squeezed his clumsy paw. "God!"

On the beach they passed within sight of the yellow raft. Teeg's body still held the memory of its wallowing sea-motion, the rise and fall of waves and lovemaking.

"We could sleep there again some night," she said.

A smile of recollection eased onto his face. "Yes, that would be good."

Waves slid up the black sand and then retreated with a sucking noise. The massive headland that formed the whale's upper jaw loomed ahead, and at its base the other colonists waited, tiny and silvery, like upright minnows. Spray from incoming breakers hid them, and then, falling back, revealed them again. Atop the headland were the ruins of Whale's Head Light, where Teeg had often picnicked with her mother, and that was where they would be taking Sol. Teeg worked at clearing a space in her mind for Sol to dwell in after his death. He would enter the catacomb within her where she kept the other lost loved ones—her mother and Zuni Franklin, her babies who had kicked in other women's wombs, the nine conspirators who had died before the escape. There was even a small place in that catacomb for her father.

She and Phoenix soon drew up to the death-party, whose silver-sleeved arms were raised in greeting. Sol lay in a stretcher on the sand, eyes closed.

"Is it Teeg?" he whispered.

"Yes, old one, I am here." The dark hands stirred at his side but could not lift. Teeg grasped each of them in turn and pressed his palms against her own.

"And the other one . . . is he with you?"

"Yes, Phoenix is here. Everyone is here."

The old man's mouth was tugged open by pain. Saliva mixed with blood drooled from one corner. Marie, bending over him, daubed it away. "Good," he rasped. "Now it is time."

Coyt hefted the front of the stretcher and Jurgen hoisted the rear, both taking care not to jostle the broken man. Teeg imagined him drowning in his own juices. Only the outer skin still held; the inner walls had given way to cancer, the cells were loosing their saltwater, the architected molecules of life were scattering into elements again.

Flare in hand to light the way, Hinta parted hemlock boughs and stepped onto the overgrown path that led up to the headland. The others followed, Teeg and Phoenix hindmost. Thickets of salal crowded in from both sides. Blackberry vines arched over the trail and caught in the meshes of shimmersuits. Soon the beach was blotted out behind them and nothing was visible ahead except darkening green. Tree roots humped the soil underfoot. Coyt stumbled once, and the lurching of the stretcher tore moans from Sol.

On a grassy ledge halfway up, they paused to rest. Gorse flickered on all sides. Rhodies glowed palely from the shadows, like luminous floral tablecloths spread over bushes to dry.

"You all right?" Teeg asked Phoenix.

He sucked in air and gazed down at the white-fringed curve of beach now far below them. "It's better up here. I feel lifted above everything."

Only the upper third of the sun still glowed between the ocean and the flat ceiling of cloud. The red light, catching the tops of waves, seemed to form a pathway of sparks across the sea. Teeg wondered how Phoenix would endure the darkness tonight, when he had no dome, no raft, no shelter of any sort.

When the march resumed, Phoenix took the front handles of the stretcher from Coyt, who seemed grateful. The hump-backed man was powerful, so lifting was no chore; but smoothing out his crippled walk to avoid jostling the litter must have been a strain.

Sensing the motion, Sol opened his eyes, rolled his head to face the sea, and whispered, "Whales . . . going north. . . ."

Bringing up the rear of the procession, with her flare lifted high, Teeg could tell from the delicate way Phoenix picked his footholds that he was oblivious to the darkness, he was wholly absorbed in the effort of balancing the shattered man. Sol in his anguish had not been able to recall Phoenix's name. "Is the other one with you?" he had asked. Yet even without a name for him, the old man had sensed Phoenix's absence and arrival. Now Teeg thought he must be comforted to have the newest wildergoer, this city man, help carry him up the darkening hill to death.

Up steeply along the mountain's flank they followed an old road-cut, now barely distinguishable from the encroaching forest. It must once have been paved, for stony lumps underfoot made the walking treacherous. From one switchback they could see down into Salt Creek meadow, where the domes of Jonah Colony, each lit from inside by a flare, glowed like jewels. The road soon led them beyond sight of the settlement, steeply up and up, and the gloom was filled with the heavy panting of climbers and ocean. The sun was a rim of scarlet. Watching it vanish, Teeg sensed the unimaginable swiftness of the turning planet.

At length the procession emerged onto the headland, the only shelf on the precipitous mountainside broad enough to support a lighthouse. Tumbled blocks of stone marked where the keeper's hut had stood. The base of the lighthouse, still faintly visible in the gloom, thrust up from the soil like a broken tooth. Teeg remembered the awe she had felt, as a child of five or six, when her mother had first led her onto this headland. The snaggle-tooth of the lighthouse had seemed huge and menacing enough for any whale. "There's no harm in this place," her mother had assured her. "The lighthouse was for guiding ships through fog and darkness." Ever afterward, Teeg had associated the ruins of Whale's Head Light with dangerous journeys.

Phoenix and Jurgen lowered the stretcher onto the grass, egg-soft, as if the old man might burst like some flimsy sack. Marie knelt over him and resumed her comforting murmur. Tired from the climb, they all stood for a spell with the forested mountain rising darkly behind them, and looked out over the sea. A thousand meters below, visible only as a faint lace of white against black water, waves smashed against the base of the cliff and boiled in rings of foam around boulders. Flares lit the grass at their feet, but everything beyond this ring of light shaded away to absolute blackness. Instinctively, the conspirators huddled in a circle around the dying man, some facing inward as if to watch over him, some facing outward as if to convoy him through the night.

Phoenix was one of those who gazed inward, toward the comforting flare. He stood half bent over, hands curled, as if he still bore the weight of the stretcher in his mind. Wind swept across the clearing and laid the grass on its side. Sol moaned.

"Let us have a fire," Marie said.

"Phoenix and I will get wood," Teeg quickly offered.

She took him by one of his curled hands and led him behind the lighthouse, toward the shaggy spruce and hemlock. Her flare lit a few meters near their feet, making it seem as if the land were being tugged past beneath them. When they reached the border of the forest, where gorse blossoms smoldered yellow and rhododendrons shone a vaporous pink, Teeg knelt to crawl beneath the overhanging boughs.

Phoenix balked, with the down-thrusting branch of a spruce against his belly like a sword. "I can't go in."

Lit from below by the flare, his face was a desert landscape, hollowed and gullied by shadows. Teeg felt overcome by a fierce love, because of the courage it had taken for him to walk even this far.

"You stay here," she said, "and I'll load you up with sticks." She hung the flare on his belt and stood on tiptoe to kiss him. Ferns stroked her sides luxuriously as she crawled beneath the feathery branches. The carpet of needles was pungent with decay and rebirth. She had to remind herself she was here after firewood, the feathery darkness was so tender against her, the branches like fingers along her body. She had only gathered a small armful of sticks when his panicked voice cried out, "Teeg? Come, *come!*"

Careful not to strain her sore ribs, she squirmed back to him through wet ferns and caressing branches. "Only a little while longer," she comforted, "just a little while, my bear." She dumped the firewood into his cradled arms, pressed her forehead against his, then crawled once more into the damp feathered woods. She made half a dozen trips, staying each time only long enough to find a few sticks, before his sobbing drew her to him again. Eventually they were both loaded down with wood and could go back to join the others.

A fire soon blazed on the ruins of the old lighthouse. The stretcher had been rigged so that Sol could recline against it, face half-turned toward the flames, half toward the sea. His white hair and beard and the black gateways of his eyes shone luminous in the firelight. Marie, his oldest companion on spirit-travels, sat by his left side. Jurgen sat near him on the right, massive and still, like a boulder. Everyone else took a place in the circle. Fire leapt in their midst and the unplumbed universe opened above.

Stillness gradually enveloped them like mist, floated them free of gravity, free of time and flesh and the mechanics of separation. It was a true gathering, their first since landing, and Teeg wept with joy.

When they had all met and fused in the depths, Marie began the death-song, lilting high and frail. Jurgen soon joined in gruffly, then Hinta with her rich keening voice, and then each one in turn around the circle, the song passing like flame from candle to candle. Teeg was not surprised to hear Phoenix catch the melody and hum it shyly. She recognized the sound of surf in it, and of wind through fir forests, the sound of rain and bird-song, of animal footsteps and plants growing.

Cracked, brittle, like a page from one of the old paper books Zuni used to show her, Sol's voice rose into the song. They were singing his death, carrying him on that journey, but they were also singing his life, all life, the grass turning green before it turned brown before it turned green, the birds flying south and then north and then south again.

They sang all night, sometimes everybody at once, always at least one voice, for the song was a fire they must keep alight through the temporary darkness. Each time Sol's voice joined the song it flickered more weakly. Teeg reached out and laid her hand by turns on the old man, or on Phoenix, wherever the current of emotion urged her to lay it. She knew from her mother that all life flamed up out of darkness, like flowers burning out of the black earth, and she was not afraid.

They rode the firelit circle like a ship into morning. Sol was the last one to sing, alone, in a voice as thin as grass. With morning light, the mountains eastward separated themselves from the sky. Westward, the horizon once again divided air from water. The universe was created anew.

Sol let the song whisper to a close. "Let me . . . look out . . . over the ocean."

He moaned when Jurgen picked him up and carried him to the edge of the cliff, moaned again as he was lowered to the grass. Marie knelt behind him and wrapped him in her arms. The others pressed close, kneeling, leaving his view open to the sea. Each one laid a hand on his quivering body.

"Whales!" he murmured ecstatically, gazing down at the morning waters. He drew breath harshly. "Dozens of them! There's a spout . . . and there!"

Teeg surveyed the calm, spoutless ocean. The dying man's eyes, darker and more vast than the night they had all journeyed through, already beheld another world.

"See the flukes! And there's one breaching . . . look! . . . the white markings on the head. . . ." The breath rasped in his throat. "And the calves . . . are with them! See . . . the little ones . . . the young. . . ."

He was twitching and heaving beneath their hands. Marie hugged him and soothed, "Peace, my darling, peace."

The breath kept rasping like a saw in wood. Then presently it fell silent, the tremors dwindled away, and the old man grew still. Teeg imagined the last walls and dikes within him giving way. The elements he had borrowed for a spell and had carried around in the shape of a man were returning to earth. She stroked him and let the tears come.

All morning they sat with the body, high up there on the shoulder of a mountain, where sky-eyes could observe them. They kept very quiet, listening to wind and ocean. From time to time someone would speak out of the silence, recalling thankfully some episode in Sol's life: how he had recovered plutonium from breeder reactors to keep it out of the hands of terrorists . . . how he had taught one friend or another to spirit-travel . . . how he had baked bread and made a gift of it in his callused hands . . . how the spirit had bubbled up in him and set him dancing.

When no one else was moved to speak, they remained for a while in silence. Then Marie undressed the body and they all took handfuls of grass and rubbed the black flesh. With branches dragged from the woods they built a pyre on the foundations of the lighthouse. From the fire they had kept going all night, each one took a brand, pressed it to the newly-gathered wood, and the funeral blaze licked up around he-who-had-been-Sol.

A beacon for travelers at sea, Teeg thought. Or for the health patrollers. But there was no avoiding the fire, whatever the danger. They had to see him off on his journey. She stole a glance at Phoenix. There was a look of transfiguration on his face—whether from horror or ecstasy she could not tell.

The burning took a long time, armful upon armful of branches collected from the mountainside. Rain began at mid-morning, kept on through noon and late into the afternoon, hissing in the flames. The sun was touching the ocean by the time Marie declared the burning finished. Rain cooled the ashes quickly. Each one thrust a finger into the charred remains and smeared a black streak across the forehead. The rest of the ashes they scattered in the grass, on nearby trees, by handfuls onto the ocean and into the breeze.

Then at last they could go down the mountain, to Jonah Colony, home.

EIGHTEEN

An expedition like this might have made sense for a young woman, blessed with stout legs and sound eyes, thought Zuni. But for me it is utter folly, in all likelihood my last folly.

She was resting at a bend of Salt Creek where the current bared a sweep of water-smoothed stones. The rock on which she perched had the melony shape and milky whiteness of a dinosaur's egg. Having already stumbled across a Roosevelt elk and the pawprint of a bear this morning, she would not have been surprised to feel the stone cracking beneath her or to see reptilian skin gleaming inside. The muscles of earth were quite capable of heaving forth anything you could imagine.

A dinosaur would feel at home in this dripping rainforest. Rain pattered on the hood of her parka, but she paid it no mind. The things of the world had already lost their edges in her blurred sight, so the added blur of rain made little difference. With the present moment crackling before her, why mope about the past? The valley of cinders, that burnt-out place she could no longer think of as home, lay nearly two days of walking behind her. The sanitation port lay three days farther back. Not a bad trek for these old pins, Zuni thought, rubbing her knees. Just beyond this bend, she remembered, the land fell away along a fault, the creek leapt over the brink of an escarpment and tumbled into a pool below. From there it meandered across a meadow, sliced through the coastal ridge, and emptied into Whale's Mouth Bay.

By closing her eyes Zuni could summon up that landscape, for she had dug clams and danced in and out with the breakers there many times as a child. Now she was reluctant to peek into that meadow for fear she would find it empty, or—worse yet—find the charred remains of a settlement.

All the tangled skein of my life narrows down at last to this one frail thread, she thought. Nothing to do but pull it and see what is tied to the other end.

She rose painfully and peered at the sky. If there were HP gliders snooping around up there, someone with better eyes would have to spot them. In any case, nobody's eyes were sharp enough to locate the spy satellites, which did the keenest watching. Let them watch. Delicately, as if tasting the breeze, she stuck out her tongue at the sky.

Roots snaggled from the bank like half-buried arms and legs, and these she held onto for balance as she hobbled along the creek. Limbs dipped overhead, each one strung with moss like pale green gauze hung out to dry. Old man's beard, she recollected, what a lovely name. All the venerable trees with their green whiskers.

The salt tang grew stronger and the roar of the falls beat louder. Behind the next clump of trees the sky took on that vague going-on-foreverness which signified the ocean. No use holding back now, she decided, hastening to the brim of the escarpment. She squinted down into cottony mist, corrugations of fluffy whiteness like clouds seen from above. Fog smothered the meadow and thrust like spears into each tributary valley. No sign of a colony. Maybe they hadn't settled here after all? Maybe they really had drowned?

Clinging to the lip of land, peering down into fog, Zuni stubbornly fought against despair. There is a way to survive, she told herself; there is always a way to survive. I will live in a hollow tree and eat blackberries and converse with the owls.

She lowered herself over the brink and picked her way downward from ledge to ledge. These falls were higher and wilder than the falls of Wolf Creek, so Zuni was soaked through long before she reached the bottom. Lower down the mist thinned, revealing the ghostly boundaries of the meadow. Still she could see no signs of a settlement. At the base of the falls a pool caught the plummeting waters. She stood there, catching her breath, watching the surface churn and buck. The spectacle transported her back to childhood, and she half-expected her lumberjack father to come tramping up with a clam-shovel in his hand and a blade of grass in his teeth.

The settlement, the settlement, she had to remind herself. This land kept seducing her into memory.

Skirting the pool, one eye on the agitated water and one on the ground, she came to a slab of shining blackness. Oregon mud, she thought. But why such a neat stripe of it? No end in sight. Too broad for jumping over. She thrust one boot forward experimentally onto the blackness, and was astonished to find it held her weight. With a quickening excitement, she squatted down and touched the gleaming surface. It was glass, etched like snakeskin. For a moment she feared it might be the melted ruins of something, more of the HP's handiwork. But no, with that careful etching, it must be a walk.

Forgetting her weariness and her aching joints, she limped swiftly along the black pathway, shouting, "Hello! Hello!" and expecting any moment to bump into some-one—Sol perhaps, or Marie. Maybe Teeg would be the first one! How amazed they would be to discover their old Zuni come a-calling!

Without seeing anyone, she soon came to a ring of domes, each feebly lit from inside, ghostly, diaphanous as a bubble. A larger dome bulged from the center of the ring, like the pale snout of a whale.

"Hello!" she cried, aware of the sappy grin on her face.

They must be here, she thought impatiently, jerking open the airlock on the nearest dome. Inside she found hanging ferns, sunken tanks glimmering with minnows, rolled sleepsacks. No one answered her calls. Where the devil were they? Hiding? Not dead, surely. They wouldn't dare, with the colony built and me here propped up on sore knees. In the entryway to the large central dome she found ten pure white shimmersuits hanging from pegs, limp and sumptuous, like the pelts of snowbeasts. Nearby was an airshower. She eyed it longingly; she was filthy from her trek, but too tired for the shower just now. She contented herself with stripping off her sodden antique pants and shirt, rummaging around in a nearby sleepcamper until she found a worksuit that looked to be the right size, and putting it on.

Arched tunnels led her from dome to dome, through workshops and greenhouses, past a solar kitchen and a battery of sunscoops. Through portholes she noticed hydrogen tanks and the fretwork tower of a windmill. Most of this survival equipment she recognized; it had been standard for many years on longer repair missions and construction projects. Some of it she had designed herself, ages ago, before realizing that only a web of cities could safely quarantine humankind.

Why ten shimmersuits, she wondered, and why ten sleepsacks? She had only kept nine bundles of cards in her rocket-covered lunchbox. Who was the tenth conspirator? At the doorway of each sleepchamber she paused to look inside, identifying the occupants by the accumulations of personal things—Marie by her trowel, Coyt by the pillow he used to brace his humpback in sleep, Jurgen by the leather tool belt he had kept oiled and limber through all these decades of plastic, Sol by the ivory comb he used for straightening his beard. Zuni lingered in Sol's doorway, her eye caught by the air-cushions, rolls of gauze, basin: the equipment of a sickroom. She felt a lurching in her heart, as if Sol were one of her children fallen sick. Weren't they all her children?

Each tunnel eventually led her back to the central dome. It was apparently their meeting place, with a flare at the center and white pillows around the circumference and a snowy vault overhead. Zuni understood only the haziest outlines of their group mysticism, but she found it easy to imagine spirit-work in this hushed, uncluttered place. She withdrew respectfully, without crossing the threshold.

Outside in the meadow she discovered that the rain had quit. The sun hovered near the horizon. No one visible anywhere. Perhaps they were off gathering something— dandelions or ginseng or seaweed. Who knew what wilder-goers might take it into their heads to gather? Or her noisy arrival might have scared them into hiding. Maybe the health patrollers had caught up with them and hauled them away for rehabilitation? No, no, the HP would never have left the colony intact. Sickness then? Poisons waiting here all these unpeopled years? Attack by an army of wolves? But where were the bodies?

Hobbling along and brooding, she soon found herself on the beach. Except for knobs of stone that showed through like vertebrae, the sweep of sand was bare. What might have been bathers floating in the surf turned out, when she limped over for a look, to be driftlogs. A mewing gull flapped down to investigate some bit of sea wrack, then flew away. Greetings, thought Zuni. High up the beach she discovered their empty raft, and in one of the caves she found the scraps of crates. Husks that they had left behind.

She collapsed onto a log and sat numbly watching the surf crash against upthrust rocks in the bay. When her strength returned she would go back to the settlement, wait for them there, live on alone if need be until whatever had spirited them away came in search of her. Whatever it was had better be ready for a fight. For now, she would sit here on the edge of the continent, peeling the damp white hair from her face, licking salt from her lips.

Twice she closed her eyes, to soothe them, and the second time lengthened into a nap. When she woke the sun was squatting on the ocean like a fat rooster. The tide lapped at her log seat. Maybe they're back, she thought excitedly. She was just twisting round to spy along Salt Creek toward the meadow when she noticed pinpricks of fire on the headland, away up where the lighthouse used to be. She blinked, not trusting her eyes, but the sparks kept burning. Could they be automated signals of some sort? Fires? No, they flickered and jounced, like flares carried through woods. Over the pounding of her heart she strained to hear any sound, but there was only the surf and wind through marshgrass.

Whoever carried the lights was angling down the mountainside toward the beach. Any path inland would have to pass near her. Hide, she thought, until I can see their faces. Yet like a donkey her body refused to budge. No more fleeing, said her bones. Sit here on this log and let whatever might come, come.

The twin lights, drawing close to her, seemed to glow more brightly as the sky dimmed. They were flares, she could see that now, bright solar bulbs carried aloft by a column of walkers. In the circles of light she counted nine figures in shimmersuits, gleaming like mercury. Except for the gritting of boots on sand, they were absolutely silent.

Motionless on her log, merging with the darkness, Zuni watched them caterpillar toward her. To her bleary eyes their faces looked as featureless as balloons. The slender one with dangling braids who carried the foremost flare might be Hinta. The hunch-shouldered one who rolled like a ship when he walked might be Coyt. Hope swelled in her, nearly buoyed her off the log. She was about to cry out. But where was Sol's unmistakable face, the zebra pattern of white beard on black skin? She squinted, straining to see. No, Sol wasn't there. Then who were these strangers? A health patrol to come sterilize the settlement? Another band of exiles?

Zuni was shrinking back into the shadows just as the trailing flare drew even with her. The woman who bore the flare halted for a moment to pick up something from the beach—a shell or bit of rock—and drawing the light near her cheek she studied the find in her cupped palm. In that instant Zuni recognized the bald mushroom head, the cratered moonface, the squat body.

"Marie!" she called out of the darkness.

The woman's hand fell limp, dropping whatever prize it had discovered, and her face swung blindly in Zuni's direction. "Who's there?"

Zuni tried to stand, but her knees would not unbend. Stupid legs!

"What is it? What? What?" The others crowded around Marie, a knot of astonishment. The twin flares bobbed and jerked over their heads.

"Somebody called my name," said Marie.

"I'm here. Here!" Zuni cried. "Come get me. I'm rusted solid."

Their voices babbled in consternation. Marie waded forward, searching for this impossible voice. But a smaller body darted past, arms outstretched and red hair flying, and in the next instant Zuni was flat on her back in the sand, surf licking her ears, with Teeg pawing her like a puppy.

"Zuni! You can't be here! Did you drop out of the sky? Come, sit up, let me help you, there." She tugged and shoved at Zuni, pummeling her with affection. "Ach, my rib! Never mind. Everybody come see what the tide washed in!"

Their bent heads formed an inquisitive circle above her as Zuni sat, giggling and weeping like a schoolchild, with Teeg's arms about her.

"My lord, my lord, it's really you," Marie said wonderingly. She touched Zuni's cheek, as if to test whether she was an apparition.

"What's left of me. I'm about worn down to a frazzle."

"However did you get here?"

"I hiked."

"From where?"

"Cascade repair station."

Again the babble of consternation. Over one hundred kilometers!

"How did you know we were here?" It was Jurgen's voice, rumbling, suspicious.

Zuni allowed herself a sly smile. "You've all been my hobby for a very long time."

"But why did you ever leave the city?" asked Teeg.

"For the same reasons you left. To see the mountains again, the forests, the ocean. To see how things are growing now that people are locked indoors."

"Did you come by yourself?" Jurgen reared over her. Dear cantankerous Jurgen. A bulldog at heart.

Zuni laughed. "Who would be crazy enough to come along with me?"

Jurgen hunched down and shoved his great bewhiskered mug close to her. After a moment's glare, a grin split his face. "You are an old fox," he said, pressing his forehead to hers. "I can't believe you're really here. But I'm glad."

When they had all finished greeting her, Marie scolded, "Now Teeg, quit smothering the woman. Let's take her home. Where's the stretcher?"

"Oh fiddle! I can walk!" Zuni waved them aside. They stood back respectfully. But when, after a half minute of straining, she could not persuade her legs to unbend, Jurgen swept her up, light as a doll, and laid her gently on the stretcher. She was too bone weary to protest, or to ask why they carried a stretcher with them or where they had been all day. A slender man with the raggedy beginnings of a beard, a man she did not know, bore the front of the stretcher. Was he the mysterious tenth conspirator? And why were there only nine in this procession? Who was missing?

Teeg pranced alongside, chattering the whole way to the settlement. Once there, she tucked Zuni into a sleepsack, murmuring, "Rest now, love."

Zuni teetered on the brink of sleep, held back only by a sense of loss to which she could give no name. Then she recalled who was missing. "Sol came with you from Oregon City?"

"Yes." There was an unwillingness in the girl's voice. "Where is he?"

Teeg brushed the salty strands of hair from Zuni's face. "He died this morning."

Zuni felt the sudden loss as if someone had carved a hole through her belly. But she was not surprised. She had known about his cancer. "He was a lovely man," she whispered. "So gentle. Remember how he would embrace you with his eyes when he spoke?"

"You were mates?" Teeg asked softly.

"For a little while. Long ago."

Both women kept still a moment, feeling Sol's presence. Finally Teeg said, "That's where we've been since yesterday, up on the headland singing him through."

"He's buried up there?"

"Cremated. It's what he asked for." Teeg sat on her heels and stroked Zuni's face. "I guess it's what I want after I die, to go right back to earth."

Sol . . . ash? All life was a burning, Zuni thought, a fire in the cells defying for an instant the ultimate cold of the universe. In the Enclosure, he would have been frozen after death, against the hope of some future cure. But out here there were no resurrection vaults, and death, when it came, might as well be celebrated with a final fire.

"We've put you in his sleepchamber," said Teeg. "You don't mind?"

"I'm glad."

The fingers took up Sol's ivory comb and untangled Zuni's hair. "Do you need anything, old one?"

"No, child."

"Would you like me to stay with you through the night?" Zuni was unable to keep the amusement from curling on her drowsy lips. "No, no. Nothing frightens me here. This is where I've wanted to be."

Teeg's fingers at last withdrew from her face, and Zuni slipped away into sleep, her body a constellation of stars.

NINETEEN

"It's simply exhaustion," Marie pronounced over Zuni's fretful body.

The wildergoers were all crowded inside her chamber in the morning, eager to learn why the city-builder had come into the wilds and whether she could be trusted to keep the secret of Jonah Colony. Each had reason to be grateful to her, for help in getting jobs or schooling, for years of kindness. But she was an architect of the Enclosure! What could possibly drive her outside? Seeing her twitch and mumble, however, with her famously neat bun of hair now a wreck of whiteness on the pillow, they saved their questions.

Watching her from the foot of the sleepcushion, Teeg felt like a bear in the fairytale, gaping at Goldilocks. What improbable visitor is this, dozing in our midst?

Tests had shown low blood-sugar, but no concentrations of toxins. Hinta prescribed rest and broth, then like the others she returned to the labor which Sol's death had interrupted.

While Teeg nursed Zuni through the next day of shock, Phoenix kept stopping by the door to peek in. Teeg would gesture for him to stop gawking and come in, for God's sake, but always he held back, awestruck, like a pilgrim at a shrine. You'd think he was paying a visit to Michelangelo. The worshipful look that had always come over him whenever they spoke of the architect exasperated Teeg, for whom Zuni was no legendary figure, but merely a person, crotchety and fond of teasing, a surrogate mother with a face shaped like a wedge of pie, eyes buried in creases from her habit of squinting, and a mind that made light-year leaps.

Now pale and hollow-cheeked against the pillow, this face had aged by seventeen years since Teeg had first glimpsed it. The memory of that first encounter was painful. Teeg had just left her mother at the sanitation port, arm bravely uplifted, to visit her father inside the Enclosure. "Only for a couple of weeks!" her mother called reassuringly. Her father looked ridiculous when he met her in Oregon City, with a video crooner's mask plastered on his puss and a bright red wig perched like a throw-rug on his skull. "I've brought a friend to meet you," he said by way of greeting. The friend was a slight, vigorous woman who fixed Teeg with an intense gaze before bowing. Even back then, at age sixty or so, Zuni was already white-haired and her face was a map of delicate lines, like frost on a window.

"Architect Franklin will care for you when I am forced to leave the city," her father explained stiffly.

Teeg felt a sickening loss of balance, as when the floor of a glider lurches beneath you. "But I'm going back outside with Mother in two weeks."

Her father's many-faceted eyes looked in every direction but hers. "That was a misunderstanding. The eugenics law requires you to stay inside."

Teeg looked pleadingly at the woman, who raised her eyebrows and asked, "You would separate the child from her mother?"

"To preserve her from the wilds, yes I would."

"There are worse fates than living in Oregon," Zuni observed.

Those words had roused in Teeg a glimmer of affection for the woman, an affection which swelled over the years into love. After that first glimpse of Zuni, Teeg had to wait seven years before being licensed to venture outside the Enclosure. By then her father had frozen in the waters off Alaska, and her mother—according to the health patrol—had drowned in the Columbia River.

While Zuni lay in the sleepchamber recovering from shock, Teeg studied every branching in the delicate frost-pattern of wrinkles on her face. It might have been the map of an imaginary country. Words bubbled up occasionally from the old woman's sleep. What few sentences Teeg could make out had to do with birds and cages. "It's all right, love," Teeg soothed, petting her. "You're with us now. You're free."

The coma of exhaustion gave way to gentler sleep, and sleep feathered away to wakefulness. Phoenix was lingering in the doorway, round-eyed, when Zuni came fully awake. A glance from her sent him scampering.

"Who's your rabbity friend?" Zuni whispered. She squeezed an upraised finger against each side of her head, to simulate rabbit ears, and she made a small O of her mouth to imitate his startled look.

Teeg was overjoyed to hear her voice. "Oh, Phoenix? He's my partner. He thinks you were one of God's advisers at the Creation."

"Ha! Wait till he gets a good look at me. A half-blind old crone. Half-dead, too, when you lugged me in here last night."

"Night before last," Teeg corrected her.

Zuni hummed. "Well, I truly am a lazybones. Didn't sleep much on the way out here. Damned beasties kept running off with my gear."

"What sort of beasts?"

With a grunt Zuni sat up. "Elk or mice or bears. It might have been anything, for all I could see. Mutant grasshoppers! Ambulatory mushrooms!" Teeg laughed. A new alertness came into Zuni's face. "Since when did you have a partner, and a citygoer at that, from the looks of him?"

"Since about ten months ago. I was hiking on the pedbelt one morning and he popped out of his door." Exactly like a rabbit, Teeg admitted, now that Zuni had supplied her with the image: a frightened rabbit with chocolate eyes and a gaping circle for a mouth. While Zuni sipped broth, Teeg proceeded to tell her about wooing Phoenix.

Zuni listened with merry eyes. "And so you turned him into a mystic?"

"Of sorts."

"And he joined your—what do you call them—ingatherings?"

"How did you know about ingatherings?" Teeg asked with surprise.

Zuni gave her evasive Buddha smile. "I told you, I've made a hobby of observing you all. Who nudged you together into this work crew to begin with?"

Teeg pondered this. "You *built* the crew?"

"Building conspiracies is a messier business than erecting cities."

"You knew all along we were coming out here?"

"I certainly hoped so. That's why I put you malcontents together."

Scattered memories of things Zuni had said to her over the years, small gestures of discontent, suddenly took shape in Teeg's mind like birds flocking for spring migration. "You've been planning to come back out to the wilds, all this time?"

"In my heart, I never left."

"But your architecture," Teeg protested, "the Enclosure . . ."

"That was my way of helping make sure there would be some wilds for me to come back to. And haven't things

grown wonderfully?" Zuni grabbed Teeg's arms and drew
herself upright. "The earth was sick, with a disease called
people. So I helped put us in quarantine. Inside the bottle,
as you liked to say so bitterly."

"I never blamed you."

Zuni gave her an appraising look. "No? Perhaps not. But
you hated your father with a fury."

"He *was* hateful."

"For helping build the Enclosure? Would you prefer to
do without it, and have everybody traipsing around outside
and fouling the planet?"

There was silence, while Teeg savored the bitterness she
had felt since childhood toward her father. Hating him was
bound up with loving her mother and loving the wilds. But
if his work had been necessary? If the Enclosure had been a
blessing to Terra?

Zuni's legs suddenly buckled and she slumped to the
cushions. Weakly, she asked, "Will you help me shower,
child? I don't have the starch back in me yet. And I'm so
filthy you could scrape me and use it for potting soil."

"Oh, Zuni, of course! I'm standing here like a light-
pole."

After the two women spun beneath airjets, Teeg massaged oil into Zuni's back, where skin slid over a rack of
bones. "We'll have to fatten you up on algae," Teeg said
mischievously.

Zuni made a face. "Thanks, but I'd rather stay scrawny."

Oiling her own skin, Teeg was reminded of bathing in the
ocean with her mother, who took this same unself-conscious
pleasure in nakedness. Life inside the Enclosure, where
bodies went cloaked in gowns and desire was fenced in by
rituals, had been a torment. The only relief had come from
Zuni, who scoffed at the sexual taboos as she scoffed at all
the other pieties of the Enclosure.

"Father hated having a body," Teeg mused. "You could
tell by the way he covered it with any old rag. And the way
he let himself go to blubber."

"Because he was fat and sloppy, you say he hated his body?" The creases about Zuni's eyes showed amusement. "It was distasteful to him. A clumsy animal for transporting his brain."

"He was rather keen on making love," Zuni observed mildly, stuffing her arms and legs into a crisp shimmersuit.

"*Father?*"

"To which I can testify from personal experience."

"With *you?*"

Again Zuni flashed the Buddha smile. "It is a very old habit of the race, my child. And on the whole a pleasant one."

Teeg was flabbergasted. That walrus of a father wallowing in bed with elegant Zuni? Impossible! "You were conceived artificially," her mother had assured her. "Your father never touched me, not once, not even with gloves."

Trailing Zuni back to the sleepchamber, where the older woman lay down again with a sigh, Teeg kept repeating, "Father? *Father?* With *you?* I don't believe it. And even if it's true, I still say he loathed the wilds. He thought Mother was crazy for staying outside."

Zuni crossed arms on her chest and spoke with eyes closed. "He was certainly the most indoors person I ever knew."

"There! So don't pretend he was some kind of hero for building the Enclosure. He didn't care a damn about saving Terra."

"Has it ever occurred to you that Terra used him and your mother and all the rest of us to preserve herself?"

"Used us . . . What are you saying?"

"I'm saying what you know intuitively. Terra is an organism, and like any organism it has evolved methods of protecting itself. The body rejects alien tissues, germs, infection. How? It seals them away. Suppose Terra has sealed *us* away inside the Enclosure?"

"You mean . . . thought it? Willed it?"

"Does the body need to think about infection? Reflex serves extraordinarily well."

"But we're talking about centuries of effort—"

"An eyeblink for Terra."

"—and millions upon millions of people, the whole population of the planet cooperating to—" Teeg hesitated, overwhelmed by the idea.

"To do what?" Zuni asked drowsily.

"Seal themselves away," Teeg whispered. Kneeling beside Zuni, who seemed to float on the cushion, she was astonished by the thought. Science's yearning outward into space, religion's yearning to escape matter—could all that have been the self-preserving ruminations of Terra? And was all of human history—at least since the decline of nature-religions and the rise of cities—a prolonged healing process for the planet? Was industrialization only a fever, succeeded by the calm years since the Enclosure?

There were a hundred questions to ask, but Zuni was asleep, the creases about her eyes still gay.

As the colonists went about their work, transplanting ferns and wildflowers into the shelter, gathering cuttings of trees to root in the nursery, they kept one eye cocked at the sky, like nervous robins tugging at worms. Health patrollers could plummet down like meteors, swoop down like hawks. The wildergoers had lived with this knowledge since escaping the city. But these days they kept even sharper lookout for catastrophe. Sol's death and Zuni's arrival disturbed their collective life, as rocks break the current of a stream.

Sol had brought a spiritual intensity to every act, to stirring soup or fixing cybers as much as to ingathering. He had also been their communications expert, who was to have assembled equipment for monitoring the Enclosure's transmissions. By patching into the nearest land cable, he would have supplied Jonah Colony with data on climate, oceans, sun activity, toxin levels. From the air he would have plucked news about spy satellites. He had grown so weak by the time of the landing at Whale's Mouth, however, that he could merely scrawl instructions for assembling the communications gear.

At the moment everyone was too busy to puzzle over the crates of communicators. Once Jurgen's wild crayfish joined the trout and bluegill in the tanks, Indy began experimenting with algaes and waterlilies, to get the right mixtures of plants and fish. Water from the tanks circulated through troughs in the greenhouse where lettuce, squash, and several dozen other vegetables were sprouting. Earthworms, frogs, wasps, flies, predatory mites and spiders were painstakingly collected from the forest and loosed into the greenhouse. Indy had her heart set on lizards and praying mantises, but none were to be found. Marie brought two green snakes dangling by their tails. Teeg and Phoenix searched the meadow until they had gathered a flask's worth of ladybugs. The small islands of plants inside the colony now stirred with tiny creatures. Crawling into bed one night, Phoenix thrust his bare toes against a frog, and leapt up howling. On subsequent nights he always shook the sleepsack, to see what tumbled out.

Construction of a library completed the outermost circle of domes. Jonah Colony took on the shape of a flower: the meeting dome in the center was surrounded by an inner ring of sleepchambers and an outer one of workchambers, like concentric rings of petals. The musty green smell of vegetation spread everywhere through the shelter. In the stillness of the meeting chamber one could hear the flap of fingerling trout leaping in their tanks. People and other beasts provided carbon dioxide and food for the plants, which provided food and oxygen in return. Frogs and insects gobbled pests. Fish tanks absorbed the day's heat and gave it back at night, so the temperature varied only a few degrees from noon to midnight. The life of the place, like its shape, was a nest of circles.

A few days after Zuni's arrival, when Phoenix and Teeg

were returning with bundles of conifer seedlings dug from nearby slopes, he paused, studying the many-humped shelter, and said, "Do you ever worry it might just grow until it becomes a city?"

"Then keep on growing till we've built the Enclosure all over again?" said Teeg. Terra healing herself: she remembered Zuni's words.

"Don't you worry?"

"Sure, it could happen." She twirled the bundle of seedlings, letting the rootlets, fine as hairs, whip against her throat. "Deep down maybe we all want to build an incorruptible world. Build utopia . . . heaven. That's what drove my father."

"But how do we keep from shutting ourselves inside again?" asked Phoenix, obviously troubled. "You see, ever since the vigil at the lighthouse and Sol . . . I've been thinking, if he could let himself *go* like that, into the wilds, so peacefully, then I should be trusting enough to *live* here."

"Then why're you so upset?"

"Because every time I go back inside the shelter I think how easy it would be to just *stay* there, like on a starship, and never come out."

"The starship is a machine," Teeg countered.

"And what about the colony?"

"It's an organism. Frogs and ferns and microbes. It breathes the air, takes in water and seaweed and dirt. All the doors invite you to walk outside. Everywhere we turn it reminds us we're part of earth."

"I suppose so," Phoenix muttered skeptically.

In exchange for the materials of life, the colonists repaid the land with mind, the attentions of consciousness. They had agreed early in their conspiracy to help reforest the nearby slopes, especially with nut trees and fruits and hardwoods, which would provide food and shelter for beasts. Accordingly, three domes in the outer ring of the colony were fitted out as a tree nursery.

As soon as Zuni regained her strength, she made her way there to admire the bold twiggy shoots marked *walnut* and *cherry*. Teeg found her bent inquisitively over Phoenix, who was on his hands and knees planting apple seeds in an earthen flat. The snowy hair was knotted once more into a meticulous bun, and her cheeks, though sunken, were tinged with rose. Evidently she had put Phoenix at ease, for when Teeg arrived he was jabbering learnedly about the germination of appleseeds.

"It takes them so long?" Zuni mused. "Do you suppose they spend all that time thinking about the sun?"

Phoenix beamed up at her. "And about breaking into blossom."

"I see you've made friends," said Teeg, approaching them.

Phoenix balanced on his heels, fingers dingy with potting soil. "Zuni was telling me about her father's orchard."

The older woman smiled a welcome. "Curious man, my father. He spent all day cutting down trees and most evenings tending the ones he had planted."

Teeg had already heard about Zuni's ashen homecoming, so she could guess, from the bruised look around the other woman's mouth, that Zuni was remembering the valley of cinders.

"Curious man," said Zuni, gazing vacantly. "All those trees. Gone."

To draw her back, Teeg asked, "What do you think of our plans for reforesting?"

"Plans? Oh yes, for the trees. A splendid project. I only wish I could see well enough to tell a crabapple from a redwood."

"Here, you can do these by feel," Phoenix said, and he poured appleseeds, glittering like bits of fire, into Zuni's palm. She imitated his motions, poking a hole in the soil with her index finger, dropping in the seed, covering it over.

Her pleated face held a look of absolute concentration and delight.

Not wanting to disturb the rhythm of their work, Teeg stood by the outer wall of the nursery, watching a spider perfect its web in a clump of eelgrass. Patient architect, this spider, building nets in hopes the universe would fling some morsel its way. Teeg was reminded of her mother, who had been an architect in reverse, patiently dismantling buildings and entire cities, unweaving nets. The newsfax had even invented a word to describe her profession: Judith Passio— Anarchitect. The day she drowned in the Columbia, the obituary had been titled: FAMOUS ANARCHITECT AC- CIDENT VICTIM IN WILDS. If she *had* drowned. For all Teeg knew, her mother had been lasered by the HP. Impulsively, she asked. "Do you suppose she really did?"

Zuni looked up quizzically from her apple planting. "Who did what?"

"My mother—drowned herself."

Phoenix broke in, "What's the point in getting yourself worked up again?"

"Of course . . . your mother." Zuni shifted from a kneeling posture until she sat with legs straight before her. She gave Teeg one of her appraising looks, the stare an architect would give to a roof truss. Her soil-blackened hands hovered in the air near her face, like those of a surgeon waiting for gloves. "All I know is what I read in the newsfax, plus some few hints from your father."

"What hints?"

"Oh, he used to complain about how restless you were during those early years inside the Enclosure. 'Why shouldn't she be restless?' I'd say. And he'd say, 'If only her mother were erased, she'd forget about going outside.' "

"Erased?" Teeg repeated, horrified.

"He wasn't very delicate when it came to speaking of your mother."

"So you think *he* sent the patrollers after her?"

"He might have." Zuni hesitated. The knees of her

shimmersuit were dusky where she had massaged them with her apple-planting hands. Before her critical gaze, Teeg felt like a girder whose strength was being judged. At length Zuni said, "Or he might have dictated the story to the newsfax."

Teeg blinked, stunned by the implication. "You mean . . . *made it up?*"

"It's possible. Your father was an inventive man."

"She might not even be dead?"

Phoenix interrupted, "This is crazy! Seventeen years in the wilds—"

"Maybe she never drowned? She could have been living out here all this time, in Portland or wherever—and you never even *told* me?"

"Teeg, love," Phoenix said hurriedly, "nobody can survive seventeen—"

"She could be *up* there," Teeg said bitterly, "and even on repair missions I've never been able to force myself to go anywhere near Portland. It was too painful, the picture of how she died. Gliders swooping down and stunners blazing and her leaping into the river. I couldn't have stood seeing the place where it happened." She looked sharply at the other woman. "But if it didn't happen?"

Zuni pursed her lips. "I've always wondered about that myself."

"But you never thought of sharing your doubts with me until now."

"Oh, I thought about it." Zuni reached out a hand and Phoenix helped her to rise. Leaning on him, she flexed each knee experimentally. "I simply didn't want you to come charging out here all by yourself, looking for someone who probably isn't to be found. If you'd gone to Portland and found only ruins? What then? Suicide? No, you're too precious for me to risk destroying you with false hopes."

"But now with Jonah Colony for a base, and somebody to go along—what's to keep me from going?"

"Absolute madness!" Phoenix interjected.

"What's to keep me?"

"Nothing I can see," Zuni replied mildly. She carefully poured the remaining appleseeds into Phoenix's waiting palm. "Save me a few," she told him, "so I can help you again tomorrow."

"Of course, as many as you want."

Tugging at his neck, Zuni lowered his forehead until it touched hers, and when she let him straighten again he smiled as though he had just glimpsed the heavenly fields. "And if our impulsive one over there," she said, nodding at Teeg, "should take a notion to go hunting her mother, promise me you won't let her go alone."

He nodded vigorously. Zuni limped away toward her chamber, brushing her fingers lightly over the seedlings as she went. Phoenix gazed after her with an expression more nearly resembling adoration than anything Teeg had ever seen on a human face. She had seen the look on dogs, long ago when people still kept them as pets, but never on people.

"I suppose you'd rather die than break your promise to her," Teeg said.

"Promise?"

"About going with me."

He turned despairing eyes on her. "Going where?"

"Why, to Portland."

TWENTY

Phoenix knew better than to hope Teeg would change
her mind. Might as well hope Salt Creek Falls would
change its direction and tumble uphill. No sooner get my
feet under me here, he thought, than she's itching to go
somewhere else. Portland, ye gods. What could be left of
the place, twenty years after its dismantling? Moss-covered
rubble and tons of plastic. Maybe it was all cinders, like
Zuni's village, like the hundreds of blackened townsites he
had viewed in satellite photos.

"I have a concern to make a trip," Teeg announced in the
stillness following that night's ingathering. "I am moved to
seek my mother, to find out how she died. Or if she died."

Everyone let that soak in for a while. The ingathering,
Zuni's first, had been the clearest since the landing, so there
was a good deal to absorb. Phoenix sat on his mat in a
clairvoyant stupor. Each of Teeg's words, as she explained
her mission, drifted before him like a tiny glass animal.

Surely they would say no, you can't go, it's a crack-
brained scheme. But no sooner had Teeg finished speaking

than everyone was agreeing to her plan. "It would be good for you to wait until the crops are established," Marie was saying. "And the ribs will take another four weeks to mend," Hinta cautioned. "And of course you won't go alone," said Jurgen.

"Teeg needs one companion," Zuni pronounced in her mild, queenly way. Her milky gaze settled on Phoenix. Me? He mouthed the question at her, finger shoved like a pistol against his chest. She nodded. "I'll go with her," he said.

Everyone murmured quick assent to that, as if he were the logical one to go. They probably figured I'm the one they could most easily do without. No irreplaceable skills here, he conceded. Just two hands and an eye for patterns and a brain full of dreck from the city. Ought to paint them a cityscape on the roof up there, he thought, something to remember me by. Towers and pyramids of lights, pedbelts curving like the paths of comets, stately citizens in masks and gowns everywhere you look.

He finally understood that Zuni had devoted her life to building those cities, not because she hated wilderness, but because she loved it. She had wanted to put humanity in quarantine.

In a moment of boldness, after the others had left the meeting dome for bed, Phoenix asked her, "Do you believe they'll stay inside the Enclosure forever?"

"A few others might slip outside, as we have," she replied. "Not enough to harm the wilds. But the future of the species, I'm afraid, is inside."

"Afraid?" he repeated. "Isn't that what you wanted?"

"It's what I believe is necessary." Netted and cross-hatched with wrinkles, Zuni's face showed deep emotion. She turned away from the flare at the center of the chamber and looked up through the dome, which was still transparent in the mild evening sunlight. Following her gaze, Phoenix saw the humped green hills, the fretted crowns of fir trees, the rouged sky over the ocean. "Necessary," Zuni repeated softly, "but it is a terrible price, to lose the earth."

Salt Creek Falls kept tumbling down, never up, and Teeg stuck by her determination to visit Portland. The weather continued rainy for days.

"Are we going by raft?" Phoenix inquired one morning, eyeing the perennial gray clouds through the porthole of their sleepchamber.

"By the end of May it will clear, you'll see," Teeg assured him. "It always did when I was a kid."

"When we were kids the climate was totally different. The polar ice caps were twice as big as now, and the rainforests hadn't been cleared. The equatorial air exchanges and the jet stream have been oscillating like crazy."

"Thus spake the weatherman," she intoned.

"Maybe I don't know anything else, but at least I know climate."

"You wait."

They waited, and of course she proved to be right. During the last week of May the vault of clouds cracked open, revealing an expanse of pure and radiant blue. Teeg was never one to crow over victories, so Phoenix merely pretended he had known all along the clear weather was coming.

Jubilant over the sunlight and the new access of electricity that it provided, Coyt began tinkering with the communications equipment. Marie was the only one who could decipher the notes that Sol had scribbled in his dying hours, so she sat on a packing crate and read aloud while Coyt, his humpback and withered arms slick with sweat, plugged instruments together. After three days of electronics and head-scratching they managed to coax a little static from the speakers. Since all messages within the Enclosure traveled through glass filaments or laser corridors, it was a delicate business tapping into the system without being detected.

Meanwhile the twigs in the nursery, a mountain's worth

of trees, were bursting out in tiny green flames. Endive and tomato and chard, each put up its telltale leaf from the black humus of the greenhouse. The fish doubled in size, doubled again, browsing in their broth of algae and larvae. The sunshine brought on blooms of algae, some twenty different kinds. Even without a microscope Arda could tell them apart, each by its shade of green, its smell, the feel of it between her fingers. Phoenix liked to watch her gliding among the fish tanks, a large-boned woman who moved with the sluggish grace of an undersea creature. He couldn't help thinking of her as the one fertile woman in the colony.

Now that the weather was fine most of the wildergoers spent the mornings outside, adjusting the windmill or tending the circular garden or gathering seaweed for the bio-digester. There was an unspoken agreement that everyone would keep laboring until Jonah Colony was securely established. As he grew accustomed to the chaotic land-scape, Phoenix would often pause in his labors to study the meadow or forest. "Keep still," Zuni told him, "and you can see it growing." Back in Oregon City, Teeg had promised him the same thing about the terrarium. Watch until you disappear, she had instructed him, and then you will truly be part of the earth. It was one thing to surrender yourself to a boxful of dirt and vegetation inside Oregon City, however, and quite a scarier thing to surrender yourself to a whole planet.

Which direction was Portland, anyway? When he asked Teeg she waved her hand vaguely northward, toward some impossible-looking hills. And how far was it? "A few days," Teeg replied. "Two hundred kilometers, I should think," Zuni told him honestly. When his eyes widened at the news, the architect reassured him, "Most of that's on the Willamette River, riding the current until it empties into the Columbia at Portland."

That information was soothing. Ride the current. Get into the little raft, the blue one for rivers, and coast in style to Portland. Nestled in the sleepsack that night, balancing on

the brink of sleep, he was suddenly jostled by a thought.
"The Willamette flows north to Portland, right?"

Teeg replied groggily, "Rivers only flow in one direction
as a general rule."

He sat bolt upright. "Then how do we ride it back all
those murderous hundreds of kilometers?"

"Find another river."

Was she teasing? He pictured them stumbling from one
river to another, always a little off course, until they wound
up in Florida or Indiana or some other godforsaken place.
"What if we pick the wrong river? Suppose it dumps us in
the Gulf of Mexico?"

"We paddle around South America until we come to the
Strait of Magellan," she replied, sitting up, "then we
shinny up a vine and travel back here through the tree-
tops." The sleepsack drooped around her waist. The skin of
her throat and breasts shone creamy in the feeble glow of
the flare. "Actually, we'll use airjets to shove us upstream.
No problem." She stretched luxuriously.

"I guess I kind of woke you up," he apologized.

Teeg idly stretched the pale belt of skin around her
ribcage where the tape used to be. Judging from the
acrobatic intensity of her lovemaking lately, Phoenix assumed the ribs were fully healed. "Oh," she yawned,
"what's the middle of the night for, except sitting around
and chewing the fat?"

"Chewing fat?" he repeated with disgust.

"It just means talking. An expression I learned from
Zuni."

"You learned a lot of stuff from Zuni. Half the things she
tells me—about hermit crabs and Earth Mothers and
whatnot—sound like things you've told me."

"That's me—Zuni's little echo."

"I can see how her voice would get inside your head and
stay there."

Teeg grew thoughtful. "I carry a lot of echoes from my
mother, too."

He was seized again by the thought of Portland, that impossible destination, as doomed and unreachable as ancient Troy. The air of the sleepchamber, thick with the breath of plants, felt clammy against his chest. Something moved with tiny clicking footsteps in the nearest tub of ferns. "What will we eat all that time?"

"Mushrooms and bearded moss."

"Seriously."

"Seriously," she replied, taking his hand in hers, "my hero is once again a wee bit nervous about Teeg's adventures. But Teeg has delivered him safely to gameparks and oil tanks and Oregon beaches, has she not? And she now solemnly promises to deliver him to and from Portland in one piece." With that she spread his cupped palm over her left breast.

He grinned in spite of himself, leaving the hand on her cool, cushiony flesh. Heart mountain. "I like it when you're serious."

"Look how easy it will be." Using his index finger as a pointer, she drew an imaginary map on her torso. "Here's Whale's Mouth Bay," she said, touching his finger to the pit of her arm. "We climb the coastal ridge about here," skimming up the curve of one breast, grazing the nipple, "then along Salt Creek into the Willamette Valley, like so," down the slope between her breasts, "ride the river thisaway," over stomach past naval, "wriggle through the brush," into the curled thickets of her pubic hair, "until we arrive at our destination where the two rivers meet," she concluded, leaving his alert hand at the joining of her thighs.

Miraculous geography, he thought, forgetting about Portland, slithering down beside her into the pouch.

By the middle of June there were snow peas and lettuce and early squash to vary the diet of algae. Phoenix gaped hungrily at the innocent trout, but Arda assured him it would take months before any of the fish would be ready for eating, and the first ones would not be trout, anyhow, but the dark bewhiskered catfish. Jurgen netted some halibut and gigged some flounder from the raft. Indy's tests showed they were too contaminated for eating, however. Even with her bad eyes, Zuni proved to be the shrewdest at locating mushrooms and clams, some of which turned out, by Indy's tests, to be safe.

One afternoon at low tide, Phoenix was mired halfway to his knees in the muck of the bay, helping Zuni dig clams. She probed with her shovel, bent down to retrieve a clam, plopped it in her mesh bag. Although she still napped at midday, she was fully recovered from her trip, and when she was fresh she could work Phoenix into the ground. Her eyesight was very poor, had always been, she told him as they rested on their shovels. "Maybe that's why I've seen things in such large patterns. Cities, Enclosures, starships."

What did she see, he wondered, when she rested on the shovel and tilted her face toward the tree-fringed cliffs? Could she tell that lichens scattered like green snowflakes over the black rock? Could she make out the white glint of gulls sailing in and out of caves? And what did she see when she closed her eyes and tilted her face to the sun? In its full glare her wrinkles vanished and she looked momentarily like a tow-headed girl. In those moments of sun-gazing her beauty was troubling, because it was accessible, it was the loveliness of a woman who could have been his lover.

Phoenix tried to break the spell by asking her, "What do you see when you face the sun that way?"

Zuni turned to him, eyes still closed. As the sidelight caught her cheeks, the wrinkles spread across her skin like fissures, and she became safely old again. "I listen for things. Like the grass growing . . . the moon spinning. Like those sea lions calling in their caves. Hear them?"

Leaning on the clam shovel, feet mired in mud, Phoenix listened. Surf. Gulls. Sizzle of wind through spruce trees. Purr of Salt Creek Falls back in the meadow. Then he heard the faint barking, like children calling to one another at a great distance . . . sea lions. In her first breathless report about Whale's Mouth Bay, Teeg had described hearing them. And now he had been here six weeks, with their chatter constantly in the background, and only Zuni's words made him notice. "Yes," he replied, "like kids in a gamepark."

"It sounds as though dozens of them have survived." Zuni bent for a clam, dropped it into her bag where it clicked against the others. "That's remarkable, on a diet of poisoned fish."

Phoenix groped in the muck but found nothing. With a luscious sucking noise he lifted first one boot then the other, picked a new spot, bent over again. "What's still alive, do you think? What's going to make it?"

"It will take hundreds of years to know for certain. Most of the large creatures, the ones high on the food chain, are probably doomed."

"Is it going to be the dinosaurs all over again?"

"Let's hope not. Remember the dinosaurs were starved out when the debris from an enormous meteor blocked sunlight for a few years, upset the photosynthetic cycle. Thousands of species died out along with the dinosaurs." She swept an arm toward the green-fringed coastal hills. "Plants don't care so much about our poisons, as long as they get rain and dirt and sunlight."

Finding a clam, Phoenix hefted its rough, prehistoric weight in his palm. "Don't you think we should be keeping records about the weather and birds and such?"

"Why?"

"So people will know what life was like back here in the last third of the twenty-first century."

"You think if we weigh fish and count bird's eggs, that will tell them what life was like?"

"At least it would help. And then we wouldn't just be drifting along from day to day. I mean, ever since we came out here, I've been wondering what everybody would *do*, once the colony is all fixed up."

Zuni gave him a bemused look. "Making music isn't enough for you? Or painting, telling stories, building sand castles, meditating?"

"But I mean useful things."

"Like planting trees?"

"Exactly, something that would make a difference to the earth."

"Then we could blast a few canals," she suggested soberly, "level the hills a little bit, pave the meadows to keep down weeds . . ."

Exasperated, he said, "No, that's not what I meant at all."

"But don't you see it's our compulsion to do something visible, to fix things up, that has nearly ruined the planet? Nature is infinitely complex, and our actions are pathetically simple. Can't we just let things alone for a while? Sure, plant trees, but be humble about it. If we can just live lightly on earth, not harm things, and grow deeper—that's a great deal."

Zuni's stare held him transfixed. Even knee-deep in mud, with the bay yawning around him, he felt more than ever like a city man. Would he ever unlearn the impulses that had created the Enclosure? Should he?

In the way she had of seeming to read his thoughts, Zuni said, "The earliest sea creatures that floundered onto the beach took a very long time to get used to the land. And their bodies never forgot the sea."

"Like I've floundered out of the city into the wilds?" said Phoenix.

"I've floundered a bit myself. Don't think it's an easy thing for me to shake off forty years of dreaming about the Enclosure. Look, I still carry it with me." From her waistpouch she plucked a tiny wire ball on a chain. "It's a model of the Enclosure, you see, with silver wires for tubes and beads for the cities." She dangled it close to his face. "The glass kernel inside there is Terra."

A deep longing came over him, for the orderliness, the

security, the bustle of Oregon City. But immediately he thought of the oppressive crowds, the costumes, the numb days at work followed by frenzied nights of chemmie-tripping or eros parlors.

"Teeg and most of the others have never wanted anything but the wilds," Zuni added, swinging the silver globe hypnotically before him. "They've always regarded the Enclosure as an abomination. So life is a bit more complicated for you and me, Phoenix. We recognize the beauty of inside and outside both." She pocketed the globe and twisted shut the neck of her clam sack. "Don't you suppose we've dug up enough of our little friends for one day?"

Phoenix nodded. Discovering this bond with Zuni had moved him deeply.

They waded inshore, the mud clinging to their boots. The bags of clams thwacked against their legs. At the mouth of Salt Creek they stepped onto a glass walkway. Zuni tapped the black surface with her shovel and said, "You see? Just fixing things up. Keep the trail from getting muddy. Next thing you know we'll roof it over."

Phoenix studied the wrinkled geography of her face to make certain she was teasing. Then he played along. "Yes, we could do with a gamepark or two. Then block out the sun and get some decent lights in here."

"And a disney," said Zuni.

"Certainly. With plastic shrubs that never lose their leaves and flowers that don't fade and some mechano-bears and deer and such that stay out in the open where you can see them. None of this sloppy wild stuff."

They both laughed. Zuni curled her arm about his waist, light as a birdwing. They continued on that way, blotting out the landscape with mural-screens, erecting syntho-stands at every bend in the path, covering the meadow in one vast bubble, filling the purified air with synthetic smells and tastes. By the time they reached the colony's entrance lock, they were both staggering with laughter.

Teeg, who was pulling her boots off at the entrance, blinked at them and said, "What have you two been eating?"

"The bread of understanding," said Zuni. "Haven't we, Phoenix?" She hugged him against her side with one of those bird-light arms.

"Loaves of it," he agreed.

Teeg looked from one giddy face to the other. Slowly a grin spread over her features. "Sure, mother and child return from playing on the beach, dizzy with joy. I remember that."

TWENTY-ONE

Patience, patience, Teeg kept reminding herself. You have waited seventeen years, you can wait a few days longer. But she grew more and more edgy as the trip to Portland was delayed, first by rainy weather, then by a series of mishaps at Jonah Colony. While testing dirt samples, Indy cut a finger and fell ill with blood poisoning. She had no sooner recovered than Jurgen came down with a fever, broke out in a rash, and spent three days writhing on his sleepcushion while Hinta and two helpers pinned him down. Soon after his fever broke, Arda discovered all the bluegill floating belly-up in the fish-tanks, casualties of some chemical imbalance, and several people had to go out hunting for wild stock to replace them.

And so departure was put off day by day. Phoenix seemed glad of the delay. "Give you time to think it over," he told her. She thought of little else. Every kilometer of the route was mapped out. She could visualize each range of hills, each river and thicket, right up to Portland. But there she drew a blank. What would the place look like? When she had first arrived in Portland with her mother, the city had been abandoned for three years. Here and there a roof had caved in, weeds and saplings had burst the pavements, fires had devoured a few old neighborhoods of wooden houses. But most of the city was built of metal and plastic, and so had endured, which was why her mother had been sent there. Dismantling a city, her mother used to say, was like plucking a chicken, and then carving the meat off its bones, and then whittling away at the skeleton. There was very little left of Portland at the end. Since the wooden houses were useless, they were spared along with the brick-paved streets. Most of the stone buildings were framed in steel, which meant they had come down, and the towers came down, wires and pipes were dug up from the ground, every appliance that had not been stolen was melted, thousands of abandoned vehicles were shredded, and the city at last was stripped bare.

Teeg carried both these images in her head—the city with its avenues of glinting towers, its domed malls, its monorail tracks gleaming overhead, its quaint wooden houses . . . and the city carved clean to the bone. Why had her mother chosen to settle in such a place? Maybe it was for the hills full of wild roses and rhododendron, or for the snowy crown of Mt. Hood looming up to the east and the Columbia surging massively by.

At length everyone in Jonah Colony was healthy, including the fish. Teeg packed tent, sleepsacks, a fifteen-day supply of food, medicines, and filters, and last of all the river raft. It was all she could do to persuade Phoenix to stop tagging after Zuni long enough to try on his backpack.

"What's a small boulder on a back like mine?" he bragged, tottering about the sleepchamber with the bulky weight on his shoulders. "I figure I'll last about a kilometer per day lugging this thing."

"Which would get us back here a year from this fall," Teeg observed dryly.

"Of course, we could just stay home and save ourselves all that trouble."

After driving him away with a scowl, she transferred some of the gear from his pack to hers, to make the going easier for him. Journeying to Portland was her obsession, and she regretted having to saddle him with it; but the others were right, she would be foolish to go by herself. She would also be very lonely. The thought of making love in their tent on some forested ridge, with no breathing soul except rabbits and possums nearby, kept her in a mild fever of excitement.

Each night during the last week of June she waited for the word of permission to emerge from the ingathering. Once Jurgen regained his strength and Zuni opened fully to the spirit, the nightly meditation became rapturous. In the great chamber, circled about a pale yellow flare, they quaked and trembled on their mats. No one, least of all Teeg, wished to break this potent spiritual circuit. Yet the burden of her journey lay heavy upon her.

On the last night of June, after an especially powerful gathering, Marie announced: "I am of a mind that Teeg and Phoenix should go now."

Jurgen spoke out gruffly: "Yes, go in peace and return in peace."

The word of agreement passed quickly around the circle, like a flame passing. When all had spoken they held hands for a moment in silence, to let the decision settle.

Afterward, everyone offered them advice for the journey. Don't cross a light corridor or you'll trigger an alarm in Security. Don't signal us except in an emergency. Don't taste any water without filters. Wear a breathing mask if you must tramp through boggy land. Watch the radiation detector and steer clear of heavy concentrations. Never let one another out of sight.

When the others had withdrawn to their sleepchambers, Zuni stayed behind to sit a few moments with Teeg and Phoenix. Her face still shone with the peacefulness of the ingathering. The lines in that face were like the grain in wood, Teeg thought, or something softer than wood, like folded cloth, like the surface of a creek.

Presently the older woman said, "No matter what you find in Portland . . . you will come back to tell us? Not just stay there?"

Having brooded for weeks on this question, Teeg said, "But if Mother is there?"

"That's not likely, and you know it."

"But if she is?"

"She may be a stranger to you. Time has forced each of you down many separate branchings of the path."

"If she's alive, she can't possibly be a stranger to me."

As the two women spoke, Phoenix shifted his attention from one to the other, like a spectator at swat-ball.

"If you choose to stay with her," said Zuni, "you'll break our circle."

"I'll mend hers by going there."

"Perhaps, perhaps," Zuni answered skeptically. "Just remember that some wounds are slow to heal. Some never do."

Teeg imagined the older woman was thinking of her home village in the mountains, where lasers had left a scar of cinders and bubbled glass. "I promise to come back here, at least for a while," Teeg said, "no matter what I find in Portland."

"Me too," said Phoenix.

His slightly crazed, devoted expression was that of a queen's fool, willing to follow his mistress to triumph or disaster, and Teeg realized that was exactly how she and Zuni had been treating him. A feeling of tenderness swept over her.

"Teeg, you are fortunate in love," Zuni said, kissing foreheads with Phoenix.

"You sure are," said Phoenix with delight.

In the morning Teeg discovered Phoenix stealthily moving gear from her pack into his own. His body, whittled down by months of training inside the Enclosure and by weeks of labor out here, was thin but muscular. His movements had lost most of their city awkwardness, and he was growing more beautiful to her every day. What she liked most right at the moment were the muscles in his back, flexing as he bent to stow her things in his rucksack.

"You'll catch a cold traipsing around like that," she murmured, opening her eyes as if just waking, "and then what earthly good are you?"

He turned to her, naked, and it was evident that his body had been dwelling on something other than a journey. They made love swiftly, fearfully, and Phoenix clung to her in silence long after climax. What was he thinking? What happened to last night's carefree fool? Who was this quivering child she held in her arms? His weight against her was a bag stuffed with mysteries.

Later they air-showered, then joined the others for breakfast. Everyone seemed glum. Because we're breaking the circle by leaving, Teeg realized. Coyt added to the gloom by reporting that he had overheard scraps of HP broadcasts: something about exiles and camp and the garbled name of a bay. He had tried in vain to catch the drift of the message, but the receiver would only pick up advertisements from the commercial channels. It couldn't possibly be us, he announced without conviction.

His news was received in silence. Even Jurgen, whose good spirit was normally as abundant as his flesh, pushed the food around on his plate and kept mum. Teeg was afraid the trip would begin that way, in gloomy silence. But as hands reached out to help them shoulder their rucksacks, Marie began the traveling song. Voice after voice picked it up, as they had picked up the song for Sol, and like the death song this one had the sound of rivers in it, the sound of wind through trees, the sound of earth's movements. With this melody in her ears Teeg led the way up Salt Creek to the falls. As she and Phoenix climbed the rockface, the voices merged with the sound of water.

From the top of the falls, looking down at the flower-shaped cluster of domes in the meadow, Teeg waved. Tiny figures waved back, then scattered to their various labors. One stayed behind longer than the others; Teeg knew her by the blaze of white hair. The old woman did not wave, but just stood there with face uplifted.

"She's found a daughter after all these years," Phoenix said, "and now she's afraid of losing you."

"I know," said Teeg.

Diminished by distance, Zuni might have been a fleck of foam. The whole of Jonah Colony might have been froth on the meadow. The slightest breeze, and everything would vanish.

As if reading her thoughts, Phoenix said, "I wonder if there'll be anything here when we get back."

Teeg shaded her eyes and studied the sky over the ocean, searching for the long-winged silhouettes of gliders. Blank sky, of course. The powers that swept down on you rarely showed their faces ahead of time.

"Who knows?" she answered. "Will the world still be there after you blink?"

Phoenix shrugged, or perhaps he was merely balancing his pack. Pointing upstream, he said, "Portland, two hundred kilometers," and set off walking. They retraced the route Zuni had taken, along Salt Creek to its junction with the Wolf, past the burned-out site of her village. Even loaded down with backpacks, they made better time than she had, reaching the repair station after three days. The sight of the gleaming travel-tubes, these outflung arteries of the Enclosure, was unsettling after so long in the wilds.

Knowing better than to invade the protector fields, they gave the station a wide berth, hiking northeast across the broad valley to meet the Willamette River. Teeg was grateful for the flat land after three days of scrambling along creek banks, grateful, after so many kilometers of worming through thickets or ducking under the boughs of trees, for the meadow flowers and grasses that stroked her thighs.

She and Phoenix took turns breaking a path. When he led, he would turn around occasionally to ask with his eyes whether he was heading in the right direction. She would point out the way and off he would trudge, the bulky pack swaying as he walked.

Near nightfall of that third day they struck the river, too near nightfall to risk launching the raft. Once the tent was inflated and the sleepsacks unfurled, Teeg went roving in the meadow to gather flowers while Phoenix heated algae-patties. Late bees hummed in the weeds. Off to the west, where the coastal hills rose like the spine of a sea serpent against a fiery sunset, two birds called to one another: Here I am, where are you? What other beasts filled the night with secret language? Teeg wondered. Except for a sluggish ground hog, three rabbits, and a clutch of squirrels, no four-leggeds had crossed her path.

Teeg loaded her arms with spiky purple flowers—Joe Pye Weed? was that what her mother had called them?—and was just standing up when she saw a dark head lifted above the grasses some few dozen meters away. She almost dropped the flowers. Narrow and long, with great shaggy whiskers, the head examined her. Who could it be? A renegade who'd avoided the HP all these years? A mutant? A bear? She was about to cry out—cry something, Help! or Hello!—when two pointed ears twitched forward on the shadowy head. Teeg flinched so violently the armful of flowers shook. The creature's head waggled. Suddenly Teeg realized that what she had taken for bushy whiskers was a bunch of grass caught sideways in a narrow jaw. Deer! She held very still, not wanting to frighten the animal, wondering how to signal Phoenix to come look. With stately movement the deer turned away from her and ambled toward the river. For a moment the dark body was visible against the even darker, glassy water. Seen thus dimly, it looked perfect, no tumors, no misshapen limbs. The only other deer she had ever seen had been crippled. This one pranced nimbly along the bank.

"Phoenix, look!" Teeg cried, wanting him to glimpse the creature before it disappeared.

Stately and elegant even in flight, the deer went bounding away, tail raised, easily leaping over the tallest weeds. It made scarcely a sound.

Moments later Phoenix came crashing to her side, axe in hand, puffing ferociously. "What's the matter?"

"A deer," she said.

He peered in the direction she pointed, but the creature had been swallowed by darkness. "A deer?" He repeated the word as if it were the name of a mythical beast, a unicorn or griffin. "Is it dangerous?"

"No, it's the gentlest creature," Teeg answered. Yet she trembled. There were not supposed to *be* any deer. The teachers had said so. But if deer—what else might thrust its head from the tangled weeds? Maybe a bear, to go with the pawprint Zuni had found?

After supper, while she and Phoenix sat on the bank watching the river flex and sway with the last gleams of daylight, the trembling seized her again. What was the trouble? Reminders of death could shake her like that. But why quake at this reminder of life? Like the deer with its ears pricked delicately forward, its muzzle lifted to catch a hint of anything stirring, Teeg strained all her senses to discover what lurked ahead.

"The river looks like skin over muscles," Phoenix said, touching her shoulder, "like about right here, or here," trailing his fingers along her throat, "or here," gently massaging her back with both hands.

Teeg grew still under his fingers, heavy and powerful and calm like the river. While they made love she imagined the river entering her, filling her, and she became the river, there was only the river, surging and surging toward the sea.

Sunlight shone lemony through the polyfilm bubble of the tent. Teeg was able to savor the exquisite morning only briefly before scuffling noises outside drove her from the

sleepsack. The racket came from Phoenix, who was locked
in a three-way wrestling match with the aerator and raft, and
was evidently losing.

"How does this infernal thing go?" he demanded.

Teeg disentangled him from the clinging blue fabric,
spread it out on the river bank, and within half a minute had
the raft inflated. "Like so," she said.

Phoenix stared at the gossamer craft as if she had
conjured it out of thin air. "Why did you bring me along on
this expedition, anyway?"

"For your cooking," she replied with a straight face.
"You do wonders for algae." When he appeared to be
genuinely downcast she felt a sudden swelling of love for
him. Hugging him, she babbled, "And for your rabbity
looks, your delirious ways in the sack, the great moony face
you get when the world surprises you. For the way you dote
on Zuni, for carrying half my gear in your rucksack, for
taking off that stupid mask and wig and coming out here
with a wildwoman like me. That's why."

He looked at her with an effort of soberness, but the
corners of his mouth pushed upward. "Is that all?"

"If I listed them all, we'd never get to Portland."

The Willamette carried them toward Portland on its
brawny shoulders all that day and the next and the next.
Phoenix squatted in the front of the raft, Teeg in the stern,
piloting them around snags and rocks. From repair missions, she was familiar with the buoyant craft and with
stretches of the river. Unlike the larger ocean raft, this one
was roofless, allowing them to see in all directions. The
shore was mostly overgrown with alders and brambles, but
here and there a meadow opened, aflutter with grasses and
bright midsummer flowers.

It was hard telling how many unburned towns they
passed, for these were smothered with vegetation and nearly
indistinguishable from the surrounding fields. But the
scourged places were easy to count, nine of them, for each
was a heap of slag and bubbled rock where nothing grew. In

three days on the river they floated past eighteen spots
where the soil was bare and chalky. Dump sites, possibly, or
spills. Phoenix kept a tally in his notebook, where he also
recorded the changes in radioactivity levels.

Twice they glimpsed deer, at dusk. Teeg imagined she
saw wolves or hulking man-like beasts on the hills near the
river, but invariably the shapes turned out, in the binoculars, to be rocks or bushes. Every now and again the raft
would startle a beaver or muskrat, which plopped into the
water and swam for cover. Occasionally a great blue heron
would lurch into the air on its ungainly wings, or else sit in
dignified composure on its fishing rock and eye them coldly
as the raft drifted by. Smaller birds stitched the air
constantly with their flight, tree to tree, bank to bank.
Watching them, Teeg imagined the air over the river was a
garment the birds kept in good repair.

Each evening they tethered the raft and made camp on the
shore, while the sun burned down in a vast conflagration
behind the sea-serpent mountains to the west. Teeg ate
facing east. She doubted whether she would ever be able to
look at the sunset again, or at fire, without remembering
Sol's burning.

The third afternoon on the river, Teeg guided the raft to
shore early. When Phoenix raised his eyebrows questioning-
ly, she explained, "The map says there's only two more
bends before the outskirts of Portland—or what used to be
Portland—and I want to be fresh when we get there."

By massaging her back that evening Phoenix tried to
soothe her, but she could not relax. All night her mother's
face kept rising into consciousness like a balloon. The lips
moved, but Teeg could not hear what they said, could not
even tell whether they spoke angrily or lovingly. Meditation, riding her breath, summoning the inner light to the
center of her belly—none of these exercises brought calm.
When at length she slept, dreams of swooping gliders and
raging fires exhausted her.

In the morning she blinked awake to find a grotesque

antlered face leering down at her. She immediately buried herself in the pouch and screamed "Phoenix!" The beast roared and she screamed again, and then she stopped yelling as she recognized the roar . . . the laughter. Flopping the covers back and glaring, she cried, "Phoenix, you idiot! You nearly scared me to death!"

The familiar goofy mug grinned beneath the antlers. "Look what I found snagged in a bush," he said, inclining his skull to display the horns. Clumsily strapped to his head with tape, they wobbled as he moved. "What do you call a male deer?"

"Buck," she answered, still angry.

"Some buck lost these. Big fellow, too. Look at all the points."

The rack was indeed a fine one. Teeg found herself admiring the way the points curved up gleaming, branch after branch, like a candelabrum. But she was reluctant to give up her anger. "You look ridiculous."

"I know it." He grinned and grinned, as if determined to drive all the night-fears out of her.

Phoenix wore the antlers while he fixed breakfast, still wore them as the loaded raft glided into the river.

"Will you take those stupid things off, so I can see what's ahead?" Teeg demanded crossly.

Without answering, he undid the tapes and stowed the antlers away. Then she felt bad, knowing he only clowned to distract her from brooding about the journey's end. But she did not want to be distracted. She had been circling back for too long to this place where her mother had died—or had not died—to give up brooding about it now.

They rode the current in silence. By and by a small stream entered the Willamette from the east. That would be the Clackamas. The snow-scarred peak of Mt. Hood reared up farther to the east. Sunlight dazzled on its frozen slopes. She had seen the mountain often on repair missions, yet each time it seemed to loom up fresh from the underworld, uncannily majestic and remote.

Mind the snags, Teeg thought. She gave her attention back to the river. Noticing Phoenix's profile, she realized that he had been turned sideways in the raft for an hour or more, contemplating Mt. Hood, with the worshipful look he had shown when contemplating Zuni on her sickbed.

He startled her by speaking. "What do you suppose that noise is?"

At first she heard nothing unusual. Then gradually she distinguished above the river sounds a harsh croaking, like the gasping of some enormous beast. She remembered the deer, with its ears pricked forward, listening. What waited?

TWENTY-TWO

Whatever was groaning apparently did not feel much need of breathing. Phoenix calculated it was likelier to be a machine than a beast, for what beast could bellow so mournfully without pausing to inhale? Still, in the wilds you could never be sure. Mutants cropped up all the time. Who knew what roomy lungs some of them might have? Maybe he should put on his antlers and go frighten the thing into silence. Nothing like a fierce pair of horns to stiffen the old backbone.

"It's getting louder," he observed, twisting round to glance at Teeg. Her haggard look unsettled him. What if it *was* a beast? "Maybe we should pull over?"

"It's probably just a drone they put in to scare people off the river."

"What people?"

"Anybody. Us, for example."

"Well," he admitted, "I think it's done a pretty good job on me." His playfulness did not erase the pinched look from her face.

According to the map that lay crumpled over his knees, they were passing through the suburbs of Portland now. But there was nothing remarkable on the shore, except some queer mounds of brush and saplings. Did they cover the ruins of buildings? Where the first bridge was supposed to be, crumbling cement piers thrust up from the river. Grass and brush had rooted on the crowns, where electric shuttles used to run. How odd, to have lived in a city that was open to the sky, with plants actually growing in the yards.

The groaning swelled louder, breathless, a voice brimming over with anguish. Merely a contrivance to scare us, he reassured himself. Meanwhile on both shores appeared the fractured skeletons of what must have been wooden houses. Beams and cross-members, some joining at right angles and some tilting dizzily, formed a latticework through which ivy curled. Ferns rooted on every flat perch of wood. Moss furred the rotting timbers in green. These house jungles were interrupted occasionally by areas of stony desolation, heaps of slag where no hint of green showed.

"This is pretty close to downtown," Teeg said. She had to raise her voice, because of the interminable moaning.

With a nudge on the tiller she guided the raft to the left of two islands. These must have been dumps, for they were cratered and barren. Chunks of what might have been pavement, maybe a river promenade, were visible through weeds on the western bank. Beyond, the shells of a few brick buildings stood roofless, disintegrating. Vines and ferns spilled forth at every window opening. Farther west the ground of the city rose over a series of knobby hills toward a heavily forested ridge. Phoenix imagined he caught a flash of light from there, a fiery wink. What? Probably sun on newly cloven rock.

"What's up there?" he asked Teeg, pointing at the ridge.

He had to ask the question a second time to get her attention, and even then she spoke haltingly. "Used to be Washington Park. Rose gardens . . . disney . . . observatory . . . Japanese gardens. All the bluebloods and moneybags lived there."

With another sway of the tiller she guided the raft into a side-channel. Immediately the groaning sounded closer.

"You have any plans for what happens when we—you know—meet this thing?" asked Phoenix.

"What?"

"I said, the better I hear this thing, the worse I like it."

She seemed to find it hard to focus on him. "Oh," she said absently, "didn't I tell you it must be some kind of wooden gears?"

"No, you didn't mention that." He had lost her attention again. Her eyes searched the banks, yet they seemed not quite to fix on anything outwardly.

Wooden gears? A piece of tree could sound so much like a beast in pain? Suddenly he noticed a gigantic thrashing movement on the western bank—a humpbacked creature—and Teeg aimed the raft straight for it, and the beast swelled up enormously and Phoenix was just deciding which point of the raft to dive from when the huge back curved neatly round into a wheel, a wooden paddle-wheel, spinning lazily in the current.

"You see, it's a water mill," Teeg announced.

Phoenix examined it with heart thumping. The great wooden wheel, perhaps twice as high as a man, stood upright, its lower paddles in the water, pivoting on an axle that jutted from a shed. The shed was also wooden, bleached and paintless, in excellent repair. It had been neatly carpentered from boards of varying grain and thickness. The nerve-grating howls issued from inside.

Kneeling on her rucksack, with arms braced against the sides to balance the raft, Teeg studied the shore intently. Her hair was drawn back tightly and knotted behind, a splash of red, making her face seem more naked, vulnerable. It was the face of a sleepwalker. Only the eyes moved.

The raft's blue lip soon bumped the shore just upstream from the mill. While Phoenix tied the lead rope, Teeg leapt ashore and hastened toward the groaning shed. He clambered after, staggering in the tipsy raft, then landing, to his astonishment, on a brick terrace. He stared down in amazement at the meticulous patterns, spirals in the middle with zigzags and stars worked in round the edges. Each brick was outlined brilliantly in moss.

Meanwhile, at the far end of the terrace, Teeg had flung open the door of the shed, and there she stood in the black rectangular opening. "Anyone here?" she yelled above the croaking of the mill. She vanished inside, swallowed whole.

Phoenix ran, but by the time he reached the doorway she had already emerged, blinking, into the sunlight. "A few bins full of grain, shovels, a broom," she hollered. "Nothing else."

Through the open door he could see wooden cogs meshing, axles spinning, two great round slabs of stone grinding against one another. The noise was deafening. "Who . . . how'd it get here?"

Without answering she prowled away over the bricks. He trotted after. "I mean, it couldn't have lasted all this time!" he shouted. She kept on toward the green mass of vegetation that crowded to the edge of the terrace. He caught up with her and jogged alongside, trying to discover what she had in mind. Just when it seemed they were about to run smack into the tangled thicket, a walkway opened, paved in bricks, broad enough for two people to march abreast. Phoenix drew up short but Teeg darted into the opening and in a moment was gone.

"Teeg! Teeg, wait!" He took a few hesitant steps forward. "The raft! The gear!" Dense bushes pressed in from each side, forming walls higher than his head. He advanced a few more paces. Still no sign of her. "You don't even know where this thing leads!" In places the thicket arched completely over the path. He faltered to a stop. The pressure of vegetation was too much.

He backed onto the terrace and sat gloomily down. She

was always scooting off somewhere, no explanation, just a cloud of dust and come-if-you-dare, Phoenix! Well, he wasn't crawling into that jungle for anything, brick walk or no brick walk. He would just stay here and wait. Camp alone if he had to.

Thinking that, he crossed over to the raft and lugged the rucksacks onto the terrace. The mill groaned on and on, setting his teeth on edge. First he sat with his back toward the chaotic forest, trying to put himself in a contemplative mood by gazing across the river at Mt. Hood. But he kept reflecting that some beast might slouch toward him from the rear and he would never be able to hear it above the infernal din of the water wheel. So he spun around and faced the vegetation. But then who knew what slimy beast might fling a tentacle out of the river?

After more than an hour of facing first one way then the other, and still no sign of Teeg, he decided this was ridiculous. Do something. He managed to deflate the raft and squeeze it into its bag without once getting entangled. Now what? The wooden gears shrieked monotonously.

Better the jungle, for the sake of Teeg and quiet, than all night beside this screeching mill. Shouldering his own rucksack, Phoenix wrapped his arms around Teeg's pack and hugged the weight against his chest. He staggered a few paces along the path, and then, discovering his balance, plodded heavily onward between the walls of vegetation. Padded front and rear with rucksacks, he felt less vulnerable. Whatever tried to make a sandwich of him would have to open its jaws very wide.

Someone evidently kept the path open, for the bushes on each side were trimmed evenly, and where the branches arched overhead they were pruned into a smooth vault. He supposed that was reassuring, a token of human control, although he would have appreciated knowing who the pruner was.

Following the twists and turns of the brick path, occasionally sitting down to rest, he soon lost all sense of direction. Where was the river? The sun was obscured by clouds, so it was no help. His legs told him the trail had been climbing steadily. As he pressed onward, arms aching from the weight of Teeg's pack, the shrieking of the mill-gears dwindled beyond hearing. In the stillness, the jungle seemed less threatening—less, in fact, like a jungle and more like a garden. He noticed that some of the bushes were hung with pinkish, bell-shaped blossoms, lovely. Here and there above the canopy of shrubs he spied the brick shells of what might once have been offices or stores, and then as the path kept rising he spied the moss-covered bones of houses.

Eventually the thickets gave out and he found himself on the edge of a meadow. Dazzled by the open space he dropped Teeg's rucksack and stood there panting. The grass beside the brick path was cropped short, and he quickly spied the reason—sheep. They were grazing on a hillock not thirty paces away from him. Sheep were harmless, weren't they? Was it the wolf in sheep's clothing or sheep in wolf's clothing you were supposed to avoid? He seemed to remember his father once calling a cowardly person sheepish. Or was it chickenish? Goatish? He felt certain they were timid beasts, yet he edged by them sideways along the path, taking no chances. They did not pause in their snuffling and munching to so much as glance at him.

The walk rollercoastered over the pasture, following the contours of the land, rising steadily. When he topped the first hillock he turned back around to get his bearings. Far below, the river dragged its dark length through the forest, past the desolate islands of downtown Portland. Much farther away to the east rose the snowy cone of Mt. Hood. Phoenix calculated he must be standing on the ridge where he had glimpsed a flash of light, the place Teeg called Washington Park.

Where the devil *was* she? He crept along, under the combined weight of the rucksacks. The walkway dipped again, skirted a heap of gray rectangular stones, then climbed another hillock. From there he could see the pasture's farthest edge, where the land seemed to fold steeply upward, and on the highest point, looking tiny against the sky, was a house.

Even from this distance he could tell it was unlike anything he had ever seen before outside a history park. Smoke trickled from a chimney. As he drew nearer, hurrying now, he could see a banistered porch encircling the ground floor. On top of that squatted two more floors, like layers on a cake, each one encrusted with windows and balconies, and atop it all was a pointy-roofed tower resembling the lookouts on ancient ships.

Was it a monument? A museum? A bit of pre-Enclosure gimcrackery preserved for showing schoolchildren the foolishness of old ways? He had never heard of such a thing. But then, since meeting Teeg, he had stumbled onto a good many things he would never have dreamed of beforehand.

The brick walk led him beyond the pasture, through a labyrinth of hedges, the house disappearing at each turn and then reappearing again, larger and less probable. The path crossed a stream over a high-arching wooden bridge, wound through some thorny bushes that bore fragrant blossoms of red and pink and white. Were these the roses Teeg had spoken of? Suddenly he emerged from the labyrinth of flowering bushes and there was the house. He leaned back to get a full view of the bizarre structure. Like the shed down by the river, it had been neatly carpentered of bleached wood, yet the materials for it seemed to have come from a dozen different houses. No two windows were the same size, the spindles in the banisters differed wildly in shape, the roofing tiles came in all shades of yellow and red. It was the sort of house an inventive child who owned too many construction sets might have built.

There were no signs anywhere to explain this apparition. No loudspeakers. He crept forward, peeking around the edges of Teeg's rucksack, afraid to call out. He was nearly to the steps when he noticed two figures sitting motionless in the shadows of the porch. One of them stood up, silvery, and the familiar voice filled him with joy.

"So you've come," Teeg said listlessly. Her face seemed blank and her voice was drained of all feeling, as if she were in shock. What was the matter? "Mother, this is Phoenix Marshall," she said, and then, waving her arm toward the seated figure, "Phoenix, this is my mother, Judith Passio."

The other woman rose, swaybacked and gaunt, her face hooded beneath a bonnet, a somber dress cloaking her from neck to ankles. In his confusion, Phoenix dropped Teeg's rucksack. As the spectral woman stepped to the edge of the porch the rocking chair she had abandoned continued its motion. Even shadowed by the bonnet, her face revealed a great effort of restraint. Obeying the ancient rule of politeness which Teeg had taught him, Phoenix bowed slightly and reached one hand clumsily toward her. The woman pulled back, thrust both hands behind her, and announced with an unplaceable accent, "Don't touch me with your city filth."

TWENTY-THREE

Phoenix was a welcome sight as he came plodding through the avenues of roses, loaded down with two packs like some long-suffering donkey. Seeing him toil past the goldfish pools and over the Japanese bridge, Teeg felt a great tenderness. Love for her had tugged him up the brick path from the river, as it had tugged him from Oregon City and Jonah Colony. Could she stretch his love so thin it would snap? What if one time she ran away and he didn't follow?

Three hours of quarreling with her mother had left her so upset that she could only manage to offer a numb greeting when Phoenix reached the front steps. The stranger who wore her mother's face greeted him with open hostility. Vile offspring of the Enclosure, her mother had called him. But how could she look at Phoenix and find him hateful?

Teeg motioned him to a rocking chair and served him tea, ignoring her mother's withering stare. For a long spell only the rockers made any noise as the three of them sat on the porch, sipping from cups of translucent china, looking out over the formal gardens. What little there was to say, after seventeen years of absence, Teeg and her mother had already said.

When Teeg had come dashing up the walkway three hours earlier, her mother had greeted her without surprise. There was no weeping, no embrace, merely a cold, "Hello, my daughter." The thirteen others who lived in the patchwork house were off working in fields or lumbermill or brick kiln. "To protect them from contamination," Judith had explained bluntly. She alone had waited for Teeg, knowing about the trip down river, about Jonah Colony, about the escape from Oregon City. She knew all this thanks to the one piece of technology in the house that was less than two centuries old—an antique solar receiver, which monitored HP surveillance broadcasts.

Horrified, Teeg had asked, "The HP are watching us?"

Her mother seemed pleased to deliver the news. "Oh, yes. They located you three days after your supposed accident at sea."

"But why haven't they arrested us?"

"Why bother?" There was a disturbing remoteness about this woman, bonneted and gowned like a wax figure in a museum. "You're nonentities. We all are. So long as we leave the Enclosure alone, we don't matter to them."

"And this house . . . ?"

"They've been observing me since 2035."

"And that's why you quit calling me?"

Judith smiled faintly. "Exactly. By keeping quiet, I am permitted to live out here like any other dumb beast."

Teeg felt the betrayal like a slap. "You let me believe you were dead?"

"Better that than quarantine," Judith answered tranquilly.

Nothing Teeg said could upset her composure. It was as if, living in a house patched together from pieces of nineteenth-century mansions, tending sheep and milking goats and laboring for hours at a hand loom, she had withdrawn in feeling as well as time from the world Teeg inhabited.

Now, three hours after that chilly meeting, Phoenix sat between them with the fragile teacup balanced in his hands. He looked from one to the other, seeking an explanation for their bitter silence. "Did you build this place all by yourself?" he asked hesitantly.

When it seemed clear she was not going to answer, Teeg said sharply, "It won't hurt you to talk with him."

Judith sighed. "In the beginning, yes, I worked alone." She rocked as she spoke, her voice carrying that faint rustiness one sometimes heard among returned space colonists. "By and by other exiles drifted through, labored on the mansion a while, then drifted away or gave up the ghost. There are fourteen of us now."

"Gave up the ghost?" said Phoenix.

Teeg translated: "Died."

"Of what?"

Once again Judith sighed, as if speaking to this cityman were a terrible labor. "Infections, bites, exposure. Cancer, mostly."

"You have no medicines?"

"Herbs, yes, and ointments." Judith studied him from beneath the awning of her bonnet. "But you mean—what is your word?—chemmies, don't you? Manufactured poisons. Those are available only from the Enclosure, and it is far better to die than to have any dealings with that place." She eyed him contemptuously. "If you were not hopelessly contaminated yourself, you would understand that without being told."

"Mother, you promised," cried Teeg.

"It's all right, child." Judith drew her lips tight, regaining her composure. "Soon he will go back to his own kind and you will stay here where you belong."

She seemed intent on this madness. In those hours before

Phoenix came laboring up the hill like a donkey, she had outlined Teeg's future. The returning daughter would exchange her shimmersuit for a woolen dress and linen bonnet, discard her watch and detector belt, seat herself at a loom. When Phoenix arrived, she would send him away, back to Jonah Colony with his gear and his corrupting city habits. "Send him away?" Teeg had replied incredulously. "I see your years in the Enclosure are not so quickly scrubbed off," Judith had said. "Therefore I will give you the length of the afternoon to get rid of your cityman."

Perched on the front of his chair, still balancing the teacup as if, tipping, it might explode, Phoenix groped for something polite to say. "You must have hunted all over to get the parts for this old house."

"While I was dismantling Portland," Judith answered coldly, "I had the foresight to store building materials and books and various items of furniture up here in Washington Park."

"Tools and nails and everything?"

"No nails. There is no metal anywhere in this house, and no plastic."

Phoenix twisted round to gaze in through the parlor window. Teeg recognized in his movements the same eager curiosity that had driven him onto the pedbelt months ago to talk with her. "Do you suppose I could . . . see the place?"

The gaunt figure rocked several times, as if weighing his request. Then she stood up and pronounced, with a note of distaste, "Very well. But you will not be able to appreciate our life."

"I'm used to ignorance," Phoenix said, rising and handing Teeg the treacherous cup. "I'm an expert at failing to understand."

Teeg had already toured the house, but she followed them anyway, fearing what her mother might say to Phoenix. In the entryway hatracks and umbrella stands flanked a moon-faced grandfather clock. The ornate hands proclaimed ten o'clock, and thus were either five hours slow or nineteen hours fast. The parlor was crowded with overstuffed couches and chairs, their velvet upholstery neatly patched. A threadbare carpet spread its faint purple design over the floor. A ponderous oak table, gleaming with oil, occupied the dining room. Unlit tallow candles leaned from wooden sockets on the walls. In the kitchen a fire seethed beneath an iron pot. Mutton stew, her mother explained. Except for the pots, everything visible was of wood or stone, including the sink and counters and the trough that fed water from a spring. Bundles of weeds hung upside down from the rafters. The other ground-floor rooms were filled with potters' wheels, looms, heaps of wool in various stages of preparation, woodworking benches, and other primitive equipment which Teeg did not recognize and Judith would not bother to identify.

The interior of the house was as much a patchwork as the exterior. Doorways shrank or expanded from one room to the next. The flooring was a crazyquilt of shapes and colors. The wall paneling and stairway spindles changed pattern several times on the way to the first floor.

In an upstairs bedroom, where oil lamps and potted ferns and doilies occupied every flat surface, the handmade dress and bonnet intended for Teeg hung limply from a bedpost. Seeing them, she felt a panicky desire to run outside into the woods. Her mother passed over them in silence.

On the third floor were a north-lighted studio and a library. Easels held half-finished copies of antique drawings—knights astride muscular horses, maidens cradling infants. The bookshelves were filled with guides to horticulture, bee-keeping, wood-heat. Among works of literature, Teeg recognized no title more recent than Rousseau's *La Nouvelle Héloïse*—a pastoral romance, three centuries old. For that matter, hardly anything in the house seemed to date from a time more recent than 1800. She remembered her mother proclaiming that the steam engine and railroad had corrupted the earth. So why not turn history backward until those fearful inventions—and every other premonition of the Enclosure—had been erased? When Phoenix, marveling at the leather-bound books, reached out to finger one, Judith warned, "You will touch nothing in this house." His hand snapped back as if singed.

By means of a spiral staircase they mounted through the roof into a watchtower. Teeg had been surprised, on first visiting this room, to find it strung with antenna wires, to hear the blather of a receiver, and to see a crude telescope aimed out one window. "Our one concession to modern technology," Judith had explained, nodding at the electronic device, "so we can listen for our enemies." This time, with Phoenix along, she made no explanations, merely standing back with arms crossed over her chest and one hand on each shoulder, as if guarding herself from the devilish influence of this cityman. She had informed Teeg that none of the others who lived in the mansion would return until Phoenix was gone. "You wouldn't expose your disciples to a leper, would you?" *Disciples?* The word left Teeg deeply troubled.

Even without the telescope, one could see from the tower all the way down to the watermill. Trotting along that brick walkway, buoyed up by hopes of finding her mother, Teeg had not realized what a climb it was. Now she felt as heavy as Mt. Hood, which shimmered in the distance. Clouds had sliced away the mountain's base; its peak seemed to hover in mid-air, like an intruder from the underworld, a mountain of the mind.

"Now you've seen everything," Judith said to Phoenix, "but have you understood anything?"

Not waiting for an answer, she led the way back down the spiral stairs. Through one of the staircase windows Teeg spied several figures ambling between outbuildings. Three or four looked to be men, dressed in gray cloaks with full beards and hats as broad as their shoulders. Another three appeared to be women in dark flapping gowns, their faces shadowed under bonnets and hair swinging in braids down to their waists. The panicky, smothering sensation rose in her.

When Phoenix paused to look as well, Judith blocked his view. "Keep your eyes from them," she said harshly. He flinched as if struck.

Teeg was furious with her mother. "Do you think he's a wizard, to hurt them with a look?"

Judith turned a calm and queenly face to her. "You must go change clothes, then give your metallic garment and all your city gadgets to this man. He has seen that you will live comfortably here, and now he must go back to his own kind."

His face twisted in confusion, Phoenix backed down the stairs.

"He's not going away," Teeg cried. "We're partners . . . joined together."

"He is diseased."

"With what?"

"With the Enclosure."

"But I keep telling you, that's superstition. He's come into the wilds, hasn't he?"

"Yes, and if we let him stay here, he will soon have machines roaring and domes rising and the same calamity will befall us again."

By now Phoenix had descended to the ground floor. Teeg could hear him dragging the rucksacks across the porch. "Phoenix!" she called. "Wait, I'll make her understand!" She ran downstairs in time to see him vanish among the roses, the packs scuffing behind him like corpses. She cupped hands about her mouth to call again. But remembering the baffled look on his face she knew he would not come back, and so she let her arms fall and kept still.

In a moment her mother's icy voice crept over her from

behind. "Good riddance. Now go take off those city things."

"Mother . . . listen, I can't understand what's . . ."

"You are home, my daughter. You will obey me."

"He's a harmless, gentle person," Teeg insisted.

"He has lived all his life inside the Enclosure."

"And I've lived half mine there."

"With your robot father and that Zuni woman."

"So does that make me diseased?"

Judith studied her dispassionately, as if examining a patient. "I cannot be sure yet."

Teeg was too shocked to reply. From the first chilling encounter on the porch, when her mother had refused to embrace her because of the shimmersuit, Teeg had prayed that the suspicion would be temporary. A chasm had opened between them in seventeen years, but surely it could be spanned. Wasn't this the same woman who had taken her hunting for seashells, taught her to wait patiently for deer, filled her with love of the wilds? How can she fear me? Teeg wondered. Yet at every turn of the afternoon Judith revealed deeper and deeper layers of dread, a dread of the city as profound as any citygoer's dread of the wilds. Each detail of the house, the gardens, her clothes, even the studiously antiquated language she spoke was a denial of the Enclosure. She was trying to erase the last three hundred years, and would tolerate nothing which reminded her of that banished epoch.

Almost despairing, Teeg forced herself to keep talking, for fear her mother would regard silence as acquiescence. "If we stayed a few days, so you could see how harmless he is . . ."

"He will not stay even one night within walking distance of this house," Judith announced firmly.

"But what can he hurt?"

"My disciples have their orders."

Images of the dark-robed figures lurked in Teeg's mind. "To do what?"

Seated once again in her rocker, Judith swayed easily. "To see that your cityman and his paraphernalia are in the river before sunset. Whether he goes willingly or not."

There was no sign of Phoenix above the fountaining arches of the rose bushes. Could he hear them from there? Lowering her voice, Teeg said, "You're so filled with hate I don't recognize you."

Even this did not ruffle the older woman. "What you see as hatred I see as wise precaution."

"It's pig-headed intolerance."

"I have labored to build this estate. Over the years I have turned away every threat." The smile flickering in the shadow of the bonnet looked artificial. "I make no exceptions for you, simply because you are my daughter."

Memories from the afternoon crowded Teeg's mind, stifling her—blood-soaked dirt out front of the slaughter-house, weeds hanging from the kitchen rafters, a film of soot on tables, her mother's woolen skirts dragging the floor. "But what have you built? You're living an antique fantasy."

"It is a good life."

"You can't go back. You can't wipe out the last three centuries."

"Can't I?" said Judith, with a lilt of amusement in her voice. "And what do you suppose you and your friends are doing in that tidy little settlement at Whale's Mouth Bay?"

Teeg thought longingly of Jonah Colony, its domes radiating from the center like daisy petals, a frail organism sheltered in the bowl of hills. Was it true—were they going backward? Were they trying to relive the past? No, no, they weren't denying the modern world. They were adapting its technology to a gentler existence. She did not want to be a pioneer woman, inhaling smoke in dingy rooms, gnawing roots, chasing goats over the countryside, brain grown numb. She wanted to live lightly on the earth, in harmony with its rhythms, all her senses keen and her mind alive and her spirit awake. With deep conviction she said, "We're not going back, we're going onward. We're gathering up all that's useful and beautiful from our history and carrying it forward into a new life."

Her mother gave the feigned smile again, as if to say, A wise woman must be patient with a naive one. "It sounds very grand, my child. But you delude yourself. By bringing machines out here, you condemn yourselves to the same path. The Enclosure waits in your future."

"That is fatalism."

"It is the truth," said Judith. "The only salvation is in the past."

Gazing at the tranquil face, framed in its linen bonnet, with the archaic house rising floor after balconied floor overhead, Teeg realized that one *could* go back, and in the same moment she knew she would never follow her mother into that stifling past. Too pained to speak, she jerked her head from side to side, like an animal balking at a cage.

"Come, my daughter." Standing, the older woman grasped Teeg by the wrist and drew her out of the chair. "We will soon cure you of your attachment to the city and to this cityman."

"I don't want to be *cured*," Teeg panted.

Tugging firmly, the mother said, "Come upstairs, child. We will dress you properly."

The mother-lure was so powerful that Teeg actually followed her to the threshold of the parlor. Then a great panic seized her. She yanked her arm free. "Let me go!" she cried. Backing away, she joggled the hatracks, tumbled the umbrella stand. "I can't breathe. . . ." She upset a rocking chair, backed down the porch stairs, still jerking her head and panting for breath.

Judith watched her calmly from the front door, like a woman composed for a portrait. Only her lips moved, but Teeg could not hear what they were saying. Could they be offering words of peace? A bridge flung across the seventeen-year chasm? Teeg held her breath, straining to hear. ". . . sad to discover the infection so deep in you, my child," her mother was saying. "You are lost, lost . . ."

Teeg did not want to hear any more. Her boots thudded on the bricks as she hurried away. She had to find Phoenix and leave here, quickly, before she smothered. The rucksacks were leaning against a rose trellis, but no Phoenix. Had he gone? Driven down the hill by hatred? The disciples! In a frenzy she hunted through the rose garden, through the labyrinth of hedges, fearing any moment to stumble into those dark-robed disciples. And then at last she found him, in the Japanese garden.

He was bent over the goldfish pool, his nose only a few centimeters above the surface. When she drew near him, panting, the goldfish scattered and he looked up with an expression of anguish. "It's all right," he said, "I understand. I'll go."

She gasped and gasped to catch her breath.

His crouching body trembled. "She's your mother, right? And who am I?"

"You're my . . . partner," she managed to say, "and you're not . . . going anywhere . . . without me."

Conflicting emotions swept across his face like tremors after an earthquake. "You're going back to Jonah?"

"Yes . . . both of us . . . right now."

His eyes grew wide. "But your mother?"

"She has her world, I have mine."

She grabbed his hand and led him running past hedges, pools, rock gardens, to the trellis of roses. She did not mind the weight of the rucksuck as they hastened down the hill. In the pasture Phoenix turned round to look at the antique house. But the sight of it was too vivid in Teeg's mind, and the image of her mother, framed there in the doorway like a pioneer woman in a daguerreotype, was too painful for her to need another look, and so she hurried on between the neatly trimmed thickets to the river landing.

The shrieking of the mill greeted them. Within a minute Phoenix had the raft inflated and the rucksacks aboard. Teeg huddled on the brick terrace, exhausted, watching him labor.

"How does this infernal air-drive go?" he asked her. He was trying to jam the cylinder backwards through the motor mount.

"Help me in," she said wearily. Clinging to him, stepping off the terrace into the raft, she felt like another piece of baggage. With a great effort she mounted the air-cylinder. "There, like so. Now cast off."

The current swept them sideways. Within moments a dense cloud of bubbles swarmed behind the raft, nudging them sluggishly upstream. Teeg knew the watchtower of the house would be visible, high on the ridge of Washington Park, a wink of light. She would not let herself look for it. Better the single sharp pain, the brutal amputation, than one small cut after another.

Portland slipped by along both shores—brick husks of buildings, mossy skeletons of houses, concrete abutments like broken bones. The forest of Portland.

Phoenix kept looking round at her, searching her face intently.

It was hard for her to concentrate on the river. At sunset, darkness seemed to rise rather than fall, like a murky fluid gathering in the forest, pouring across the countryside, engulfing hills, thickening upward into the sky. Thrust up where it could catch the sunlight, Mt. Hood was the final landmark to disappear, a luminous fist shoved up from the surrounding gloom.

Phoenix was scarcely more than a voice to her when at
last they pulled to shore, well upstream from Portland.
"You're sure this is what you want?" he asked.

"I'm sure," Teeg replied. "Zuni was right. Some
reunions are not possible."

TWENTY-FOUR

There was an old proverb about never looking a gift horse in the . . . what? Ear? Nose? Mouth? Phoenix could not recall how it went. Nor did he have any clear notion what a gift horse was. But he knew the proverb had to do with accepting presents humbly, not inquiring too closely into their origins, and that was why it kept springing into his mind. He was content to have Teeg back from her mother's antique house without demanding to know why she had come. The simple gift of her was enough.

"She has her world, I have mine," Teeg had explained simply. During the late afternoon on the river that was all the explanation she offered. In the sleepsack that night she was fidgety but silent, and he did not question her. He stroked her timidly, grateful to have her within reach. She kept her own hands fisted tightly against her belly, as if to squeeze the pain into one spot and hold it there.

From the look of her eyes next morning, she had not slept much. As he mouthed the algae-brew that passed for breakfast, he thought of suggesting they vary their diet with

267

some roots and frogs. Fried lichens, maybe. Any bit of nonsense to lift her gloom. He would have tried walking on his hands across the river to please her. There was something pure about her silence, however, as he imagined a field of new-fallen snow would be pure, and he did not trample on it.

When they boarded the raft Teeg occupied the tiller seat, on the unspoken assumption that she would do whatever guiding there was to be done in this partnership. But her mind was clearly not on the river. Several times Phoenix had to cry out for her to pull hard right or left, to avoid snags he could see looming in front of them. Each time he looked round at her she was brooding on something, eyes unfocused, mouth working. He offered to change places with her but she refused. Just a daydream, she said.

One of her daydreams ran them against a half-submerged boulder, very nearly tipping them into the icy river. After he clawed them back to safety with a paddle, she said, "All right. You steer a while."

Now you're in for it, he thought, seizing hold of the tiller. The air-drive spewed a froth of bubbles out behind, shoving the raft against the current. The sizzling noise made conversation difficult. From the bow the river had never looked so infested with menacing humps and ripples.

Teeg emerged from her brooding only once, to suggest they keep on going as late as possible, until nightfall if he felt up to it. He did not feel up to it, but he kept going anyway, wanting to put as many kilometers as he could between her and that bonneted anachronism up in Portland. He tried to imagine how it would feel to have your mother seemingly rise from the dead after so long and then to lose her again so quickly.

The river was a gleaming tongue of blackness when Teeg finally consented to halt for the night. "Let's build a fire," she suggested. "Give the bears and HP a clue where we are." As if the detectors needed light: once they locked onto you, Phoenix knew, body-heat was signal enough. In the glow of firelight, sun, flare, even in darkness he marveled at her. The way her tongue flicked over her lips as she ate, the way her foot kicked free of the shimmersuit at bedtime—everything she did since reclaiming him like a wayward child at the goldfish pool seemed fresh, as if she were a package newly opened.

Later, in the darkness of the tent, she broke her silence. Evidently her spirit-wrestling was over, for the words trickled out calmly. "I never dreamed she could become such a stranger. I always thought of her . . . the way she used to be when I was a child. I guess she was pretty bitter even back then. She hated Father and Zuni and everything to do with the Enclosure. But her life wasn't eaten up with saying no."

Her breathing filled the tent. Waiting for her to continue, Phoenix tiptoed a pair of fingers along her ribs.

Presently she resumed: "The most I hoped for was to find out how she died. I wouldn't let myself believe she could still be alive. At first Portland looked so wild—no trace of her left, I thought. Then we heard the mill and there was fresh grain in the shed, and I was running up the brickway. And there was a house where there couldn't possibly be a house. And there was this old-fashioned woman rocking on the porch. 'Teeg,' she said, as if I'd just returned from a few minutes' walk. 'Hello, my daughter.' I was so busy yelling and crying that it took me a moment to see how much she'd changed. I danced up to hug her and she drew back. 'Not in those foul garments,' she said." Teeg's voice broke under the pressure of memory. "My own mother wouldn't *touch* me."

Her grief struck Phoenix dumb. Reverently he traced a finger along her collarbone, into the shallow at the base of her throat, down the valley between her breasts. He stroked her as if the grief were a wrinkle he could smooth away.

Just when he was beginning to think she might have been soothed to sleep, she murmured: "Zuni was right. Time forces people down many separate branchings of the path.

Mother's away off over there somewhere, and I'm here.
Right here." Her leg came against his, her fingers lit on his
chest. "That's what marriage is—right?—two people keep
choosing the same path to follow."

Marriage? he thought. The word seemed as old as blood.
Journeying together. "Sounds good to me," he answered.
He could not imagine her choosing any path, even into the
ruby throat of a whale, that he would not choose also.
Terrified, maybe, and quaking—but he would go.

Her face was hot and wet on his shoulder as she rolled
against him. Hooking one arm across her back he coaxed
her all the way over, covering himself with the blanket of
her body.

For the remaining three days on the river they steered the
raft by turns. With each passing kilometer Teeg seemed
more gay. She transformed the shores into vivid tapestries
with her chatter about deerferns and sandstone and long-
eared bats. When Phoenix had his shift at the tiller she
tipped back her head and bellowed songs about shipwrecks.
When her own shift came, she crooned about lovesick
maidens. She could sing for hours, song after song, until the
Willamette Valley was peopled with coal miners and
whaling-ship captains and moonshiners and other extinct
characters.

Gradually she was escaping the orbit of Portland and
entering the orbit of Jonah Colony. Her talk filled with
speculations about the settlement. How was Zuni getting
along? And Buddha-faced Marie with her garden? The
runnerbeans should be ready for harvesting. Had the new
bluegill survived? Were the ingatherings deep, even without
dear old Sol? They're probably short-circuited without us,
eh, Phoenix?

He would grin *yes* to whatever she asked him. Half of it
he could not hear because of the constant buzz from the air-
drive. Her gaiety was all that mattered. Each time he
imagined his love for her had grown as vast as it possibly

could, her red hair would blaze in the sunshine or her quick
body would twist round to behold some passing wonder on
the shore, and his love would swell a little more.

In the evenings he inflated the tent and built a fire while
Teeg collected nosegays of flowers. After splashing and
scrubbing with filtered riverwater, she went blissfully
naked, but Phoenix always wriggled back into his shimmersuit. Though he realized the patrollers could only track him
as a tiny spark in a cyber-field, just as he had once tracked
clouds, still he could not quite shake the feeling that he was
being watched. Observing his modesty, Teeg remarked,
"You can take the boy out of the city—but can you take the
city out of the boy?"

Probably not, Phoenix admitted to himself later, in the
dark of the tent, in her arms. I will always be a halfbreed
with muddled heart, caught midway on a bridge between
the city and wilderness.

When at length they reached the point on the river where
they had first launched the raft, they shouldered the
backpacks and headed overland. There was no need to give
the repair station such a wide berth, since the HP knew of
them already. Teeg declared she did not care a fig about the
patrollers or their snooping satellites. Her mother had
explained that little bands of wildergoers were kept under
observation all over the globe, the way you observe a
bacterial culture in a petri dish to see if it will spread or
wither.

"By watching us they keep tabs on the condition of the
environment," she said.

"But suppose they find out all they want to know about
Whale's Mouth, and then decide to haul us away to
quarantine?"

"Why would they want all of us malcontents back
inside?"

"They could just burn us out," Phoenix suggested
bleakly.

"And waste perfectly good test animals?" Teeg walked

ahead of him on the trail, flinging answers back over her shoulder.

Phoenix slogged along, unconvinced. A few minutes earlier they had passed the charred site of Zuni's home village. The blackened image of it was seared into his mind. "Still," he persisted, "they're watching us, and they could descend on us at any moment."

"Sure they could. And a tree could fall on you."

"It's not the same."

"It's exactly the same." Saying this, Teeg swung round on the trail and he nearly stumbled into her. She stared fixedly into his eyes. "You're going to die, aren't you?"

Here it was broad daylight, trees festooned with bearded moss were arching overhead, Salt Creek was purling along beside him—and he was seized by midnight panic. "Eventually," he admitted.

"Death's going to come, sometime, somewhere. And what do you do about it?"

Her eyes were extraordinarily green today. Oregon eyes. "I . . . just . . ."

"You keep on living, is what you do. You can't do a thing about death, so you just nod at it, and go on about your business. And you can't do anything about the Enclosure, either. It's simply *there*, and it's going to *be* there regardless of what we do, unless humanity pulls up stakes and goes shipping off into space. So we stick out our tongues at the spy satellites and keep on planting trees and raising fish and seeking the center." She was breathless when she finished speaking.

Turning back around she continued on along Salt Creek, one boot shoving against the steep bank, one sloshing in the water. Phoenix scuffled behind, the rucksack tipping him first to one side, then the other. It seemed intolerable to him, never knowing from one hour to the next whether the black gliders would swoop down from the sky. But Teeg was right, death was also intolerable, an outrage, and yet he kept on living. Was the Enclosure inevitable? He could not accept that. Deep down he still wanted to save humanity from the Enclosure, even though Zuni had insisted that the desire to make things over was the root of human ills.

Let things be, Zuni had told him. Seek to live truly yourself, and others, seeing you, will do likewise. It sounded very noble. But if they could not see you? If they were locked inside their opaque bottle? What then?

Whenever he was tempted to despair, he remembered his own example—Phoenix the wary, the reluctant, the befuddled cityman. I have made the journey. Here I am. It is possible to break free.

They heard the purr of Salt Creek Falls for half an hour before they reached the brink of the cliff, where water fumed down into the meadow. Zuni had told them about arriving at this same point and seeing only fog. Phoenix imagined what she must have feared. He felt as though he had spent his own life venturing out and circling back, always hoping to find the beloved face, the familiar place, waiting for him on his return.

There was no fog this day. Jonah Colony was luminously visible. It radiated from the center of the meadow, gossamer domes and fretwork towers and pathways of glass, seeming as vulnerable as ever. The sight of it made him feel the way he always felt when he noticed the delicate blue veins under the skin in Teeg's wrist.

Lifting her voice to be heard over the bluster of the falls, Teeg cried, "It's still there!"

The look of exaltation on her face was so intense that she seemed to cast a light around her. The same passionate look had set his heart dancing months ago, when she first loomed into view like an unpredicted planet on the pedbelt outside his door. She was the original green-eyed siren. He vowed to follow her into blizzards or quicksand or gaping jaws. For the moment he merely had to trail after her down the steep path beside the waterfall and across the meadow.

Someone must have spied them coming, for welcoming faces crowded out of the domes—Marie with a smudge of dirt on her cheek, Coyt holding a chunk of circuitry, and Zuni with her cobweb of wrinkles tugged into the shape of joy.

Five voices spoke at once. Foreheads kissed, palms touched, hands eased them out of their backpacks. The talk was a jumble of Portland and seedlings and health patrol and broccoli.

Mention of the HP rang alarm bells in Phoenix, who asked, "Where are the others?"

"Up at the lighthouse," Zuni replied, waving her arm in the direction of Whale's Head.

At mention of this everyone suddenly grew hushed, and Teeg said anxiously, "Someone's died?"

Zuni beamed, like a child trying to contain a secret. "Oh no, quite the opposite."

"What's that supposed to mean?" demanded Teeg.

"Come see." Zuni grabbed her by the hand, Marie grabbed Phoenix, and Coyt limped after them on his uneven legs. Along the creek to the beach, over the squishing sand, up the lighthouse trail—even without the rucksack Phoenix was beginning to feel misused by gravity. Along the way, Teeg reported on her mother's transformation. Like a visitor from the past, she said, my own mother, a stranger, keeping sheep and disciples in an eighteenth-century house. Zuni and Marie, two wise old ones who had swallowed quite a lot of bitterness themselves, were consoling her.

Coyt was telling Phoenix how the receiver had finally picked up HP broadcasts, from which they had learned that Jonah Colony was already on the surveillance map. "It turns out there's places like ours all over the earth. And they just watch us, like they'd watch a radiation spill or an earthquake fault."

Still finding it hard to believe, Phoenix said, "After all our secrecy, and risking our necks in the ocean—they don't even *care*?"

"Don't give a damn, apparently, so long as we mind our business," said Coyt. "We've talked with some colonies that have been going since the Enclosure. Twenty-six, twenty-seven years, and the HP's never touched them."

"You actually talked with them? Other exiles?"

Phoenix could hear the pleasure in Coyt's voice: "It's not easy, let me tell you. Most of the old colonies have got pretty crude equipment. And the HP jam my channels about as fast as I generate them. But a few words get through."

A network of wilderness settlements, an anti-Enclosure: the idea delighted Phoenix. Maybe they could spin another sort of web around the planet, a web of dirt paths and rivers instead of glass tubes, connecting tiny settlements like Jonah Colony, open to weather and the shimmering universe. Unlikely, but possible, and that was hope enough to live on.

Teeg was just recounting her meeting with the deer, much to Zuni's delight, and Phoenix was wishing he had brought his antlers along, when they reached the grassy shelf where the ruins of the lighthouse stood. Jumbled stones, wind-bent shrubs, mountain rising steeply behind, ocean spreading out forever beyond the lip of land in somber green. For Phoenix the place still burned with Sol's presence. The grass owed a measure of its brightness to his ashes.

At the edge of the cliff, where the land fell away dizzyingly a hundred meters to the breakers, the other five colonists sat facing the sea. Like a rock in the midst of them, Jurgen held binoculars in his great paws. Hinta, yellow hair tugged back to keep the wind from blowing it across her mouth, was speaking close to his ear. Indy, Josh, and Arda pointed at the ocean and talked gaily among themselves.

What were they seeing? Phoenix wondered. Birds? HP gliders? Ships?

"Look who came back!" Zuni sang out.

Startled, the five turned round, and their faces broke open with pleasure. Come, come, they waved, handing binoculars to Phoenix and Teeg. "Out there," said Jurgen, pointing, "where the greenish patch of water looks like it's boiling."

Phoenix gazed through the binoculars. Blank water. What on earth was he supposed to see?

"There it goes!" Teeg cried. "And another!"

Everyone was yelling and leaping on the brink of the cliff, and Phoenix was staring himself blind at empty ocean. He lowered the binoculars in dismay. What on earth? Zuni came over then, sat him down on the grassy lip of the continent, and with her fingers on his cheeks she aimed his gaze delicately, saying, "Look there, bright eyes." At last he saw the spouts, five of them . . . six! . . . like tiny fountains. Broad flukes thrust above the surface, waved mightily, then swept downward, stroking the ocean, with a movement as delicate as Zuni's touch on his cheeks.

"Whales!" he said wonderingly.

"They've found their way back," Teeg said with joy.

"Did they ever lose it?" said Zuni.

Afterword

Although filled with futuristic gizmos, *Terrarium* was hammered out on an ancient typewriter, the kind powered by fingers. I began work in November 1978, the month of my son's first birthday and his first solo walk, a couple of months before my daughter turned six. The keys kept jamming on the typewriter, and baby Jesse kept thumping on the walls of the ticky-tacky house we were renting in Eugene, Oregon. The bedroom where I sat dreaming of the Enclosure was not big enough to swing a cat in, as my father would have said. The only window, set high in the wall, revealed a slab of sky, more often gray than blue in that season. I holed up there in the mornings, while my daughter was away in kindergarten and my wife rode herd on Jesse. Then around noon each day, Ruth lowered her guard, and Jesse used his new legs to stagger down the hall to my room. He pawed on the door and babbled in his own invented language, every day the same message: Come on out, Daddy, it's time to play. He pawed and babbled until I quit typing, then he raised his volume until I opened the door and hoisted him into my arms.

Every afternoon, rain or shine, we did go out and play. We strolled the sidewalks of Eugene, sat beside fountains, paused in parks to examine ferns and bugs, watched herons hunt along the Willamette River, patted the trunks of trees, contemplated clouds. Home from kindergarten, Eva often joined us on our rambles. With Jesse swaying in the backpack, we hiked in the nearby hills, my feet laced into the cracked leather boots that I would loan to Zuni Franklin for her own hike through the Oregon woods. Like the young Teeg Passio, Eva posed questions and made up stories about the creatures we met, while Jesse sang in the backpack and kept time by swatting me on the head or yanking at my beard.

So my life was divided, like the world of *Terrarium,* half indoors and half outside. I earned time in the open air with my children by putting in solitary time at the desk. I had the luxury of writing and fathering all the livelong day because I was on leave that year from my job as a teacher at Indiana University. The move from our settled home in limestone country to this temporary home in the country of spruce and fir was as liberating and bewildering for me as the move outside proved to be for Phoenix Marshall. The novel was on my mind in the afternoons as I roamed with the children, and the children were on my mind in the mornings as I wrestled with the novel. Jesse and Eva tugged my thoughts into the future. What sort of earth would they inherit? Would they suffer from nuclear war? From pollution? From hunger? When they were my age, would they be able to breathe the air or drink the water? Would they have confidence enough to bear their own children? If so, would those children still be able to see whales or wolves? Would they meet any wildness at all?

On weekends during that year in Oregon, Ruth and I often bundled the kids into our rusty Fiat and drove out through green mountains to the coast, where we moseyed along the edge of the sea. The bay we visited most faithfully was known as Devil's Elbow, named for the volcanic rocks that rose like charred bones from the waves. When I sent my conspirators there to found a colony, I changed the name to Whale's Mouth Bay, but everything else about this haunting place I kept the same—the meadow and creek, the headland with its lighthouse, the bearded moss, tidal pools, and cobbled shore, the dark and looming cliffs riddled with caves.

On other weekends we drive up the Willamette Valley to Portland, to walk along the riverfront where Phoenix and Teeg would come upon the groaning mill, or to admire the roses and rhododendrons in Washington Park, where Judith Passio would establish her pastoral community. I borrowed pieces of Judith's patchwork house from the handsome home of Charles and Ursula Le Guin, with whom we stayed on several trips. Their hedges and flowers, multiplied a thousandfold, would lead Phoenix up the hill to his reunion with Teeg. I have long since apologized to Ursula and Charles for dismantling their beloved Portland, a city I admire; but Judith needed some ruins, and so I chose a place whose contours I knew.

When we stuck around Eugene on Sundays, we usually worshipped with the Society of Friends, those Christian mystics known to the world as Quakers. Their religion appealed to me then and appeals to me now because it is communal, it dispenses with doctrine, it seeks the source of all Creation in a holy center. It is also risky, because, instead of hearing God in the silence, you may hear only the Id, or the grumbling of your belly, or the static of the day's news. My conspirators derive their own religion from the Taoists and Buddhists and Sufis, as well as from the Quakers. Like the spiritual seekers in all those traditions, Teeg and her companions hunt for the holy ground together, in suffering and celebration, in work and prayer, and in the greater life of nature. Without some shared faith, I figured, no community would long survive in the wilds.

Who can trace all the sources of a novel? The pedbelts of Oregon City owe something to the conveyors of a Louisiana factory where I drove a forklift during my college summers. The domed city itself is an exaggeration of the shopping malls that I first encountered in Indianapolis, consumer nirvanas hermetically sealed against weather and history. Teeg's glass tank, brimming with plants, is a smaller version of a terrarium that I saw, years ago, in Chicago's Museum of Science and Industry. The fossil that she gives to Phoenix resembles one I found in an Ohio creek bed. A visit to Disney World lurks behind my image of the appalling gameparks. The chemmies derive, of course, from the drugs sold over the counter and on the street in our own society, but they also derive from booze, that elixir of oblivion, which destroyed my father. Behind Zuni's glimpse of her Oregon village burned to cinders by the health patrol, there are images of torched villages in Vietnam. The grief that Zuni feels over the desolation of her beloved country is the grief I felt over the flooding of my childhood landscape by a government dam. I could trace a public or private source for every detail in the book, from Teeg's bare feet on the opening page to the California gray whales on the final page; but I see no need to multiply examples. When I pluck at any line in *Terrarium,* I am liable to find it connected through memory to the whole of my life.

At the end of our year in Oregon, I had not quite finished one full draft of the novel. We camped our way back from Eugene to Bloomington, the roof rack of our Fiat loaded with playpen and trunks, my files stuffed with photographs and notes, my mind filled with images of mountains and rivers and ocean.

We pitched our tent in the Badlands on a night when Jesse was cutting a new tooth. He was so fretful that I gave up on sleep and eased him into the backpack and the two of us went out walking under a full moon. Soothed by moon and motion, he soon grew quiet, riding along with his fingers hooked into my hair. I could have walked forever among those dazzling hills, in that splendid light, with my boy on my back and this ground under my feet. From the pressure of his grip, I could tell when Jesse was looking this way or that. I found myself gazing through his eyes, and they were utterly clear. Stone, snake, burning bush. We walked in beauty, my son and I. We saw that these Badlands were unmistakably good, as the Lakota had always known. What we glimpsed there, I realized, was a glory that runs through all places and all creatures. No words could ever capture it. Yet no story could ever be true without witnessing to this beauty and power.

Back home in Indiana, I kept dreaming of Oregon. Over the next three years, while the nuclear arms race accelerated and the environment deteriorated and my children grew, I completed the first draft of the novel and then a second and a third. Those were the early years of Ronald Reagan's presidency, when the Secretary of the Interior announced that we need not preserve the forests because God would be coming soon to end the world; when the Secretary of Agriculture declared that we could replace topsoil with chemicals; when the head of the Environmental Protection Agency approved of drilling for oil in wilderness areas and along the continental shelf; when the President himself remarked that trees are a major source of pollution and that, in any case, when you've seen one redwood you've seen them all. I was at work on the fourth and final draft of *Terrarium* when President Reagan unveiled his Strategic Defense Initiative, which soon became known as the "Star Wars" plan, and which he invited us to think of as an invulnerable shield over our vulnerable heads. It was a time when anyone who loved the earth might well have despaired.

I struggled with despair, for I did not see how we could keep on piling up weapons, using up oil and iron and ozone, annihilating other species, paving the soil, fouling the waters and air, adding to our own swollen numbers, without eventually rendering the earth uninhabitable for our descendants. I still do not see any way of sustaining the industrial binge, let alone of extending that binge to the whole globe. There were just over four billion human beings, many of them wretchedly poor, when I began making notes for *Terrarium*; as I write these lines, the human population is nearing six billion, and the number of those suffering—from starvation and pollution and war—is rising even more rapidly.

The novel was finished in 1984, a year rendered ominous by George Orwell, and it was first published in 1985. Reading *Terrarium* again on the occasion of this new edition, I find that the most disturbing trends I projected into my imaginary future have, if anything, only intensified over the past decade. More and more people jam the world's highways and cities, fill the countryside, crowd out other species. More and more drugs ease our aches and compensate for the madness or futility of our lives. We keep transferring our talents to machines, leaving less and less meaningful work for humans to do. Our impulse to create an enclave where nothing can harm us, an infantile paradise where we need only eat and play, has achieved an apotheosis of sorts in the Mall of America. Our enclosures become ever larger, more sumptuous, more perfect refuges from the planet. We move ever deeper indoors, into the sealed boxes of our houses and offices, into domed stadiums and air-conditioned cars. Within these boxes, we retreat farther and farther into the twilit zone of television, tapes, and cyberspace.

Although I set my story in the twenty-first century, I only used the future as a screen for projecting enlarged images from our own time. I had no difficulty believing that we could poison the planet, but I never for a moment believed that we could save ourselves by building and inhabiting a global network of enclosed cities. Even if we knew how, we lack the will or the means to carry it out. All the resources of our nation have been required to sustain a handful of astronauts for a few weeks in cramped capsules, and even those resources have not always been sufficient to keep the astronauts alive.

Seven years after I began fashioning the Enclosure out of words in a rented room in Oregon, engineers began constructing Biosphere 2 out of glass and steel in the Arizona desert. This cluster of greenhouses, covering 3.5 acres and fitted with the best technology money could buy, was designed to be a self-contained system, within which humans could live and work indefinitely, growing all their own food and recycling their wastes, insulated from the outside. The developers believed that such bubble shelters might one day enable us to colonize other planets, or to survive in the degraded atmosphere of this one. *Terrarium* had been in print for more than five years when the first group of colonists moved inside Biosphere 2. The press followed this endeavor with much ballyhoo, at first announcing visionary hopes, and then, as problems emerged, confessing doubts. There were hints of illness, malnutrition, stress. There were reports of squabbles among the eight colonists. An injury forced one of them to sneak outside for medical treatment. The filtration system broke down, and technicians had to pipe in fresh supplies of air. Scientists who had neither money nor reputation invested in the project began to speak of it as a tourist attraction, a technological fantasy, a hoax. Whether hoax or bold experiment, Biosphere 2 has demonstrated that we are a long, long way from knowing enough to build a substitute for earth.

To gauge how much time has passed since I hammered out the opening lines of *Terrarium,* I need only look at Jesse, who is now seventeen years old, with his own downy beard. He is an inch taller than six feet, and he weighs 195 pounds, far too heavy for me to hoist in my arms or tote in a backpack. But he still tugs my thoughts into the future, and so does Eva, and so do the students who gather in my classes, the toddlers who chase dogs down our street, and the babies whose faces beam from the arms of my neighbors. I am still trying to imagine how we can insure that the earth will remain a home for them, and that it will not become, like Venus or Mars, a hostile planet.

For all my worries, I wrote *Terrarium* with a sense of hope, and on rereading the book I find that hope renewed. The earth remains fertile and resilient. No matter how far we have retreated indoors, we are inseparably bound to the earth through our senses, through our flesh, through the yearnings and pleasures of sex, through the cycles of birth and death. Like Phoenix, any of us may wake up to discover where we truly dwell. Like Zuni and Teeg, we may labor for what we love, no matter how many voices tell us to give up. Like the colonists gathered on the Oregon shore, we may use the wealth of human knowledge to build communities that are materially simple and spiritually complex, respectful of our places and of the creatures who share them with us. We may seek holy ground together. Even in dark times, we may keep telling stories, witnessing to a wild beauty that we do not invent, a power we do not own.

Bloomington, Indiana
Spring 1995